# GUARDIAN OF MONSTERS

## A PI URBAN FANTASY

### SLEUTHS OF SHADOW SALON
#### BOOK ONE

## CATHERINE STINE

**Konjur Road Press**
*Forays into Fictional Magic*

**Guardian of Monsters**
*A PI urban fantasy*
Sleuths of Shadow Salon Book 1
by Catherine Stine

Cover by Christian Bentulan/CoversByChristian

**Synopsis:** Celestine, artist intuitive and witch, opens Shadow Salon, a
cover for her PI business in Savannah, Georgia with Luna, a winged
mermaid and water mage. They use clues in Celestine's art to solve the
bizarre murder of housemate Ray, whose supernatural stalker is now
hunting Celestine and will destroy Savannah if he's not stopped.

For news of books, events and sales subscribe to Catherine's newsletters
or visit her website at catherinestine.com

**Other Books by Catherine:**
Theater of Curses (Shadow Salon Book 2, '24 launch)
Witch of the Wild Beasts
Witch of the Cards
Secrets of the Mermaid
Alpha's Revenge
Pictures of Dorianna
Fireseed One
Ruby's Fire
Refugees

**Readers say:**

"Supernatural twists, devious villains and romance galore!" - Reader

"Action-packed, emotional thrill ride!" - Electrifying Reviews

"Full of creativity, imagination & original concepts" - Fluttereal Flight

"Characters you want to hang out with!" - Holly Kowitt

✺ Created with Vellum

# CHAPTER ONE

Celestine settled onto a paint-splotched chair in a studio at the Savannah School of Art and Design and peered around with curiosity. About fifteen other students filtered in and took spots arranged in a semicircle around a set of wooden risers someone had pushed together.

She'd signed up for a four-class intensive to bulk up her handcrafted illustration skills. This school in Savannah had a stellar reputation. She was already adept at the Wacom pad and digital pen, but she had particular reasons to go out armed with only old-school pencils and markers.

While she waited for class to begin, she studied the others. In walked a woman with purple braids and what looked like silk paisley pajamas, a guy in a tight tank with a crown tattoo circling his neck, and a woman in a white tutu with white lipstick. Celestine chuckled to herself. Artists were flashy dressers who gave zero fucks. Back in Red River, she was practically the only one with tattoos, much less full sleeves of roses. Her almost-waist-length jet-black hair pulled back by sparkly combs, and her penchant for dark lace halters, made her stand out even more. So being surrounded by likeminded folk here was sweet.

The tattoo on her left arm concealed an irregular patch of skin that she shaved to conceal the hair that grew wild— a genetic gift from her father Wayland, a wolf shifter. She was an advocate for those on the fringes, but it served no useful purpose to advertise her inner wolf. Better to keep her nighttime magic safe until needed.

Her gaze settled on a tall, lean man walking in with a lithe gait and a distinctive sandy mane framing his angular face. He wore a crisp white button-down shirt, as if heading to church or someone's wedding. It was at odds with his moss-green shorts and long canvas rucksack bouncing on his wide shoulders. He put his gear on a seat behind her. While listening to him unzip his pack, she raised her head to the air-conditioned swills. It was September in Savannah and as hot as a bee sting in a firepit. Even at four p.m., it had to be pushing a hundred degrees.

She'd passed new studios, though this one, with its chipped cabinets and rough-hewn floorboards, was pleasingly "seasoned," as her dad would say, or "decrepit" as her mom, Stormy, would say.

Celestine had left her hometown in Red River, Louisiana, a year ago when she was twenty-four, and though she missed her folks, she'd settled into a small room above Bay Street, courtesy of her dad's old biker buddy Ray, who owned a leather shop downstairs. The noise from the street was constant, raucous, lively. And the smell of Ray's tanned leathers was pungent, but she was getting a deal on the rent, so who was she to complain?

Plus, Ray paid her to paint images on the leather wallets and belts and encouraged her to exhibit her art in the shop. She'd already sold two pieces—the first of a heron in marsh grass, the second of a statuette of a girl in Bonaventure Cemetery. The sales made her happy and had Ray bragging about her as if she were his own grown daughter. He wasn't exactly the fatherly type, more a hardened biker who plastered wolf and skull decals on his black vest and had a few pirate-style gold teeth. With the drawings she hung, she had to be careful not to apply her magic or the buyers would get an unexpected jolt. She wasn't selling spells, just pictures, though she told Ray one day while they worked that she could see herself doing just that.

"An enchanted art gallery. Can you picture it?" she mused.

"If you're anything like your dad, you could sell the hell out of art or freaking spells or anything you set your mind to," Ray had said. "After all, he sold a horde of coyote shifters on a war that wasn't their own and won your mom over from the enemy camp in the bargain."

"Ha! I've heard that star-crossed saga during many a bedtime tuck-in." She and Ray had laughed together, and she painted designs on ten wallets that afternoon.

Celestine's attention returned to the art studio as an older man she figured was the professor entered the room. He had silver hair and blue eyes under his spectacles. He stepped onto the riser and turned to face his students. "Welcome. I'm Professor Gray, and in this illustration class, we'll go through some notable techniques of both digital and classical methods. Today, we have a live model, and as I requested, we'll be drawing on vellum with graphite. Everyone get to the art store?"

Celestine and some others raised pieces of smudgy graphite. She briefly worried she'd be clumsy at it after years with the digital pen. Back in Red River, she had designed a tarot deck in Photoshop for old Nola Jaye, the turbaned reader who sat in front of her parents' apartment complex. That is until... she shook the memory away.

Out came the model, a zaftig lady wearing only a flowered shawl. She sat gingerly on the risers, unwound the shawl, and twisted her legs and hips in a reclined sitting position supported by her chafed elbows.

Celestine set about to do her best rendering, lightly framing in the woman's contours and then gradually sharpening and shading as she assessed the scale of torso and the angle of the woman's bent arms.

At the juncture of the legs, a swell of energy rolled through her, and her fingers moved like stubborn children, bucking authority, pushing the pen in a different direction than she wanted them to. This happened every so often. But did it really have to happen on the first day of this class? Magical energy tickled her fingertips as if ants crawled on them. Old Nola Jaye would've called it prophecy. Ironic. Celestine tried to move her pencil against the growing current and felt a series of hard pinches along her drawing arm. The energies seemed to hate it when she resisted them, so she sighed and let them—whoever they were—guide her pencil, not to legs and feet but a single curving line.

Nola Jaye had tried to explain the forces to her in a two-card oracle pull. The Magician and the Wheel of Fortune. These were the cards Celestine picked over and over and over. "A seer," Nola had muttered, and nodded sagely as the opaline jewel on her turban glinted.

"What's that mean?" Celestine had asked when she was only seven, then at ten, at thirteen, and nineteen.

"You predict things."

"How?"

"You'll see," was Nola Jaye's cryptic reply.

"What if I don't want to predict things?"

Nola Jaye just shook her head.

At twenty-two, Celestine found out exactly how she would predict things: a drawing she did, preceded Nola Jaye's demise by three days, of an overturned coffee mug and a bloody turban. Too specific to write off to chance.

It took them a year to find Nola Jaye's murderer after they found her dead on the pavement, her turban unwound and soaked through from the wound Nola Jaye had sustained from falling headfirst onto the asphalt. They tested the remaining liquid in her overturned mug. Turned out to be a powerful poison from a superstitious rando who hated supernaturals. An angry neighbor who used to spit on the sidewalk as he walked by her on his way to work at a real estate agency. There were lots of folks who hated how supes had poured out of New Orleans and spread over the Red River Valley. "The Devil's folk," they would hiss. As far as Celestine was concerned, folks who murdered old ladies were more the Devil's folk, even if they did attend church on Sundays and every day in between.

She glanced down at the graphite lines her hands were automatically drawing and took in a sharp breath. Then she looked over at Professor Gray across the room. He was bent over a student's easel. Suddenly, he met her gaze and raised one curious eyebrow. Awkward! The force emanating from her was undeniable. She shouldn't have sent it toward him. Now he was likely to question what was unfolding on the page, just as she was doing. Chill bumps rose along her back.

It wasn't the Prof who was suddenly standing by her shoulder, though. It was the lean blond-haired man with the green rucksack. What the hell?

"So, you think she looks like a mermaid, do you?"

"Not exactly," Celestine said, waffling. Indeed, the woman she'd drawn had a tailfin. Also wings. What the hell times two!

Blond Hair looked closer. He smelled of forests. Of mint and midnight soil. "Who's that man sprawled by her feet, and why are his eyes missing?"

"That's my business," Celestine answered rudely. "Shall I go look at your drawing and grill you?"

"Sure," he replied, amusement in his tone. "Take a look."

She got up. He'd drawn the model in competent strokes, yet he'd jettisoned the black graphite for colored pencils of jade and gold. Celestine sniggered. "The model looks like a tarnished statue—verdigris all over." *Kind of like you,* she thought as she stared at his iridescent green eyes rimmed with amber. Like a mad woodland sprite. Breezy golden energy shimmered around him, but she couldn't identify it. Her guard was up now.

"I draw it as I see it," he said simply.

"The lady on the risers doesn't have green skin," she countered. Pajama Girl, sitting to her left, chuckled. "Metaphoric, then?"

Professor Gray was walking their way.

"Life is a metaphor," Blond Hair replied with a wink.

Professor Gray now stood by Celestine's easel. He rubbed his bearded chin as he peered at it. "Very imaginative. Is that a sleeping man at your, er, mermaid's feet, or what? All the jacket decals, the gouged eyes," he noted as if to himself.

"What the flying crap?" Celestine mumbled through the hair that she'd purposely let fall over her flushed cheeks.

"Excuse me?" Professor Gray stared with crossed brows at the drawing.

"She *sees*," whispered Blond Hair under his breath.

Celestine drew in a sharp breath at his comment. Even if he knew this innately, why would he say it out loud? Who was he, really? She was too stressed to quickly sense if he had powers of some sort.

Others had filtered over and were peering at the drawing. She wondered how many people were supes. Most of her interactions with them were friendly, but she wasn't so naïve to think that there weren't rival groups in Savannah, some with nefarious missions.

In this moment, though, her concern was the drawing she was staring at with dawning horror. She'd just rendered a distinct likeness of Ray. Was this a prophecy of some sort, as Nola Jaye had said? Celestine had no clue as to who the mermaid was or why this likeness of Ray with no eyes was splayed at the mermaid's feet. She only knew she had to get out of the class. She bolted to her feet, folded the drawing into a small square, threw it and her art supplies into her crossbody bag, and then raced to the door and out.

# TWO

"Ray! Ray! Are you here?" yelled an out-of-breath Celestine as she wrenched the shop door open and crashed around loaded racks of leather jackets, pants, and belts to the area behind the counter, where they finished the leather pieces. "Ray!" she cried again, not seeing him in the back making coffee or even taking a catnap on the raggedy couch. She swallowed her rising panic.

"Wow, wow, zowie, what's all the fuss?" Ray said as he scurried out of the shop's small bathroom. "I thought the place was on fire!"

"Thank the spirits you're okay," Celestine gasped as she threw her arms around his thick leathery neck.

He gave her an uncertain return hug and then stepped back to study her. "What's going on? I wasn't aware I was in danger."

"It's hard to explain," she said, suddenly shy and ashamed of what had seemed like an appropriate response but now seemed like total theatrics.

"Try me." He gestured toward the couch. She sat and

explained about the drawing, about the Oracle card pulls with Nola Jaye over the years, about the turbaned medium's declaration regarding Celestine. Ray knew full well the bad stuff and what had happened to Nola Jaye at the end.

After all, Celestine and her parents, Wayland and Stormy, had all come to Savannah to toss Nola Jaye's ashes on the gravestones of Lionel and Lonetta—Nola's mama and daddy—side by side in Bonaventure Cemetery. Ray had invited Celestine and her family to stay with him, and before the pilgrimage to the cemetery, Wayland gave Nola Jaye one last joyride. He belted her ashes to his chopper and he and Ray bombed around the town squares and surrounding marshes.

With all of this, Celestine had never told Ray about her drawing or the old card reader's prophecy for her.

Ray let out a raspy sigh. "Well, a fuckin' toad's belch! I'm glad I'm not dead! Good you were wrong on this one, girl. Though I wouldn't mind laying at a pretty mermaid's feet."

Celestine play-slapped Ray's arm. "You're a real cutup, pirate." He'd told her he came from an old buccaneer family. She never knew whether he was fooling around or for real because he'd relayed it all with a big grin. From all she read, pirates were a thing of the distant past, when the high seas were a dangerous bet and even the British aristocracy hired privateers and pirates as black-market cops to protect their oceangoing goods and lives. But Ray did look the part with his black beard, beer belly, leathery skin, and mischievous coal-black eyes. She still recalled, when she'd first moved into his place, how she had picked up a wooden carving high on his shelf of a boat with black sails and a three-eyed logo on it.

"Don't touch!" Ray had shouted. He'd hurried toward her, batting his hands. A burst of white heat pierced her side in what felt like hectic magic. She'd dropped the wooden boat as if it burned her.

"What is it, Ray?" she'd asked, wondering whether the burst of magic had come from him or the boat.

"Some things are best left unsaid," he'd muttered, his spooked eyes showing the whites. He had since removed it from the shop, and she never again brought up the subject.

Her memories were broken by Ray's boisterous baritone. "Hey, shall we make some art, then? Not of a prophecy kind?" His beaming smile showcased his gold teeth.

"Excellent idea," she replied. "My magic's drained, so it'll just be regular flowers, stars and the like. No loaded charms."

"Sounds ducky to me." Ray got out assorted leather pieces from a bin, and they moved to the makeshift studio behind the counter. The wooden table was filled with awls, pricking irons, cutting mats, chisels, burnishers and an anvil, and Celestine's leather paints and brushes. There, people could watch them crafting the products—ogling was a popular activity for tourists and townies alike. Today, though, the shop was quiet. Even so, Celestine was surprised when Ray ventured back into dark conversation.

He spoke as he lay a hank of leather over a well-worn template and began to trim it into a pouch shape. "For real, though, I have no family, so when I croak from a heart attack or whatever, just cremate—"

"Whoa, Ray!" Celestine cut in. She wasn't sure she could take more drama. "You're strong as a bull. You're not going anywhere."

"Sure, sure." He shrugged as he trimmed another piece on the metal template. "But, uh, if I did..." He looked over at her, and she saw gravity in his normally jolly face. It was her fault he was pondering his mortality. "Look," he said quietly, "I'm not scared of death. I've dodged more than a few grisly endings by now. The days tick away. My time grows shorter. Who knows how many murderous germs and villains are out to get me?"

Celestine was speechless. She held the tiny brush in the air that she'd been sketching in a lion with and stared at Ray. "Yeah, who knows? But hey, you're here. You're healthy, and I'm so sorry I rattled you with my lousy so-called automatic drawing."

"I'm over it," Ray replied with a flip of his leather piece on the template.

"Okay, good." Celestine dipped her brush in the golden paint again and filled in the lion's mane.

They talked of lighter things as they worked—the rising popularity of artsy belts for both genders, the dwindling popularity of expensive thigh-high boots and cavernous handbags. Who had the money to blow or the shoulders of steel one needed to haul a crapload of junk? She took a few photos of him working on his leather pieces. They discussed how the food at Crawdaddy's was getting too bready, how the moon was rounding to full in two days, how tourists would never tire of Haunted Savannah tours, because people liked to be freaked out of their gourds.

They worked until the sun was low in the sky and then ordered from... where else: Crawdaddy's. Because while the oysters and crawdads might be overly bready, they were still the best thing around.

And then Celestine said she had somewhere to go.

Ray glanced at his watch with raised brows. He was one of those folks who'd never made the switch to doing everything on his cellphone. "It's half past eight," he announced. "I thought you were tired."

"Look, I'm glad you care, but I'm also glad you're not my dad. I'm a grown-ass twenty-something, and I've got noteworthy street smarts."

Ray grunted, and Celestine gave him a quick hug. "I'll be quick, pirate. I won't be back super late."

Ray grunted again as Celestine grabbed the shoulder bag she used for spellcasting that hung on a peg by her work desk. Truth be told, she was worried. Terribly worried. That drawing was frightening, and she needed to get some informed advice, fast. Celestine slung the bag across her chest and headed into the night.

Scaling the wrought-iron fence of Bonaventure made Celestine's heart pound in wild anticipation. The spirits sounded like thousands of cicadas; the flitting of souls caught in purgatory were restless, dashing shadows. Always restless. But not dangerous... for the most part.

Celestine, part earth elemental witch, part human, and part-wolf shifter, came alive in the dark. She used her night vision to navigate around graves and mausoleums and swerve around the malevolent spirits, which appeared as reddish rather than blue-tinged shadows. Though they weren't specifically after her, they could stick to her clothes and hair in their frustration and anger if she didn't steer clear.

In fifteen minutes or so, she came to the side-by-side gravestones she was looking for—Lionel and Lonetta. Celestine flung off her sandals, sat, and burrowed her feet in the grass for grounding. Then she opened her spell-casting bag and got to work.

She drew a protective line around herself and the stones and pulled out Nola Jaye's oracle deck. She placed it in front of the twin gravestones with a gift of a single peach, Nola Jaye's favorite fruit. When asking a favor, one should offer a gift, so it was for simple balance and to show respect. Then Celestine performed a slow, silent chant to raise the old fortuneteller's spirit enough to "talk" with her. She had rarely done this, but she needed direction.

She closed her eyes and was listening to the crickets sing when she felt a gentle tap on her shoulder. "Nola Jaye, is that you?"

A shiver of cold air swept by her cheeks and settled in front of her, chilling her bare toes.

"I need to ask you: What do I do with the omens? My art? What if they're right? I'm worried about Ray. How long should I watch out for him, for bad signs? And what if the drawing is all wrong? How will I know the difference? Am I wasting my time trying to get better with automatic drawing?"

An unseen hand nudged the peach, and it rolled off to Celestine's left. "What do I make of that?" she asked petulantly. This communicating with the dead thing was not her forte. She needed a ghost tracker or realm jumper for that.

A card from the oracle deck began to show a corner of itself, as if an invisible hand was pulling it out. It wobbled in the air just long enough for Celestine to see it. The Magician. Then another began to separate from the deck and rise. The Wheel of Fortune. The ones she had pulled since childhood. Both fell into her lap.

"Okay, I guess that means I'm to proceed. But, Nola

Jaye, when will the images make sense? How long should I worry about Ray? Who is the mermaid? Is she a literal mermaid or just a symbol? How can I be sure I'm interpreting any of it properly?"

A few fireflies blinked out of the inky dark. Then a horde of fireflies swarmed around Celestine, seemingly out of nowhere. Lights strobed on, off, and on in a tumultuous lightshow.

*In due time, you will see*, came a voice inside her head. *Stay alert. A persuasive male supernatural. A frightened woman. A dangerous mission.*

And then, as quickly as the fireflies had swarmed, they dissipated. The voice left her head. Once again, the crickets chirped from all corners of Bonaventure. Only one more thing happened before Celestine packed up her spellcasting tools. A crunch and a slurping arose from the grass, and when she looked down, she saw three bites taken from the peach before it rolled off into the dark.

As she left the cemetery, she felt an unsettled entity with water magic follow her. But when she spun around to see if anyone was there, the path was clear.

TURNING the corner onto Bay Street, Celestine had a heavy pit in her stomach. The blinking lights were no longer those of gentle fireflies. More like blaring red lights on emergency vehicles lined up in front of her building. EMTs were loading someone into an ambulance, but the sheet was pulled all the way over the person's head. A crowd had formed, and she recognized her neighbors. They looked over at her with shocked eyes. She ran the rest of the way, already sensing the ending awaiting her.

"Ray!" she screamed. "Ray!"

The EMT guy turned and asked if she was a relative of Ray Bartello's.

"What happened?" she yelled, tears already streaming down her face. "I'm Ray's housemate. I work with him in his leather store."

"I'm afraid he passed about forty minutes ago. He was in the side alley. Could be from the shock of, um... losing his eyes. We'll run some tests if you authorize—"

"Oh. My. God, what? His eyes? Where the hell are they? Did anyone see what happened?" The bystanders murmured and shook their heads. "Did you try CPR on him? Did you try those electrical zappers on him? Did you try everything?" she heard herself scream.

"Ma'am. We did all of that. It was too late."

*It happened as soon as I left the house. Dammit! I should have stayed in. If only I'd taken my drawing more seriously, I could have protected him.*

"He was a complete flatliner by the time they got here," some guy in a red T-shirt said. "I saw his boots sticking out of the weeds and called 9-1-1."

"I'm sorry." The EMT guy wore a sympathetic frown. "Would you like to ride along?" he asked Celestine.

"To where exactly?"

"To the morgue," he murmured. "You have ID?"

# THREE

After Celestine went to the morgue to sign the death certificate, she returned to the house and stayed in bed for two days, alternately crying and staring at the ceiling, except when she trudged to the bathroom or choked down oatmeal and tea in the kitchen.

The team of doctors had no clue as to what had happened to Ray. The gouging was oddly clean, with no notable knife (or spoon!) marks. The autopsy revealed no poisons, no stab wounds, no heart attack, or other discernible reason for his death. The eye-gouging was quite serious, though it wouldn't necessarily have led to a death from blood loss or shock in the amount of time he was prone in the alley, bleeding out. The forensic and medical team promised Celestine they'd continue to work on an answer.

In the meantime, her intuition told her this was not a robbery gone bad, though they found no wallet on him, and that it was more than a random violent attack. Ray was big, burly, outspoken, and he carried a shiv in his boots—not the type to be picked on. They had found his knife still in his boot, so whatever happened, it had happened fast, with no time for him to reach for the thing and protect himself.

The third day rolled around. Illustration class day. Celestine doubted she could handle it. Not yet. It was bad enough that the press still milled around Bay Street, waiting to interview her. Peeking out her window, she saw their cameras set up outside. Heard the chatter of reporters. God, how long would they camp out there? Someone had leaked the story about her prophetic drawing, because there was mention of it in the Savannah papers from "an anonymous source." Was it the teacher or that nosy blond-haired guy who sat behind her? If so, he would get an earful as soon as she could summon the nerve to go back. At least she had the drawing in her possession.

That afternoon, instead of going to class, she finally ventured into Ray's office, a room she had never seen. A Post-it note was stuck atop a stack of official papers on his desk with her name scrawled on it in red marker. A wave of intense sadness mixed with intense curiosity rushed over her as she sat in Ray's swivel chair and read through the first of the stapled papers.

*Last Will and Testament of Ray Bartello*

*I will my building on East Bay Street to Celestine LeBlanc.*

*I will my leather store and all the leather tools and goods to Celestine LeBlanc.*

*I will $50,000 dollars to the Save Savannah's Coastal Waters nonprofit group.*

*I will the medallion chain in my desk to my first mate, Peter Leger.*

*I will my pirate books to my second mate, Harwood Port.*

*I will my remaining estate, valued at 1 million dollars, to Celestine LeBlanc.*

Celestine drew in a long, shocked gasp and held it. Was

this really happening? Why her? Especially after she'd drawn that horrid image of him sprawled out, eyeless. She shuffled through the rest of his papers, exhaling an agonized sigh as she did.

He had left her the deed to the building and a handwritten directive to cremate him and scatter his ashes on the Savannah shoreline, off Jekyll Island. Another Post-it note requested that she read the contents of a sealed envelope for more information and then burn everything except for the will.

"First and second mate?" she muttered. "Was Ray a sailor? Was he a pirate for real? Maybe he wasn't joking."

Underneath the pile was a sealed 7x9-inch padded envelope with a simple cl on it, as Ray had mentioned in his handwritten note. She held the thing in her hand and strained to feel Ray's energy. Was this the last thing he'd done before his demise, or had he been planning it for a while? His life-force pinged off the paper, and something else—fear. So his determined action was recent, but there was no way of knowing whether it was the last one he took. Her senses weren't that attuned in daylight hours. Especially before four p.m. Her innate powers seeped out at dusk and flowed freely after dark.

A dreadful idea occurred to her. Ray could have ordered his own killing. Was that why he had all of this neatly stacked on his desk? Or did he know someone was after him? The memory of his spooked reaction to her picking up the boat carving when she'd first arrived floated in. But that had been almost a year ago. How could he possibly have known when he would pass away? Had he scrambled to put all of this together the minute she left for Bonaventure? Weeks or months before this? All were upsetting possibilities that couldn't be ruled out, though what possible reason would Ray have to fund his own assassination or have people hunt him down?

"No negative assumptions," she mumbled to herself. "Things are bad enough as is."

She got up and slid the bolt lock on Ray's office door before sitting back down and carefully running a stationery knife across the top of the packet. She drew out its contents. More papers.

A picture of a ship in a bottle and a key slid out with the last shake. And a longer note in Ray's back-leaning scrawl.

*You want to open an enchanted art gallery. Here's the means. You're like a daughter to me. I always wanted to protect you. In doing so, I held things back. There's not much time. If you're reading this, I'm probably not alive. You may be in danger as well. After I saw your foretelling drawing, I knew that my world, the one I kept separate from you, and your world are meshing. You see, I'm a pirate mage. It wasn't a joke. I have supernatural powers, and I've fought hard-won battles against formidable enemies, unseen to the mundane world. One clan of these enemies are dangerous water mages. I sense they may be back. The Devil only knows what they want this time. Find Peter and Harwood. They will tell you more.*

*Stay safe. I put up wards to protect this place, but you may need to strengthen them.*

*Love, Ray*

HER HEART PINCHED. *Ray knew. He knew his time was up. He tried to protect me by hiding things.*

No note regarding the key or the picture of the ship in glass. *Oh no. He probably ran out of time.*

She pulled open his desk drawer and pawed around. Pens and lozenges to calm the gravelly voice she'd never hear again, she thought with another intense rush of sorrow. She reached farther into its low confines and pulled out more. A silver dagger. She reached to the back of the drawer, swished her hand from left to right, grabbed onto a chain, and pulled it out. A man's heavy necklace with a round medallion on it. A picture of an island in a distinct comma shape sat in its middle. She flicked the clasp and felt like a voyeur as she unfolded the paper within and tried to read its faint notations.

*We will save the J... clan from...* What looked like a faded splotch of blood followed. She carefully folded the note and snapped it back into the medallion. It wasn't meant for her. It was meant for Pete Leger. She needed to move the packet and the medallion to a safe hiding place. Who knew if detectives would come knocking to inspect his house? Or worse. Much worse. She shuddered as she carefully placed the packet in an outside pouch and the medallion in a hidden pouch in her crossbody bag. Before she went in for questioning tomorrow, she needed to look through Ray's place for clues, for precious objects, for things she couldn't yet name.

She'd been in his living room and kitchen but not his bedroom, and she had never taken a close look at his shelves. A lingering sense of formality made her hesitate, though he'd given her permission in the notes left behind.

She stepped into his kitchen. He'd been surprisingly tidy for a single dude. His coffee mugs, pans, and utensils hung in a line over his counter. His sink was free of dishes save for an empty glass mug and a thick china mug, still half full of cooled black coffee. Celestine's eyes pricked with tears. She blinked them away. Ray's very last cup of joe. Very last gulp of ale. She pushed on.

In the living room, wicker chairs with fleece blankets

tossed over their backs sat around a round wooden spindle table festooned with a cotton tablecloth and a sculpture of two gulls. His windows were covered with navy curtains. She drew one aside and looked onto the alleyway below where his body was found. More tears welled up, and she let them roll down her cheeks.

After pulling the curtains back in place, she moved into his bedroom. His denim slippers sat by a wide red leather recliner. A pair of his reading glasses too. The bed was neatly made, and the walls were lined with paintings of whales, brackish reefs, giant turtles, and ships. She muttered to herself, to Ray, "Was one of those ships yours?"

The air, in a gentle sway, seemed to reply *yes.*

She peered closer. A tugboat, a sailboat, a large wooden craft with olive-green sails, and that same comma-shaped island on one of them. "What is it?" she spoke into the silence. "What does it represent?" This time, no answer.

She moved to the bookshelf. Books on philosophy, barrier reefs, the cuisine of Georgia, on famous ghosts and ghost tours. Her neck prickled. She was getting warm, as the kids used to say during games of hide-and-seek. Hot now...

She reached entire shelf of pirate books. That many required something bigger than her crossbody bag. She took the canvas carrier he carried firewood in and emptied the logs on the hearth. Then brushed it clean of splinters and carefully stacked the books. She studied the rest of the bookshelf. Lots of great reads, but nothing else stuck out as crucial to solving the mystery surrounding his demise.

She looked higher to see if there were any ship models that might fit his picture. None. She flung her bag around her shoulders, grabbed the heavy canvas carrier, struggled upstairs to her room, and dumped the items on her bed.

Finally, she ventured down to his moldy, dank basement. She flicked on her smartphone's flashlight and kept searching for clues. This was where his Inner Tidy ended and his Outer Slob began. A clothesline was set up with two crusty, mildewed towels on it. She sneezed, stirring up dust. Mildewed boxes lined the floor, sagging from water damage and age.

Eureka! One spiderwebbed ship in a bottle sat forlornly on the concrete next to the last broken-down cardboard box. Two spiders skittered about, frantic under the harsh light beam. She gave them a fighting chance to escape before swiping away the glittering web, picking up the bottle, and trudging up the stairs.

In her room, she hid the bottle with the model boat and the padded envelope in her dirty laundry hamper and the pirate books in her trashcan, under crumpled tissues and a banana peel. Not the greatest hiding places, but not the worst. When she had time, she'd find a better spot for them.

She silently promised Ray that she'd keep looking, though she was suddenly overwhelmed by the weight of the tragedy and desperate to get outside, to forget about stuff, even for an hour. To grab a drink or two, to eat a crappy fried meal. She slipped out of Ray's building—*Gah!* It was hers now—through the fire escape in the back. Beyond the prying eyes of the journalists out front. The sun had set, so her earth wolf powers burst out like extended claws—her night vision, her nimble gait, her unerring sense of direction. She shifted to her wolf. This way she could be inhumanly fast.

It led her through backyards and alleys, through shadowy lanes where tourists didn't travel, and to Magic Hands, one of very few massage parlors that was actually on the level and *not* a so-called happy ending joint. Yes, there were those kinds down here, even for women. What she needed even more than a stiff cocktail was some human touch, however distant the stranger.

She shifted back to human form in the dark alley and then slipped through a narrow door covered in painted graffiti hands. She greeted the proprietor, who wore crimson lipstick and a shell necklace. "Would you prefer a soft or harder touch?" asked the woman.

"Hard. My back is sore from moving stuff," she answered.

"Ooh, I've been there," the woman said sympathetically as she took Celestine's cash and gave her change. "Male or female practitioner?"

"Male," Celestine decided. "I like a guy that can sometimes relax me without sex."

The woman snickered. "I hear you. Oryn is in room number two when you're ready. Just lie down on the massage table and he'll be in soon."

Celestine knew her way to the sauna and changing room. She hung her clothes in a locker and slid into a terrycloth robe. In the darkened massage room, she wasted no time removing the robe and lying belly down on the sheeted table. Between the soft spa music and the warm linen over her aching, exhausted body, she was already half dozing when the masseur entered. She didn't bother turning around to see him, even though she hadn't had a guy named Oryn before. She would get a glimpse when he had her flip over at halftime. She'd been coming here for six months. This place had stellar, trustworthy workers who even wore masks in an extra nod to sanitary protocol.

"Lavender or unscented oil?" a tenor voice inquired, gentle and smooth, like amber.

"Lavender," she murmured.

His capable hands spread the warmed oil over her back and got to work, kneading her shoulder blades and running along each side of her spine. His touch was almost too firm, on the verge of pain, but the kind of muscle pummel that released the cortisone trapped there. Tomorrow would feel like a sweet release of cramped terror, sadness, dread.

"So, how long have you been working at Magic Hands?" she asked.

"Oh, three or four weeks."

"I'm surprised I haven't had you before. I come here almost every week."

"First time for everything. I hope it's a good experience," he said. With another splotch of warm oil, he moved on to her right leg.

"Have you worked in this field for a while?"

"I was trained by a professional, but, um, this is a side gig. One that I like," he added.

"What do you like about it?" she asked, a part of her worrying that her questions were getting too personal.

"I like helping folks free up their meridians, their chakras, or whatever you choose to call it. I believe the free movement of energy fields is essential to cognitive and, well, intuitive health."

He really had magic hands on top of his magic voice. Celestine's limbs were melting into buttery ooze, her head a frizz of soda bubbles. Her spirits were rising. Or was it the hypnotic spa music? Or the New Age-y chimes and digital birdcall that, if she were in another sort of mood, she would find irritating as hell. She chuckled.

"What's so funny? If you don't mind me asking," he said under his breath as he ran his firm hands up and down her thigh. That gave her ripples of floaty calm.

24

"Just how relaxing or irritating spa music can be, depending on one's mood."

He chuckled in response.

"You said this was a side gig," she added. "What's your main, uh, passion?"

"I like to draw. Always trying to improve my skills."

She stiffened, then felt a subtle breeze of air magic through his fingertips, most likely in reaction. Then it dissipated, and he continued with his firm run along her left calf, down to her ankles and back. Upgrading his drawing skills? That had to be coincidental. *Calm down, girl.*

"What do you do?" he asked her.

Good question. What *did* she do? Sketch dire predictions. Cut her pricey art classes. Feel guilty about it. "I've been painting designs on leather pieces. Freelance work," she answered finally.

"That's cool. So you're an artist?"

*Hmm, he wouldn't ask this if he'd been in that art class.* "Yeah, though I haven't liked some of my recent art."

"Why not?" He was kneading the nape of her neck now, freeing up energy she forgot she had.

"It's scaring me," she admitted. "It's very dark. It makes me not want to continue."

He pressed a certain place on her neck and uncorked another trapped pocket of fear and rage. His fingers paused there as it flew out and out. "Art sees everything," he said cryptically. "What are the images, exactly?"

"Of someone I cared about who subsequently died. The disturbing imagery got leaked to the press," she said sharply. She didn't know this guy from Adam. One could talk to strangers in ways one could never speak to friends, to lovers. "I hate that. I feel betrayed."

"How awful. Why would someone do that?" he asked as

he threaded his fingers though her hair and massaged her scalp. The sensation made her giddy.

Funny how the massage had put her to sleep at first but was now waking her up. Rousing her emotions, releasing the civil boundaries of dialogue. And this guy's vibe was tinted with airy energy, scented with woodsy moss. "Who knows why the dude leaked the story? For money? Attention? Maybe he's just an A-hole! I'm going to find out."

"Why assume it's a man?" he asked with a hint of annoyance.

"I have my reasons."

The masseur lifted his hands from her scalp. "Go ahead and turn over when you're ready so I can do the last part of your massage."

She complied, careful not to make the sheet on her ass twist and fall to the floor.

Settled on her back, she adjusted the sheet to rest just above her boobs. She glanced up at him—lanky yet coordinated, with an oversized cotton cap that made it impossible to see his hair. The room was dimly lit, and the guy wore a safety mask as well. There was something terribly familiar about him she couldn't quite place.

"Full disclosure," he said, "I should tell you that I think I kn—"

She bolted upright, clutching the sheet to her chest. "You! *You* sold my story to the press. You're that guy from illustration class who grilled me, aren't you? How dare you!"

"I was about to tell you I *am* the guy you spoke to in class once I realized who you were, but I wasn't sure how without interrupting the massage."

"You should've. I resent that you let me go on without letting me know."

"Sorry not to." His eyes looked sad, chastened as they gleamed from the shadows. "But I wasn't the person who leaked the story about your drawing. I would never do such a disgusting thing." He sounded genuinely pained.

"Why should I believe you? Prove it!"

"Not sure how to prove it other than to help you find the guilty party."

"Don't bother! Only that old teacher saw my drawing, so it was either you or him."

"Wrong. It wasn't Professor Gray. He's not out for attention. He protects his students. I've taken a few classes with him, and he's a good guy. Lots of people in the class saw the drawing. Besides, word spread beyond that class like wildfire after, um... your friend's death."

"See! You *do* know what happened."

"It went viral. How could I not? You cut class today, so you didn't know that your classmates were talking about it, trying to make sense of it. I have no control over that." He sighed, and in a softer voice, said, "Shall we continue the massage?"

"Hell no!" She stared at his liquid green eyes and searched for deceit. All she felt was mostly contained air magic, the escaping strands wafting her way like clouds. "What did you mean in the class when you said that I *see*? What do you know about seers?"

He glanced around as if there were predators even in this sanctuary with soothing spa music and sweet sage incense. "I protect the seers," he whispered.

"Huh? Who the hell are you anyway?" Celestine heard the nasty, accusing edge in her voice and didn't care. "I sense your air magic. What are you, and what is your real profession? Who the hell do you work for?"

He sighed and removed his cap, letting his gorgeous

blond hair fall wildly around his angular jaw. He removed his face mask as well and breathed out a sigh. "I'm a fae, so yes, I have air magic. If you want to know more, I'll tell you. You're my last customer for the night so, um..." He nodded to her hands, still clutching the sheet to her breasts. "Shall we go get a drink so we can talk in private? You'll want to step into something more comfortable than a flimsy sheet."

She let out a low guff of laughter despite her anger. "Yeah, but no funny business, fae. Because my wolf will bite your fae into shreds. Got it?"

He snickered. "Got it, wolf seer." She couldn't help but notice his sexy dimples and how his eyes narrowed to pleasing half-moon shapes when he smiled. He snuffed out the sage incense, poured her a glass of water filled with cucumber slices, and left it on the shelf by her towel. "Take your time. Is the Seahorse good?"

It was a bar two blocks away that fringe supes and young folk liked. She nodded.

"I'll meet you outside, then, down the block to the left. Best to keep a little distance between my work and my off hours."

She nodded again, and he padded out.

She lay back down on the table, breathing deeply to regain a touch of the Zen state he'd put her in with his large, sensitive hands just fifteen minutes ago. Evergreen eyes, dimples, air magic, someone who protected seers. Oh my. No matter what happened later, this was an effective distraction from her despair over Ray.

CHAPTER

# FOUR

T he masseur named Oryn cleaned up well. She studied him as he walked her way. Tight black T-shirt with a botanical illustration of a hellebore on it, moss-green shorts, this time with a black leather belt that featured a roaring dragon head buckle. Under the streetlights, his nose piercing and Roman-style copper bracelet gleamed. His green rucksack was slung over a shoulder, and he wore low-rise boots.

She wouldn't let on, but she liked how his gaze slid from checking out her breasts in her purple halter to her tight black jeans hugging her slinky hips, and up again to her hair, twisted and held with glittering combs. She was mourning Ray, her face still puffy from crying, but she was glad she never went out in public without some lipstick and a decent outfit on.

They strode in. The place was decorated with seahorses —wooden hand-painted ones; glittery ones on strings; slick, laminated images on metal. They chose seats in the corner booth, away from the chattering bar scene.

"I'm Oryn," the fae said. "Oryn Forest. We were never properly introduced." He extended his hand, but she held back.

"I'm Celestine LeBlanc. I appreciate you trying to explain things, but we're not best buddies yet. That remains to be seen."

He retracted his hand. "Fair enough. I won't take it personally."

"So, how exactly do you protect seers? Who do you deem a seer?"

Almost in answer to her question, an enthusiastic twenty-something guy with tanned skin and curly black hair bounded up to their booth. "Oryn! Good to see you here." They bumped fists.

Celestine felt the kid's rangy wolf essence right away. After all, she was part wolf herself.

"Thanks for finding my brother and me a place to crash," he said to Oryn. "Man, those urges to shift on top of being on the street were making me crazy. I need to figure out how to contain it all. Go to job interviews."

"No problem," Oryn replied. "Let me know how the therapy appointment goes."

"Sure. See you around." The guy glanced at Celestine and then back to Oryn. "Sorry to interrupt your conversation." And then he bounced away.

The waitress came over for drink orders. Celestine hesitated while Oryn ordered a margarita with lemons and blueberries. "That sounds good. I'll try one, too," she said.

Oryn had a lopsided grin on his dimpled face.

"Okay, okay," Celestine said, "I guess I got at least part of my answer about protecting supes. Do you also work at a clinic?"

"No, mainly on the street, around the neighborhood. Some of them live under a tunnel near here. I do stuff like finding them food bank sources, medical help."

"I'm sort of an advocate myself," she admitted.

"Oh? How so?"

Celestine shrugged, weighing in her mind whether to tell Oryn about how old Nola Jaye was taunted before her death for her eccentric dress and card readings. "I knew someone who was bullied in my town. Hell, I was bullied there. I developed a second sense about who would be vulnerable, who needed a helping hand. It's part of why I liked Ray. He had a soft spot for fringe types. Sometimes he gave away his leather pouches, his leather key chains. Sometimes I went with him on giveaway walks around the squares and helped. It felt good. Like we were spreading happiness, if only for an afternoon."

They paused their conversation when the waitress came to set their drinks down. Celestine fished for her wallet and felt the medallion from Ray's drawer in her bag's hidden pouch. She paid for the drink and waited until the woman walked away to pull out the heavy necklace. This would be a test for Oryn. See how he reacted. If he seemed too interested in the object itself, it would prove that he was out to exploit the situation.

"Any idea what this island is?"

Oryn studied the laminated image on the medallion's surface for a moment, then said, "Jekyll Island. It has a comma shape. Why? Whose is this?"

"Ray's," she replied, and slipped it back into the zippered stash section.

"Oh. I'm sorry your friend passed," said Oryn. "You must want to find out what really happened. From the news, it sounds like the cops have no leads yet. Can you keep doing your drawings? Maybe they'll render another clue."

So he was more interested in her, in suggesting ways for her to solve this mystery. She liked that and felt safe enough to go on. "Yeah, I hope to do more drawings, but I don't always know what they mean. How to read them. Do you have any idea why someone would want to..." She grimaced. "... cut out an eye? I haven't lived in Savannah for long. Maybe you've heard stories? Lore?"

Oryn chewed on the lemon slice in his margarita and swallowed the rind whole. Surprisingly, he didn't wince. Was the guy composed of an acidic citrus essence? Somehow, it fit with her picture of a fae, whooshing about the forest and tidal plains at night. "Eyes," he mused. "Eyes are special vehicles to the soul. Maybe some lunatic thought he could see someone's soul in them, through them."

"But why *Ray's* eyes?"

"Did Ray have a secret life? Or was he just a leathersmith?" asked Oryn.

She thought about him saying he was a pirate mage. That he ferried a ship, and the note about his first and second mate. But was she ready to trust Oryn that much? "He used to joke about being a pirate. Are there still pirates around Savannah?"

"Sure, descendants of the various clans. Do they still sail the high seas? Doubtful."

"What are the names of some clans, mundane or supe?"

"I'm no expert. I moved here about ten years ago, and pirates aren't my specialty, but, uh... Blackbeard's? Long John Silver's? I could find out."

She sniffed. Oryn seemed like a decent guy; he probably

wasn't the leaker after all. Though it was one thing to ask him questions and another thing entirely to enlist his sleuthing services. "I can do research myself."

He shrugged. "I hope you come back to class. Finish out the last couple days."

"Not sure I want to, what with the leaks, the publicity."

At that moment, two people burst into the bar. Celestine immediately recognized them. To her consternation, they made a beeline for the booth. "Hey, Oryn! How's it going?" asked the classmate in pajamas with purple braids. Tonight, she had on SpongeBob SquarePants cropped PJs with a chunky pink necklace. Celestine almost laughed out loud at the ensemble but decided it was strangely cool.

"Hi, Aline. Hey, Riley," Oryn greeted the woman and the guy with the crown tattoo around his neck. "Remember Celestine?"

"Of course!" Aline smiled at her. "Sorry for your loss. Was he your uncle or...?"

"No. I was just rooming in his house. Who in our class ratted me out?" snapped Celestine. "Do you know who told the press about my drawing? Was it one of you? Because if it was, we can't—"

"Whoa, whoa." Aline raised a hand, palm out. "The cops were all over the school after your person was found. They wanted info. I don't know how they knew you were in that class, but cops find out stuff fast." Riley nodded and Aline went on. "Anyway, Prof Gray told us not to talk. Plus, well, *shit*, we're artists. We don't blab about our own with, like, outsiders."

"Totally bad form," Riley agreed.

Oryn looked over at Celestine. "Maybe it's best to move on. To trust the art students, the teachers. You tell me you're an advocate for those on the fringe. As they say, we protect our own art tribe. Besides, your drawings are important, special. Now that we know someone leaked the story, we can protect you and your drawings more fiercely."

Celestine wasn't expecting this. She was flattered, touched. Oryn had called her art special. Maybe she *should* give the class one more chance. After all, she hated to waste money. "I do need to improve my hands-on skills."

"We missed you in class today," said Riley. "There's only two more classes. Next week we're learning tips on opaque gouache. Should be good."

"Such a great medium! It's watercolor, but you can endlessly paint over your mistakes," chirped Aline. "Want to see my supply?"

"Sure," said Celestine.

" I made this carrier myself." Aline pulled a roll of canvas from her messenger bag, untied its twine ribbon, and unrolled it. Rows of little pockets lined the thing, and in each one was a mini tube of color.

"Impressive," said Celestine, glad that her classmate was feisty and resistant to criticism. She had come down on Aline hard. "If I feel okay next week, I'll go back to class. This experience has been so traumatizing."

"We hope you do," said Riley. "We'll keep your drawings low-key."

"I give you my word, too," said Oryn.

"Me three," said Aline.

"Thanks. Hey, I'm really tired, going to head back," Celestine decided.

"Want me to walk with you?" Oryn asked. "I mean, after all of the menacing activity..."

"Thanks for the offer, but no." She appreciated their

attempts, but she needed to go slowly, to build trust organically. She gave Oryn a stern Don't Ask Again smile.

And then she walked out.

⁓

CELESTINE HAD a sense that something was amiss when she turned the corner to Bay Street. The same old tourists were lined up for nighttime carriage rides and the infamous Ghost Tours. But there was a creepy vibe, as if she was being followed. She whirled around more than once, but no one was there. She shook off the worry, walked up the concrete stairs, and began heading down the walkway to Ray's—*no, my place now*—when she heard and then saw a torrent of water coming at her along the sidewalk. Thoroughly startled, she skidded and, as water gushed higher around her, her legs gave way. She fell hard on her left hip. Her spellcasting bag went flying.

"Ugh!" she exclaimed as the wind was knocked out of her. She groped around to see how deep the water was and realized that it was dry.

Bone dry.

"Water magic," she grumbled, reaching for her splayed-out bag. "Who the hell are you?" She struggled up, rubbed her sore hip, and brushed off dirt. "Show yourself, asshole!" she shouted. "You coming for my goddam eyes now? I dare you!"

A couple on the street looked up in alarm. She ignored them. She fumbled in her bag for her door keys and had to try twice before it unlocked because her hand was shaking so much.

Inside, she collapsed in a heap on Ray's old couch in his office until her breathing calmed. And then she came up with a rather unorthodox plan. She went up to her room, collected the drawings and watercolors she had done that hadn't been sold, and brought them down. Then she pulled out the tools she needed from Ray's drawer in the storefront leather studio. She went around this studio and behind it, to Ray's office, and hammered nails on each wall.

Then she fetched her spellcasting bag, arranged the art in a small circle in Ray's office, each one propped up by a chair or cushion. She drew a protective boundary with chalk, sat on the floor surrounded by her art, and got to work.

She lit some sage and whooshed it around the art in a slow circle as she chanted a spell for protection and to weaken a water curse.

"Dry, parched, everything parched," she whispered. "Let all that is not dry who enters this place without permission become waterless as a husk, and let their magic weaken. Let them blow away and disintegrate like tumbleweeds." She chanted a few lines in Latin, using a personal charm to protect Ray's spirit and his important icons. "Guide my hand in art to reveal the clues, oh good spirit of wisdom and heart."

She heard liquid thundering that sounded like a waterfall being sucked right back to its source. The very air became a water vacuum. She had to grab onto the rug to stay in the circle because the force of the reverse waterfall, curling and drying, was mighty.

She sensed things in this house, slippery, undulating entities that wished her ill, being sucked away, too. It was a blessing that they had revealed their hostile presence in an actual water mirage on that sidewalk. It unnerved her that she and Ray had been in danger not just outside, but here in these very rooms.

When the air felt clear, she infused each painting with a charm. To ward off water magic, to alert her of its presence, to radiate protection.

She stood and rubbed her sore hip, then hung the artwork—a seagull in a salt marsh, a rendering of the Wheel of Fortune card, a beautiful spreading tree in one of the historical squares, a view of the gibbous moon between graves in Bonaventure, a portrait of Nola Jaye, and another one of Ray—on the various nails, so that each wall had an energized ward to guard her house.

*My house! My sanctuary. My magic art studio and head-quarters to solve the murder of my friend Ray.*

The paintings were alive. They hummed inside her head.

She reclined on Ray's soft couch and went into a trance, conjuring up energy for one last task before bed.

When she was literally vibrating, she rose, grabbed her drawing pad, and settled at Ray's desk. This would be her special drawing table. It still shimmered with Ray's sunny vibes, echoes of his gruff laughter. So this desk was its own protective ward. She picked up the graphite pencil and let her hand wander over the vellum of its own accord.

Her hand set a tempo and continued it even when she closed her eyes at certain points. It was a very strange experience to both be master of her drawing and, well, a devoted follower.

When her hand stopped moving and she opened her eyes, she was horrified. She had drawn not just one or two eyes, but a whole polluted sea of them. An obsessive three quarters of a page of them were connected by a gooey liquid, one eye blobbing into the next.

"Damn watery eyes!" she exclaimed. "I blocked the intruders with their foul water magic, but the mess came out in my own effing drawing!" And then, when she looked lower on the page, an even stronger horror and revulsion twisted her gut.

She had drawn a bed of lopped-off fingers, a nest of effing *fingers*. She threw the graphite pencil on the desk, grabbed her crossbody bag, and went up to her room and shut and locked the door. Put on her pajamas. Brushed her teeth. Tomorrow she had an appointment down at the Savannah police precinct to go over Ray's case. She wasn't sure how much to tell them. She thought of what Aline said earlier. *We don't blab about our own with like, outsiders.*

Celestine checked her wastebasket. The pirate books were still under the crumpled trash. She checked her dirty laundry hamper and was relieved to see the envelope and the ship in a bottle in there. Then she checked the zippered pocket in her messenger bag. The medallion was gone!

"What the fuck!" she hissed as she ran her hand over every corner of the bag. Gone. When she fell in the water mirage, her bag had been thrown off her shoulders. Holy crap! The water entity must have stolen it then. Why? What was the big deal about that medallion? Oryn had said it was an image of Jekyll Island. What would they want with a medallion of Jekyll Island? Were these nasty water sprites the same ones who killed Ray? She had felt a watery entity stalking her when she left Bonaventure to speak to Nola Jaye the other night. It had probably followed her home and been tracking her ever since. But why was it after her?

She got in bed, pulled up the covers, reached for her phone, and scrolled to the news. Her gut dropped when she read the lead story all over her feed:

*The body of a man believed to be that of sixty-seven-year-old recluse Peter Leger was found on Jekyll Island with his fingers cut off. The man was apparently the last descendant of the Legers, an old pirate family, not uncommon on the island. Neighbors say he had left his house in the tidal marshes for a number of years, before suddenly returning just a few months ago. Any information regarding Peter Leger is appreciated.*

With a sense of dread in her stomach, she clicked off the bedside light and shivered until she fell into a fitful sleep.

CHAPTER

# FIVE

"Are you related to the deceased Ray Bartello?" asked the detective, studying Celestine through bifocals that rounded and enlarged his eyes to great-horned-owl size.

"No."

"How did you know him?"

"He was an old friend of my father's."

The detective nodded and jotted down notes in his old-school yellow-lined pad. "So you were renting a room from him?"

"Yes. Well, he gave me free rent."

The detective raised his brows. "For...?"

"Because we were like family to him and him, to us." She tried her best to hide the irritation in her voice. "He was a nice guy. I also did work for him in his leather shop."

"In return for the room and board."

"No. He paid me for my freelance work. He knew that I was trying to be an artist."

"I understand you were enrolled in a four-class illustration thing at SCAD."

"Yeah." Going down the artist track could open a big can of worms about the automatic drawing. About mundanes' suspicion of supes. *It'll seem like I'm lying.* She should stick with one-word answers if she could.

"The news reported that you drew a picture of Mr. Bartello sprawled on the ground, eyeless, shortly *before* his untimely death. Is this true?" His owlish stare intensified.

"I guess so," she mumbled, glancing around at the desks piled high with papers and files. Two officers were working, obviously eavesdropping but trying not to stare. She didn't understand why this detective dude didn't take her to a private room to interrogate her. Maybe he wanted witnesses.

"You guess so?" He sounded incredulous. "How on earth did you know Mr. Bartello was going to be attacked?"

"I didn't, sir. I had no clue. The drawing was a fluke."

His cynical frown made it obvious he wasn't buying any of it. "You stood to inherit his property. Word is that he had lots of money as well. The leather business—"

"I won't be continuing with the leather business," she cut in. It came out sounding entitled, aggressive. All wrong.

"Do you have any idea why Mr. Bartello would will everything to you? Did he ever discuss this with you?"

"Nope."

"So you already have plans for the space?" the man asked coldly as he leaned forward. "Where were you on the night of his murder?"

She was speechless. He'd knocked the wind out of her. Of course she was under suspicion. Yet the thought of someone thinking she could harm a mouse, much less her beloved Ray, was repellent. But how could she explain what she was doing in a graveyard as he lay dying? It would sound shady as hell. She sighed and gave as true a statement as she could, however brief.

"I was in Bonaventure, paying tribute to another old family friend who passed." *That sounds horrible! As if my psychopathic method is to kill so-called friends and then bring them flowers in the graveyard. Too late to walk this one back.*

He jotted down notes. "Do you have an alibi?"

*Um, Ray's ghost? The murderous water entity that stalked me there and back and then tried to kill me on my own sidewalk.* "Ray, but he's gone." Her voice cracked. She was suddenly observing herself like he must be. Would the detective hear the pain in her voice? It would show that she wasn't a psychopath because she'd read they didn't feel pain. Detectives were trained to be objective, though, to take the emotions out of things, right? She could turn the tables on him, ask *him* some questions. Distract him. She sure had a lot of questions.

"Can I ask you something, sir?"

He took a sip of his stale coffee and nodded. "What's on your mind?"

"Do you have any idea why someone would want to remove his eyes? Have you ever had anyone do this before?"

He sat there, jiggling his pen between his index and middle finger. It took him a minute. Finally, he spoke. "There was a case a few years back. Turned out to be some type of hoodoo ritual." He grimaced. "People believe nutty stuff. Some folks believe the soul is in the eyes." He focused on her with his owl stare. "Do you believe that?"

"No. But yeah, eyes are pretty important. There's mention of them in the Bible and in other sacred texts, right?"

"You got me." They were silent for a moment. "I'm no

scholar, so, um, we have a researcher on it," he said. "Did Mr. Bartello have any enemies?"

Celestine thought of the shadowy water-magic stalkers and Ray's cryptic warning. Nola Jaye's warning also came to mind: *A frightened woman, a dangerous mission*. Was the frightened woman her? Nola Jaye seemed to be referring to someone else. A dangerous mission seemed a frightening inevitability. Yet how could she describe this supernatural stuff to a man who dealt only in data and facts? She didn't quite trust the mundane world, and she knew they were leery of those who dealt in magic. Was there any point of connection? Any reason to share tips? For Ray. Ray's enemies... Were Ray's killers the water mage clan? If so, *why* did they want to do him harm?

"Miss LeBlanc?"

"Oh! Sorry. I'm trying to think."

"Do you know about last night's murder on Jekyll Island?" the man blurted. He had his pen in his hand again, poised to take more notes.

Celestine tensed. "I read about it online. How horrible. Someone cut off a man's fingers! Who would do that? Do you think it's connected to, um... Ray's murder?"

"You tell me." The detective's voice had gone icy again, and he was doing his owl stare. Was this hot-cold-hot-cold switcheroo his method of terrorizing confessions out of folks? Way too obvious a ploy. But those lopped-off fingers. Ugh. She pictured her drawing of eyes and fingers and felt a roll of nausea. *Deep breaths. Keep it together.*

"Who was Peter Leger?" she ventured. "In the news, they said he was a recluse and descended from a pirate family on Jekyll Island." It was her turn to stare down the detective.

"Leger was a longtime resident of the island. He lived by

the salt marshes. Kept to himself, the neighbors said. We interviewed an old woman out there. Not so friendly. She did say he went missing for decades. Perhaps simply underground or incognito. We're looking further into it. Why do you ask?"

This might be the one thing Celestine would reveal. If it could help Ray. If it could shine any light on the case. This leap was terrifying, like jumping over a slavering shark pit and being unsure she'd make it to the other side. "Ray knew Peter Leger," she said. "Ray told me he'd been out of touch. He said that Peter had been his first mate. I had no idea Ray was a sailor, a captain of a boat. But anyway, Ray willed him a certain medallion. I suppose he wanted me to find Peter Leger and give it to him."

The detective paused from madly scribbling notes. He looked up at Celestine. "Did you? Did you go to Jekyll Island last night? Did you meet up with Peter Leger?"

She glared at the detective. "How dare you insinuate I had anything to do with his fingers being violently removed, with his murder, with any of it! It's sickening. I never had the chance to find Leger or give him the necklace because someone stole it from me last night, out of my shoulder bag. Look, I'm telling you this to help you solve the case. That's all!"

"I'm doing my job," he replied flatly. "I appreciate the information."

She tried to calm her fury at his random accusations. He was only fishing for clues, as she was. "I thought pirates were a thing of the past. Are they?"

The detective shrugged. "As far as I know. I mean, yeah, you don't see black-sailed ships prowling around and ransacking vessels. Unless it's for a film or a tourist event." He snickered. "Why do you ask?"

"I just wonder if Peter Leger's death had anything to do with his ancestry. I mean, they did make mention of it on the news, after all."

"Pirates? Who knows? I will look into it. Though I will say we weren't aware that Mr. Bartello did much sailing on any type of vessel."

"Me neither," Celestine admitted.

The man was being more civil, at least for the moment, though she knew he viewed her as a prime suspect. It was a motivator for her to investigate, to find clues that pointed to her innocence. He seemed to respect her interest in sleuthing. He put down the writing pad and stood. "I think we're done for now. Thanks for coming down to answer questions. Let me know if something comes up. And don't leave town. We may need to ask more questions as tips come in and we work on Mr. Bartello's case. Understood?"

She nodded.

"They call me Detective Wade around here."

"I'll try to keep you updated, Detective Wade."

# CHAPTER
# SIX

The trip took an hour and a half, and then a twenty-minute drive over a long causeway to Jekyll Island proper. She parked by the upscale shops in the bustling tourist area to stretch and grab a snack. Her intensive research had told her that this place had come a long way since its origin as the home of the Guale Native Americans before the French explorers arrived in the 1500s. It was officially named Jekyll Island by General Oglethorpe, who founded the Georgia colony in 1733.

The island then became a family-owned hunting club for a good hundred years before its posh transformation in 1886 as the Jekyll Island Club, a holiday resort for million-aires like J.P. Morgan and William Vanderbilt. Celestine had sighed with relief when she read that, in time, some prescient conservationists miraculously saved three quarters of it as a maritime wildlife refuge. She would head to this wild area after breakfast.

She munched on avocado toast while glancing at a couple of store windows. A few moments of peace before the bushwhack.

Hopping back into her car, she drove northward. Sandy beaches gave way to meandering salt marshes that hosted cranes and storks feeding and stretching their wings and wiry legs. She passed longleaf pines in tiny island groupings that someone on the way had called marsh hammocks. She stopped once to admire the driftwood on a random white-sand beach, then headed slightly east, into a long patch of wetland with reddish cypress trees, their ancient, exposed root systems a spooky wonder.

And then, in a mostly undeveloped span of wilderness, she turned left onto a rutted dirt road almost hidden in another thicket of pines. She had gleaned the whereabouts of Leger's last stand from the news, not from Detective Wade, who would be peeved she'd ignored his directive to not skip town. She rationalized this by telling herself that if she learned anything of note here, she would dutifully report back. Though she suspected if there was magic involved, sharing could be problematic.

She was seeking out Leger's few neighbors who knew something about him—maybe the old lady Wade had mentioned or items he may have left sitting around. Leger's cottage was off-limits, no doubt blocked by crime scene tape.

She parked a long way behind the squad cars she spotted through the trees, then pulled on her long mud boots, locked her car, and set out, weighed down slightly by a thermos of water. In her pockets were crystals she'd infused with wards and charms against hostile water magic.

She steered far from the squad cars, so if they had scent hounds, they would be less able to track her at a distance through the twisty ribbons of salt marsh. If she had just been out on any hike and not plagued by Ray's murder, this place, with its fiddler crabs just visible under the shallow parts of water, its judders of tall grasses, the constant dance of spiders and mites and dragonflies, would seem beautiful, not haunted.

After she'd hiked at least a mile without sighting anything, she became agitated with nervous irritation. Why had she wasted time stopping to eat? It was well into the afternoon, and if she lost her way back, she could get trapped in here for days, weeks. No one knew she was there. No one would come looking. Even if she did run into someone, she might startle them, prompting them to shoot her for invading their territory. Detective Wade and the news outlets reported Peter Leger had gone incognito—a whole next level of hermit. Clearly, he had not wanted to be found. Was he in hiding? If so, why? He *had* been found and killed, as she could be. She fingered the crystals in her pockets. So far, it seemed that the water-magic entities had not followed her here.

After another quarter mile, unable to stop her cycling dread, she decided to turn back. It was then that she saw lights up ahead. She picked up her pace, and a cabin came into view, surrounded by spindly pines and tall reeds.

Her heart clattered triple time to her knocks on the door. No answer. Ear to the wood. Someone was in there, puttering around. Or picking up a double-barreled shotgun. She knocked once more. Nothing. Ear to door again, and it swung open.

A woman stared out at her. Her face was a map of weathered lines and a white mop of hair, most of it flying, some strands pulled back into a messy bun. She had maybe a half dozen teeth missing. "Who are you and whatchoo doing at my house?"

"Hi, I'm Celestine. I'm friendly. Don't be scared. I'm not

a reporter. I just have a personal connection to someone who lived out here and, um..."

"Who'd that be?" The woman's eyes were filled with suspicion, and she looked ready to slam the door in Celestine's face.

"Peter Leger." The lady began to close the door, and Celestine held it open with her hand. "Wait! I knew Ray, too. Ray Bartello." The woman opened the door a crack more and looked harder at Celestine with a new curiosity in her milky eyes. "Ray who?"

"Bartello. Did you know him?"

Rather than answer, she gestured for Celestine to come in. "Wipe your boots on the mat there. I don't want no mud on my rugs."

She ushered Celestine into a cramped living room with horsehair cushions on two facing wicker chairs and a wooden table piled with chipped dishes. The woman had plants springing from various pots along the floor under a small window. Looking up, Celestine saw everything under the sun hooked onto ropes, strung around all four walls. Beach chairs, satchels filled with who knew what, an old-fashioned straw broom with a branch for a handle, cooking pots, and dozens of mismatched mugs. Surprisingly, the place smelled fresh, like mineral sea soaps.

It was a wonder that the woman had electricity all the way out here. A black potbellied stove was set out a foot from one wall, a pile of pine logs beside it.

"Sit," said the woman, and offered her tea.

Celestine accepted it, wondering in a dark part of her mind if the woman was going to poison her for trespassing.

"How's old Ray?" asked the woman, hobbling over with her own tea and taking a seat in the facing chair.

Celestine sighed. "He passed recently."

"They take us all in the end," mused the woman, not specifying who "they" were. She gazed at her hands as she wrung them. Then, looking up with a wistful expression, she launched into a memory of Ray. "He was a sweetheart, that Ray, a real looker in his day. Black hair slicked back, muscles all day, smile that could charm the pantaloons off a corpse."

It was an awkward moment, as Ray had only been dead for mere days. "How well did you know Ray?" asked Celestine. "How did you meet him?"

"Oh, Ray and I rolled in the hay a few times, though he was a good twelve or so years younger than me. I think I taught him a few things." The woman giggled like a schoolgirl. "I was a wild gal back in the day." Her laughter faded to a wistful smile. "I met him through Peter. They spent a lot of time out here in the marshes, fishing, drinking, talking about their forays. I never paid their plans much mind, though I do recall Ray talking about his ship and how he sailed it in... what's the word? A *glamour*." She frowned. "I never did learn what a glamour was, other than, say, Audrey Hepburn and Marilyn Monroe and them glamour-puss Hollywood gals."

"I know what glamouring is," Celestine offered. "It's supernaturals hiding in plain sight from regular humans —*mundanes*. They have abilities to conceal activities that are private or only relevant to other supes."

"Supernaturals?" The woman wrinkled her already-lined brow.

"People with magic. There's a whole other world than the surface one you see out there with people shopping in Walmart, tourists on vacation, lounging on the beaches, golfing."

"*Whoo*, ma'am, I try to stay far from them tourists

around here." She snickered and made a tooth-sucking sound. "It gets harder and harder. You'd think everyone and his mother wanna live out here in this marshland. But it ain't like that, no way, no how. They would die out here in one dang night. Snake bites, drowning, you name it."

Celestine took a sip of lukewarm tea. Surprisingly decent—homegrown mint? "So what was Ray's relationship to Peter? How did they know each other?"

"You ask some snoopy questions, gal. You're lucky that this here lady is in a sociable mood." She adjusted the Peter Pan collar of her faded cotton smock. "Name's Irma Mae, by the by."

"Celestine LeBlanc. Pleased to meet you, Irma Mae. So, Pete and Ray..."

"Ah, yep. Ray was a friend to Pete when Pete was in a very bad way out here. Sick, you know? And who was going to take care of folks in this forsaken marshland? No one, 'cept us, that's who! But we came out to be left alone so that's what we got."

"Who is we?" Celestine asked.

"Hermits and lovelorn drunkards and homeless ramblers. Those on the run or shunted by the world. They come here to lick their wounds and be left alone so's no one will hurt them anymore."

"Was someone trying to hurt Peter Leger?"

The woman cocked her head to one side and squinted at Celestine, as if trying to decide, finally, if she was okay or one of the baddies, despite Celestine's proclamation to innocence. Irma Mae must have made a positive determination in Celestine's favor because she went on. "There was a side of them guys I didn't want to know about. Too scary for me. I never asked questions, though I do remember some stuff I heard. Pete said he was done with the war. He was exhausted and broken. His head was all mixed up. He said that now it was won, he could finally rest."

"What war? Was he a veteran of the Afghan War? The Iraq War? Vietnam?" Celestine got out her phone and typed in some notes.

"He never mentioned those." She sipped her tea, followed by the sucking of her teeth as if to dry them of liquid.

"Which war did he mention, then?"

She reached for a toothpick on a side table and chewed on it philosophically. "A war, say forty sumpin' years ago, against evil murderers, who killed and killed and killed just 'cause they could. Some war on the seas around Savannah. For the survival of these here islands and the whole shebang. Frankly, I figured Pete had done gone and lost his damn mind. He babbled about things flying in the air and water monsters and crazy-ass shit. S'cuse my French."

"Whoa! It must've been with the supes, because there's no war that recent here recorded in any history books or online. I've done tons of research on this city and its history."

Irma Mae shrugged with a frown. "Looky here, I done told you the truth, so don't go doubting me, young lady."

"Celestine. I, um... believe you, I'm just trying to make sense of it all. So did Peter Leger ever mention what these villains wanted?"

"What does a villain ever want?" She set the toothpick down. "Power, I s'pose. Power and more power. It's a dang drug. The hateful, greedy ones never get enough to be satisfied."

For an old loner, Irma Mae sure was smart. She understood a tyrant's playbook better than most. Celestine needed names of suspects to put more pieces together. "Did Peter ever tell you any specific *names* of the villains?"

"Ooh, you got my brain all churned up, gal. I feel like I'm playing that card game Concentration."

She didn't remind Irma Mae again that her proper name was Celestine, not gal or young lady. She just needed answers. "Sorry, but this is truly important. I'm trying to figure out what happened to Ray."

Irma Mae gave her the side-eye. "You ain't with those no-good cops, are ya?"

"I said I wasn't. Please believe me!"

"Okay, okay. You're just making this ole gal nervous." Irma Mae squinted her eyes and gazed up at the line of knickknacks hanging off her rope line. "Oh, hey!" she exclaimed with a snap of her bony knuckles. "I got me one. Name was Vex Blade. Pete called him Bastard Blade. I can still hear Pete ranting away, gettin' all fired up, crazy-like. He said that Blade came within a rat's whiskers of murdering him. Ray, too. He said that Bastard Blade wouldn't be happy till he done killed every good soul in Savannah."

"Why? Why was he so angry?"

"The only other thing I remember is that Pete said that he and Ray and the boys done ruined Blade's dastardly plan. And they killed his first mate. Can't recall the name."

"Oh, wow! That's helpful. Celestine typed in more notes. "What plan, exactly?"

"Girl, you think Pete was really onto something for real?" Irma Mae looked shocked, as if she'd never once considered this. "I always thought he was talking mumbo jumbo. Tell you the truth? It all escapes me 'cause I thought he'd lost his marbles what with the stuff he ranted—sumpin' about mountains of gunk and flying swordsmen and beheadings and houses collapsing. Pete disappeared for years after he said all that. No one knew where he was. They said maybe Blade took him to hell with him. I never paid it no serious mind. Though we did miss Pete. And Ray said that since the war was over, none of the boys could stand to see each other. It reminded them of the living nightmares they done gone through. So I s'pose they all lost touch. And then..."

"Then what?"

"A few months ago, Pete was back here like nothin' ever happened. Kept his head down, seemed more skittish than ever."

"Did you talk to him? Ask him where he'd gone? Ask him why he went away for so long?"

"I tried. He refused to answer. He'd just be looking behind him like he saw a dang ghost. His eyes were sunken in. His face was death warmed over. I only saw him two or three times in the salt marshes, fishing for dinner."

Irma Mae yawned. "You got enough outta me now? You've done tuckered this old gal out."

"I think so." Celestine glanced at her notes. Took a last gulp of tea. "You sure this is all you know?"

"All I know, gal, every last bit."

Celestine got up, rubbing her left hip, still sore from her fall on the sidewalk. It was dusk outside. A shudder of fear ran through her. Irma Mae must've seen it.

"You gonna be okay hiking out? At night it's dark as tar in this marsh."

"Sure, I will," Celestine muttered, in part to convince herself.

"Well. How's about a lantern?"

"I have a light on my phone, but I appreciate the offer." She was tempted to give Irma Mae a hug, but she resisted.

The old woman had her head tilted back on the chair, already half dozing. *Must be hard to age, let alone in a harsh salt marsh.* "Thanks again. Take care, Irma Mae."

"Same goes to you, Celestine."

Curious that Irma Mae suddenly remembered her name, Celestine thought as she ventured out.

She trekked as fast as she could without tripping on ruts in the tall grass and falling into the water. What had seemed innocent and wondrous took on an unsettling aura —the calls of cranes, squeals of rats and raccoons, the piercing chirp of cicadas, the sudden rustle of a fleeing snake underfoot. Celestine's pulse pounded in her ears. She held a compass, and she glanced at it fitfully under the glow of her phone light.

About ten minutes in, her feet slid on a patch of mud, and she was walking too fast to keep her balance. She tripped and fell into the muddy marsh banks. It was almost impossible to lift her boots up from the suction of the muck, and her throat closed as panic set in. She clutched at the slimy marsh soil and crawled out on hands and knees, since there was no tree to grab onto. She would try to be more careful after this.

Finally, she saw the lights of squad cars, and her fears turned to being detected. She turned off her phone and slipped it into her bag. Tried to maneuver with the moon-glow as her guide. It would seem mighty suspicious if she was caught out here, not to mention her disregard of Detective Wade's warning not to leave Savannah.

She was distracted by this worry when she heard the roar of what sounded like a surfside breaker crashing toward her. It hit her before she could put up a ward spell or hold out her crystals. Bowled over by it, she fell hard into the mudbank. She clambered to her feet. *Must be on better guard. Have stronger magic at the ready.*

Just as she steadied herself and reached for her crystals, another phantom breaker forced her into the marsh water.

*Do something. My earth magic!*

She fisted her crystals as she treaded water and chanted to conjure a shield of dry soil, rising from the marsh like it was a narrow barrier reef.

The water entity strobed into startling view as it watched the growing mound and hesitated. A man, long blue hair and beard, heavy brow, face distorted in rage, wearing only black pants and a neckerchief stood there. A tattoo of a three-eyed red demon was imprinted across his ripped chest. One jagged scar ran down the left section of his face.

"What do you want?" Celestine spluttered.

"You, drowned!" it spat.

"Who are you?"

"None of your business, wench!" The phantom returned to invisibility. It sent another violent breaker crashing her way just as she was climbing onto her conjured soil bank.

Shoved back by its intense force, she fell off the glamoured strip of land and went under the tidal waters, gagging on brackish liquid. Another magic wave churned her up from below. Struggling to hold her breath, she gasped, and water seeped down her throat and into her lungs.

She managed to bob her head to the water's surface and sputter, "Help! I'm drowning!" She hated the idea of alerting the cops, but this magical tatted enemy wanted her dead.

Their hounds came first, howling and yapping. Two of them stood on the banks and kept up their racket. Then she saw the powerful police flashlights jiggering through the pines in her direction.

As she watched the lights, another magic breaker hit her and churned her violently downward. The next thing she knew, she was stretched out in the tall grass, stars high above in the black sky, cops leaning over her.

"You awake?" one asked.

"She's come to," said another.

She gagged, and they pitched her to her side so she could vomit up a pint of muddy brackish water. They gave her a towel and seemed to be waiting for her to talk.

"Thanks," she choked out when she could.

"Can you stand?" one asked.

"I think so. Help me up?"

A cop on each side. Eased her to her unsteady feet.

"Is that your blue Honda Civic out here?"

She nodded.

"You're in no condition to drive."

She couldn't argue with that.

"You've got keys? One of our guys can drive your car back, and later they can escort you home. Where'd you come from?"

"Savannah."

"A ways off, then."

She dug in her bag—she still had that, thankfully—and found her car keys. Forked them over. Gave them her address.

"Let's get you some water and get you to a hospital. The police will need to see you in the morning."

Hard questions would follow. For now. she was relieved to be alive.

∾

CELESTINE WOKE to the sound of bleeping machines. A nurse was taking her pulse. "Where am I?" she asked.

"Southeast Georgia Health," replied the nurse, looking at the heart monitor. "Your vitals are fine. Surprising after the state you were in last night when they brought you in."

"What state was that?"

"Your lungs were a third full of water. They had to pump it out. You had welts all over your legs from bites and deep abrasions from your struggle in the water. Looks like there were jagged rocks in there." She gazed at Celestine as if she was a miracle specimen. "Strange how fast it all healed."

"Almost like magic, huh?" Celestine joked, though she was really in no mood and wanted to get the heck out of the hospital. How was it going to happen without her car and being all the way down here near Jekyll Island? She had urgent business, but she couldn't think of exactly what it was. Maybe brain fog was one of the side effects of struggling with nasty water entities.

Oryn knocked on the open door and peered in. He grinned at the nurse and then gave Celestine a worried look. "How's Miss LeBlanc?"

"Oryn! What are you doing here?" Celestine exclaimed.

"I heard what happened." He grimaced. "The news said Ms. LeBlanc, a suspect in Ray's murder disregarded orders to stay put, and she was found injured on Jekyll Island. I inquired at the local precinct, and they said a cop drove your car up to Savannah. So, I figured you might need a lift. Bit of a hike otherwise."

Celestine was flattered yet unnerved. "Geez, Oryn, it's crazy how word spreads."

Oryn looked over at the nurse. "So, is Celestine ready to get sprung?"

"It seems the police need to talk with her first," said the nurse. "I have strict orders to keep her here until they arrive." She gave Oryn an apologetic grin. Apparently, few could resist Oryn's dimples, green eyes, and mischievous aura like Celestine could.

"Fine," he replied. "I can hang nearby in the waiting room..."

Celestine sat up in bed. She had just begun to trust Oryn, but he suddenly seemed all too interested in tracking her. Why was he so eager to help her? "Oryn, it's a thoughtful offer, but orders are orders. I'll get back home by myself. I'll be all right, promise," she added when she saw his furrowed brow.

"You should have someone to accompany you," countered the nurse. "It's not only smart, but it's a strict recommendation if at all possible. Plus, aren't you an hour and half north, up in Savannah?"

"Yes." Inside, where Celestine kept her secrets, she was relieved. Outwardly, she shrugged. "If you insist." She turned to Oryn. "I might be a while with the cops."

Oryn grinned. "No problem. I'll just do some sketches in the waiting room or check my email." He winked at Celestine.

She had to admit, the warmth of his wink gave her strength, and it told her that he cared enough about her to make sure she got home safely.

THE CLATTER of hard heels on linoleum and the dragging of metal chairs woke Celestine from a morning doze.

"Coffee or tea?" offered the nurse when she brought in

the hospital breakfast: scrambled eggs, white toast, dry hash browns.

"Coffee, thanks." Celestine glanced at the two officers making themselves at home in folding chairs as she ate. She was tired but famished and had wolfed down almost all the food before the nurse returned with her coffee. The officers had theirs in takeout cups.

"We need to ask some questions. You ready?" asked a red-faced guy with a big belly under a tight shirt with strained buttons.

"Yeah." She gulped down coffee. Black fortitude.

"What were you doing in the marsh?" asked the second, a wiry bald-headed guy.

"Trying to find someone to tell me more about Peter Leger," she admitted irritably. "He was a friend of my friend Ray Bartello. You must have heard about Ray on the news. Found him dead, without eyes, in Savannah off Bay Street."

"Yep. Gruesome thing," replied Bald Head. "Have you been to the marshes here before?"

"No."

"So you never met Ms. Irma Mae? Never up in Savannah?" asked Red Face.

*Strange question.* "Nope. She says she hates big cities. Too packed in with people."

"Did you or your deceased friend Bartello hold any grudge against Peter Leger?" he persisted.

"Look, I never met Leger. And he and Ray were good friends, so no animosity."

The husky cop leaned in, alcoholic gin blossoms evident on his cheeks. "Did you get any useful information from the old lady?" He seemed to be trying a friendlier tack.

"Irma Mae wasn't too forthcoming. Except she did say

60

Peter Leger seemed spooked when he returned. Do you know where he went for all those years?"

Red Face took a moment, clearly surprised she was now asking him questions. "Nope. We're looking into it."

"Irma Mae said he ranted about a war in Savannah, some forty years ago—so in the 1980s? Ever hear of this?"

The red-cheeked man glanced over at Bald Head. "No, you?"

Bald Guy frowned as he shook his head. Celestine's temper flared. What the hell were folks paying taxes for if these guys didn't know history, do research? She knew this was unfair, but she was terribly impatient. In a hurry for answers.

For the next hour, they asked her way too many questions. Nothing she hadn't already gone over with Detective Wade or hadn't thought of herself. Again, as with Wade, she held back on the supernatural content. What good would it do? They had no expertise with what, to them, was an unseen, unreal world. She would take that on herself. It was a burden to do alone, though. She thought of Oryn's air magic, but she didn't know him well enough yet to recruit his help. She'd just barely begun to trust him. Still, it was sweet he'd offered to drive her back. Weary again, she zoned out until the red-faced cop's next line pierced her malaise.

"Have you done more drawings... the ones that foretell the future?"

*Gah! This cop must believe in the woo-woo world enough to consider my drawings, at least with a huge grain of salt.* She wasn't his personal psychic lackey, though. These automatic images were too raw to share with anyone, much less mundanes, until she could interpret them herself. *Plus, they might make these cops suspect I'm guilty if they show something I don't even understand yet.*

"Sorry to disappoint you, no, and I can't perform on a schedule," she grumbled.

Her leeching hostility must've hit its mark because Red Face narrowed his eyes in Disapproving Dad mode. "I spoke to Detective Wade, assigned to the case up in Savannah. He gave you strict orders not to leave town. He said you understood this." What was with men who still viewed her, at twenty-five, as a rebellious teen? After this long hour of meandering interrogation, she was tired, and her patience had frayed. They could go eff themselves!

She needed to contain her anger and her earth magic before it made them more suspicious of her. Her impulsive bursts of anger, like the symbolic reveal of shifter fangs, often got her in trouble. She willed herself to calm down and be civil. "I did understand, Officer. I'm sorry. I was just a bit desperate."

He seemed pacified by her faux apology. "We'll let you off the hook here, since Detective Wade is the man assigned to your case. Just know he'll be paying you a visit when you return. And no more treks to our marshland."

Celestine hated being told what to do. "No one around here has any answers. Someone's got to solve this thing."

"Look, you're no detective," snapped the cop.

*I could be. I already know more than you, and I'm a quick learner.* Celestine LeBlanc, supe sleuth had a satisfying ring to it. If she did open a PI business, they'd never know it. Supes stuck with their own.

"I'm good at logic puzzles. Good at figuring out mystery plots well before the end of the book," she said defensively. In a gentler tone she said, "I'm just heartsick. Another man's been murdered. How many more will there be before—"

"We'll get them. It's our job. Give us time."

That was what Detective Wade had said, too. But for Celestine, it wasn't good enough. Ray's letter warned that time was likely running out.

# SEVEN

It wasn't until late afternoon when they finally released Celestine. There had been paperwork and more paperwork, another round of exams, which revealed her "spectacularly fast" recovery (supe, natch). Only her fatigue and the worst of the abrasions remained, safely bandaged. Finally, they called storage for her mucked-up clothes, which she was not eager to put back on.

Oryn was as patient as a dragonfly lingering on a leaf for a fly—waiting, waiting, and more waiting.

Outside, after an orderly wheeled her out in a wheel-chair just to be extra safe, she told him thanks and stood as the second the orderly disappeared inside. Celestine insisted Oryn not play valet while she cooled her heels under the covered entrance. He shrugged and walked her to his car in the brutal heat.

"You really didn't have to wait all day for me," she repeated for the third time.

"It's fine. Don't feel guilty. No need to thank me again."

They'd reached his car. What else: a shiny green Forester for Mr. Oryn Forest, fae extraordinaire.

She drew the line at him opening the door for her, but she was glad he'd made a run to Target for a clean T-shirt and shorts for her since her clothes were torn and reeked of marsh mud.

"Hungry?" he asked as he steered them out of the lot.

"Gosh, can you believe it, I am. You?"

"Yeah, the hospital lunchroom was uninspiring. All those prewrapped bready rolls. I kept myself busy doing sketches."

"Oh? I'd like to see them."

"Sure. Soon." When he glanced over at her, she noticed his eyes had changed to amber. Like an effing chameleon—a handsome one. And the late afternoon sun flowing in the driver's window gave his hair white-sand streaks.

"So how was the bedside interrogation? Harsh?" he asked.

"Nothing I couldn't handle." They chuckled.

"Shall we get takeout up in Savannah? Sushi? Teriyaki? Vegetable bowl?" He looked over at her. "Or what's your fancy? We could stop by my place. Eat there before I get you back."

She froze. He was going too fast. He seemed to sense her fear.

"Outside, in my *garden*," he clarified. "Look, Celestine, I'll never put any unwanted moves on you. Set that worry aside. I'm a gentleman. I just worry about you going to your house right off, what with the dangerous water phantoms and your injuries that aren't all the way healed. You said you were still tired. At least take an hour to relax." He looked her way with a fetching grin. "I have a green thumb, and my whole yard is surrounded by woods. Must be a fae thing."

When she laughed, her muscles relaxed. It *would* be good to have a moment before going back to Bay Street. "I owe you a visit after you drove all the way down here, waited all day, and are driving me back. Who does that?"

He reached out his hand and laid it gently on hers. "You owe me nothing. Ever."

His hand released tiny sparks of air, like energizing taps. The airy sparks ran along her spine and turned warm as they spread in her belly. *Too soon. I'm the one who needs to cool off.*

They chose sushi with tons of ginger, a bag of organic pita, a container of hummus with caramelized onions, and lime spritzers. He parked in the driveway of a pale-green clapboard house on a quiet lane she'd never seen, outside of the historic district. He flipped on a porch light, illuminating enormous crepe myrtles bursting with crimson blossoms and pale-yellow gardenias.

"Wow!" Celestine exclaimed, stepping out of the car.

"Only the front of my place has red and yellow flowers. The back garden's a whole different scene," he told her.

"Is that a warning?" she quipped, helping him carry the food bags through the garage and straight out to his yard. He flipped on a single patio light. The backyard was already aglow with mysterious twinkles. They placed the food on a wrought-iron table, and he led her down a stone path to his garden proper, a veritable jungle of black irises, black hellebores, and dark-blue flowers of sorts Celestine had never seen.

"I call it my midnight garden," he said, and led her farther into his wonderland of winding vines, broad-leafed and lacy plants, all dotted with purple or periwinkle or solid black flowers. Soon, they were in a narrow wood, and still his flower garden burst up on either side of the path.

His eyes lit up with mischievous curiosity. "What do you think?"

"I never knew black flowers existed. And so many in the same garden. It's like a Disney theme park, but a very dark and witchy one." They laughed.

"Fae, not witch, but yeah. Gardening relaxes me the way most use pot or booze."

"What are all of the sparkly things?" She pointed into the trees.

"My little friends. Will-o'-the-wisps. They guard me and look after the forest."

Celestine grinned. "Your *what*?"

"You don't know much about the fae, do you?"

She shook her head.

"You'll find we're a strange bunch."

She snickered. "No stranger than a part-wolf shifter, part witch, part mundane."

"Oh, you'd be surprised."

"Which tribe do you hail from? You're right that I know very little about the fae, except there are many types, correct? What's your line's particular history or lore?"

He sighed. "That's a long, fraught tale. Too heavy for the moment." Shadows fell across his handsome face as he hesitated. "I promise I'll tell you sometime. Good enough?"

She didn't want Oryn to be sad. She needed lightness badly, too. "No problem," she answered, patting his forearm. She gave out what she hoped was a freeing laugh.

He gazed at her and then smiled up at the trees. His responsive laughter was like coming upon a waterfall after a grueling mountain hike.

"Oh, she's only a friend," he said to the air.

"Say what?" Was he bonkers? "Who are you talking to?"

"The forest sprites, the will-o'-the-wisps," he replied with an absolute straight face.

"You talk to them?" she asked incredulously. "What did they ask?"

"If you were my special person." He looked down toward his boots.

"Oh." *Awkward*. She'd walked right into that one.

As if to recover from the embarrassment of the moment, he said brightly, "Want to see what a little air magic can do?"

She remembered the dinner waiting for them on the table, yet she was so curious about his offer that she wasn't ready to eat. "Sure, show me."

His energy burst out spring green and spicy and electric as he stretched out his arms, closed his eyes, and chanted something under his breath. Lifting his head to the upper branches of the trees, he intoned something else, which sent the trees to swaying, and visible eddies of wind, like whirling dervishes, began to spin around them. Pink, lime-green, and violet wind eddies. He mumbled something else and reached out his arms. The tiny will-o'-the-wisps approached in airy ribbons, dancing and spiraling at his command. Hundreds of them alighted on him, his shoulders, his chest, clinging to his back and shorts.

"Show-off!" said Celestine affectionately. Truth be told, she was studying Oryn with new fascination, and something less pure—through an unexpected shimmery glaze of desire. *Good fucking goddess! He's a grown-up sexy-as-hell Peter Pan with not just one Tinkerbell but a whole army of fae at the ready.* She tamped down her surge of lust but kept on staring.

"Want some sprites sent your way?" he asked with a low chuckle, as if he could read her mind.

"Um, uh..." Too late, they were off, spiraling back into the garden, settling on the black flowers and on the tops of the swaying trees.

He made a wide circling motion with his arms and then lowered them with force to his sides. The wind calmed, the trees became motionless, the sparkling, colored wind eddies dissipated.

"Holy crap, Oryn, I'm impressed," she admitted. "You're better than the fucking Northern Lights."

His eyes did the half-moon curve that meant he was flattered and pleased. "I try," he said simply. "It makes me happy."

"That's cool."

"Hey!" he said. "Shall we eat?"

She nodded. They wandered back up the garden path and opened the takeout feast. Sat across from each other on the wrought-iron chairs that matched his table.

"If your light show is that amazing, I would imagine your protective magic is also impressive," she said.

"It can be effective, and complementary to earth magic. One amplifying the other."

Was he suggesting they join forces? She let that one sit. She might find him sexy, and he'd proved himself trust-worthy so far, but she needed to slow down. She felt vulnerable after that salt marsh attack, and her wounds ached even though she'd put on a brave face. In the past, she tended to jump in fast and then panic and abruptly retreat. She was trying to grow the hell up. It wasn't fair to flip-flop all around, even with a friend. Was Oryn a friend yet? She'd only known him, for like, a minute.

"What are you thinking?" he asked her.

She chewed on her pita and hummus. Wiped her hands, grinned at him. "How I think you're an upstanding guy. How I think we could be friends."

"Upstanding? Like standing up?" he quipped. "So, we aren't friends yet?"

"We are, kind of. I just want to be careful, make sure I'm not leaning on you because I'm going through stuff."

"I get it. Friend." His eyes switched to amber, to warm, patient understanding. The will-o'-the-wisps twinkled brighter and then flew off to perches in the far garden.

They drove to her place. The reporters had thinned to maybe five, who pressed toward Oryn's Forester as he parked.

"Oh geez," grumbled Celestine, gathering up her mud-caked bag.

"I can at least walk up to your door with you."

"I won't turn that down. I've been sneaking out my back door since—" She sighed. "I can't avoid them forever."

Mics were thrust in her face as she stepped toward the front stairs.

"How do you feel about Ray Bartello's murder?"

"Do you have a statement for the press?"

"Is it true that your drawing predicted Bartello's death?"

"Why would you draw him eyeless?"

"Are *you* the murderer?"

She waited until that last crappy question—more an accusation—to say anything. Then she stared at the reporter. With scalding rage contained in a deceptively quiet hiss, she said, "Ray Bartello was a good friend of mine. I'm heartbroken by his passing."

She glanced at Oryn for moral support. His slightly narrowed eyes seemed to say, *Go slow, you don't owe them.* She agreed. After the supernatural attacks, she was not going to hint that she knew a damn thing, because the more that bad entities knew she was trying to figure out the case, the more they would try to maul, even kill her. Oryn gave a faint nod, his eyes tinting green. She went on.

"I know nothing about how this happened. You could camp here for days, and I still couldn't tell you more. The proper place to provide any tips or leads is to the Savannah Police." As she pushed through the group, Oryn walked slightly behind her, since the reporters were busy photographing them together, no doubt fuel for salacious media.

"How do you know Miss LeBlanc? Are you dating her?" some ballsy reporter asked Oryn. He didn't answer.

"Did you know Ray Bartello? Did you or Miss LeBlanc have a fight earlier on the day he was found?" asked another.

"Can you tell us anything more about the case?" asked a third.

Oryn face wrinkled in disgust. "Look, Miss LeBlanc needs peace. She's said what she can. Yes, we're friends, not that it's your business," he added sharply. "You may as well go get some sleep. Camping out here won't get you what you seek." He swept his arm around Celestine, and they hurried up the stone stairs leading to her place.

Oryn stopped on the stoop while Celestine unlocked the door. "So, I'll see you at class tomorrow? Will you be okay?" he asked. "If you want, I can cast a few air wards around the house so you can get a worry-free night's sleep. Otherwise—"

"It's not your job to protect me," she said, gazing up at him and realizing how very much taller he was, next to her five-foot, seven-inch frame. *Good goddess, the man must be six and a half feet tall if he's an inch.*

"Okay, up to you," he replied, turning to head down the stairs and Bay Street.

She almost shouted "See you in class," but that would only tip off the lingering media sharks. She'd have to picture her brain padlocked with a clamp on her mouth to contain her impulsive banter. She waved to him instead. She lowered the earth wards, went inside, and promptly raised and strengthened them.

She hung a closed indefinitely sign on the front door. No way she could run a leathercraft shop right now, or ever. She had loved working on the pieces with Ray. It wasn't that she was into *leather*, per se, mostly the art part and chatting with him. She began to work off her anxiety by sorting out Ray's leather items and putting them into large canvas bags. There were big shoulder bags, vests, high boots with rivets, hair fasteners, bucket hats, and belts. So much time and money and effort he had put into this place, only to perish. That was life—sometimes long and easy, other times short and violent, with a big question mark at the end. She hoped she could at least replace the question marks on his passing with solid answers and karmic justice for the bad actors.

She put most of the items in a large hall closet, except for a bag of leather pouches and two dozen backpacks near the front door to hand out on the street, so she could carry on Ray's charity work. His caring generosity was mind-boggling, both to her and to the street supes. This gave her a spark of joy amidst the pain. She also didn't need the awl and the loads of leathercraft tools, so she hauled what she could to a corner of the den. Hopefully, she could sell them. Gradually, the front room was cleared of inventory. It would take more time to really clear the space enough to start an art gallery, though she could begin to picture the wall space, where the desk would be, the information table.

A real gallery! Wow! She felt another burst of happiness imagining it. What would she call it? She loved dreaming up names, but this one would take a moment.

She wandered into Ray's old office and sat. Chin in palms, elbows on the massive oak desk. She opened a journal and jotted down notes before exhaustion slowed her mind and her limbs more than they already had.

• *Irma Mae knew Ray and Pete. Pete described a supernatural war in what would have been the late 1980s, early 1990s. One of the enemies was called Bastard Blade. Ray and Pete stopped them. Find out how and why!*

• *Water entities tried to drown me. Must improve my earth magic defenses and spells.*

• *No more hospitals!*

• *One of the water phantoms showed himself. Thin, enraged, blue-bearded man. Said he wants me dead. Why? And what does he want besides this? Is he on a mission or does he just want to destroy those who work for the good? What is their good that he deems bad?*

*Drawings:*

• *Who is the mermaid with wings?*

• *Why did I draw eyes and lopped-off fingers? A case of aimless gore? Or do these body parts serve some dark purpose? Find out!*

Celestine woke at three a.m. with her pen still in her hand and a terrible crick in her neck. She had fallen asleep at the oak desk, bent sideways. She rose and stumbled to Ray's den couch. Spread a fleece throw over herself and sank into another fitful sleep. She dreamed of bloody floating fingers and of choking on brackish water.

Then, buoyed by a sudden glow of stars that flickered around her like a vessel of spring lightning, she drifted into the night sky.

CHAPTER

# EIGHT

S he walked in and chose a seat. The class parted to let her by, as if she was some kind of royalty or a curiosity so strange that it was perilous to get too close. They continued to steal peeks while she set up her paper and paints.

Aline took the spot to Celestine's left and settled in. She unrolled her handmade paint container and strung it up on the easel. Today, she was dressed red harem PJs and a long red top. Riley took the seat behind Celestine. Oryn sat to her right. He smelled of pine sap and the lilies in his midnight flower garden. His grin and his ever-changing eyes, tinted gold under the unflinching studio light, drew her in. It was unsettling to be such a curiosity yet sweet to be flanked by what she now understood to be her protectors—two mundanes and one fae.

"Today, we will work in opaque gouache," explained Prof Gray, and proceeded to demonstrate how to mix, apply, and—after waiting only minutes—overpaint, since the gouache dried so quickly. A water-based medium that was endlessly correctable was an amazing thing. The Prof had set up two choices of still life on a long table: one of colored glass bottles and the other an arrangement of books and feathers.

Celestine chose the bottles. She liked how the light shining through them formed multicolor patterns so that, for instance, the blue bottle also had pink and gold and green reflections. She mixed her paints and said a silent charm to ward away the Prof from her easel. He eyed her from across the room but stayed put.

If he managed to break through her invisible guard, she had a plan.

When her hands began to tingle with supernatural energy, she willed them to just draw the bottles at hand.

*Damn, can't you wait to do this until I'm alone in my home office?* Her fingers stubbornly ignored her. *Okay, it must be important. I give up.*

As a double precaution, she flipped over the top page of the drawing pad when he wasn't looking and simply drew underneath. Her paintbrush moved of its own accord, this time with flowing color. Once she gave in to it, Celestine was electric with energy. Oryn looked over, clearly feeling its aura. She gave him a smile and then a warning shake of her head, and he focused back on his own work.

This time, she kept her eyes open as her automatic drawing unfolded. A piece of unusual crockery with not one, not two, but three spouts. On the surface, there were what looked to be sea creatures—ones she had never seen in any marine biology or science book. She trained her mind to float like the enchanted vessel in her dream, to leave room for her hands to move any which way.

She heard the drone of the Prof's voice and looked up. Oh no, he was coming her way. With all of her psychic strength, she willed her hand to stop and flipped the paper over, back to the rendering of the bottles.

He frowned and grunted when her unseen force stopped him. It looked almost cartoonish, as if he had bounced off an unseen trampoline standing at a ninety-degree angle. He tried to circle around it. Same result. An amused murmur welled up from the students.

Celestine stood and asked the Prof very politely if she could speak to him briefly in the hall. He agreed, walking the other way out of the room to avoid the magical barricade.

"What is it, Miss LeBlanc?" Confused annoyance lined his face.

"As you must know, I did a drawing last week that got leaked to the news. Someone here must have talked."

"Perhaps. I'm aware of what happened."

"So I'm feeling quite vulnerable, which was why I skipped our last class. I want to learn the techniques, but, um, if you could just leave me be in these last two classes, give me space, I'd truly appreciate it. I'm traumatized. I can't feel safe if folks are talking to the press."

The Prof stroked his beard. His look of irritation faded. "Well, I want you to know I wasn't the one, Miss LeBlanc. I will honor your request, though."

"Thanks."

His smile was sincere. "I wish you the best." They filed back in to probing stares, including Oryn's.

"It's okay," she whispered to him when she settled back in. "Your painting of the books and feathers is cool, by the way. Nice range of greens."

Oryn grinned and looked back at his work. Aline, on her other side, didn't even look over. *Impressive self-control.*

Celestine's hands vibrated with even more energy as

she flipped the paper back over and launched into another automatic drawing. She burned for it, her psyche and hands on fire. This one was of a key, and next to it were a few scruffy, angular rats and some dead flies in a dark square of space surrounded by wall. Yuck. WTF! Was this the same key that had fallen out of the envelope?

She looked closer. Hard to say, but when she got her drawing home, she could compare the indentations. The hot prickling in her hands lessened and finally stopped, like a gas stovetop being flicked off. She heaved out a deep breath and rubbed at her sore hands. Wiped away sweat on her forehead. Winced at a surge of pain in her shoulders. This automatic drawing thing took a lot out of her, and *gah*, especially in public. She needed a nap or a massage or both.

The price a supernatural paid for magic.

At least she had her next set of clues. She just had to figure out the coded imagery. Why couldn't her hands jot down clear sentences, obvious directions? *It would be too easy for an interloper to intercept and beat me to the solutions.* Nothing like answering her own questions.

She flipped over her paper to the still life for the rest of class. Beautiful glassware and a drawing that might even be good enough to put up in her future gallery.

Class was over. Surreptitiously, she removed the automatic artwork from under her vellum pad, rolled it up, and stuck it in her messenger bag. Oryn was asking her if she wanted to hang out. Aline was securing her canvas paint stash with the tie and asking Celestine if she liked working with the gouache. Riley was being quiet and hanging by Aline's side. Were they a couple? Seemed to be.

As they had at the start, the rest of the students studied her without coming over to talk. Had they sensed the magic barriers she'd set up for the Prof, or did they just know to steer clear? After all, not just one, but two people connected to Celestine were dead. They were probably scared of her! She would keep that misconception going if folks kept giving her a wide berth.

"Hang out?" Oryn asked her again.

"Um, how about later? At the Seahorse." She gave her friends an apologetic grin. "I need a nap in the worst way."

They figured out a time. And then Celestine hurried out before she lost her resolve, because Oryn's pull rivaled the strength of the magic that had shuddered through her hands.

BACK INSIDE THE Bay Street house, she raised the wards and ran upstairs to her room. She hung up her gouache painting of the strange three-spouted pottery decorated with sea beasts of a type she'd never seen. Later, she would have time to stare at it and try to figure it out.

A second wind drove her to fetch the key and compare it to the one in her other drawing. She collected the items she'd hidden in the temporary hiding spots. Good, the key was still in the padded mailer. She held it up to her rendering, comparing the notches. A match!

Now, where would rats be? She cringed at this off-putting section of her painting, and at how nasty the rats looked—yellow eyed, maws open, ready to bite, mangy. Most vermin lived in basements. She went downstairs and tore around the dank space, searching for sections of wall that might hold a secret lock box, examining the packed dirt floor under her feet for false sections, trap doors, uneven areas. Nothing but lots of spiders and cobwebs.

She blew out a breath of frustration. "Think, Celestine,

think!" she grumbled. "Where else do rats hang out?" She needed to buck up and put her squeamish side on hold. "The attic? Too hot. In the walls? Not enough food. They like to *eat*," she mumbled. "The pantry."

Still fueled by pure adrenaline, she tore upstairs to the kitchen and peered behind all of the dish shelves. Nothing unusual there. Next, she went into Ray's old-school walk-in pantry. The wooden shelves were still filled with jars of rice and pasta and cans of beans and soups. She forced herself not to get all choked up on memories of them sharing dinners in his kitchen. Instead, she methodically moved all of the goods off of each shelf to see if anything was concealed in the wall. Nothing on the top shelf but weevils, she realized, when a swoop of her arm came away with the gross critters stuck to her sweaty skin. The next shelf down was cleaner, but the walls behind the dry goods were solid —no hidden drawer in the wall. The next shelf down, more of the same.

Finally, she was on her belly, peering under the lowest shelf and shining her phone's flashlight around the confines of the crawlspace. She saw no lines that indicated a built-in drawer or anything of the sort. But just when she was about to give up, she spotted the smallest of vertical notches that just might be a keyhole.

Craning her neck and twisting her torso at a very uncomfortable angle, she reached forward. The moment the key touched the keyhole, a screeching pierced her ears, followed by a rampage of chittering, slavering magical rats, their pink tails switching and slapping her arm. One bit her hard on the ear, and another, squealing loudly, took a bite out of her chin on its way out of the pantry.

"Ow!" she yelled, rubbing her chin and feeling warm liquid. "You ugly shits!" She shimmied out of the space and looked at her reflection in her phone's tiny mirror. She winced at her bloodied chin and ear. Her eyes darted around the kitchen. No rats. Ray's magical guards had disappeared. *You wanted me to open the secret drawer, but you forgot to remove your own ward from the stash!*

Gawd, if she went back in there, would another round of vermin attack her? She had no choice but to try again. Whatever was in that wall had been quite special to Ray.

Reluctantly, she again got down on her hands and knees and shimmied in on her stomach, key in hand. Cautiously, she reached forward. The instant the key touched the keyhole, her hand and arm were punctured with what felt like nails and broken glass. She pulled back, wincing. *Bloody hell! Ray, how am I supposed to know what your ward is or how to lower it?*

She tried again, with the same painful results. At least there were no more rats coming at her. This time, she didn't pull her hand back but tried desperately to push in the key. Not happening. Not until Ray's dangerous ward was broken. A sense of doom overtook her, and she stayed on the floor, belly down, in desperation.

She was a witch, and a witch could divine things, she reasoned. Although most of her magic had so far revolved around earth spells, not divining. Maybe it was time to stretch, to try new things.

She wriggled out of the crawl space and went into the kitchen. Picked out actual jagged bits of glass and washed and bandaged her cuts and bites. Odd that while the rats were specters, the glass was real. She wondered if magical rat bites required a rabies shot. As much as she hated going to the doctor, she supposed it was worth a rabies test to be safe.

Ray had enough dirt in his houseplants to filch a cup for

power poultices. She mixed soil, a pinch of damiana from her herbal stash box, and a corner of a paper from Ray's den with his handwriting on it. She added a small azurite stone for visioning powers, some mugwort for protection, and a tablespoon of peanut butter as a binder. Pummeling the mixture as best she could with one of Ray's hammers for softening leather, she reconsidered selling his tools. They just might be useful for other spellcasting recipes, and for weaponry!

She rolled the gritty poultices into little balls and zapped them in the microwave to harden them. Then she lay on the couch, and popped a poultice power chew in her mouth. *Gross!* The peanut butter flavoring was barely noticeable compared to what tasted like the gunk on the bottom of her boots when she trekked in the marshes. She chewed, gagged, and swallowed. Then she shut her eyes, settled in, and mumbled a divining charm.

*Please let me see in my mind's eye the ward Ray Bartello used to lock the secret drawer. Open a guide to his unique magic. Allow me to help my friend Ray in this way. It was his desire that I get the key, that I open the drawer.*

She descended deeper into the trance. Again, as in her dream, she traveled there by what looked to be Oryn's twinkling will-o'-the-wisps flickering around her to create a celestial boat. Moving into a dark, enchanted realm, she could see Ray standing up ahead, on a far shore. He was talking to someone, though she couldn't see who or hear his words. She called to him. Nothing. He did not look her way. She uttered the chant again, slower. Then in her mind, his words came.

*Rats come first, biting, scratching! Nails and glass shards next to injure all interlopers and thieves. This charm remains firm until one who knows me says their name and says they come in love.*

"I am Celestine LeBlanc, and I come in love," she whispered. "I come in love and friendship to solve your murder."

The twinkling vessel sailed her around the dark realm, and when she lost sight of Ray in this fantasyscape, she willed herself not to panic. For if she did, the spell's undoing might fail. She willed herself to have hope that she would return to consciousness with her mind intact, for she was unfamiliar with this type of magic.

She traveled up in glowing rings, each one like the bottles in class, casting colored reflections. Then she was awake and brimming with purpose.

Dizzy upon rising, she took a minute. When her balance was steady, she ventured back to the crawl space. Wriggled in on her belly and shone the phone's light on the low section of wall. This time, the key fit in the vertical notch with only a spark of electrical current to her arm. She turned the key and pulled open an almost flat drawer.

In it were lots of dead flies as in her rendering. But also, a leatherbound journal the size of a small paperback with the comma-shaped Jekyll Island stamped on the front! She gasped. Flipping through, she saw Ray's unique backward-leaning scrawl on the pages, though large sections were missing. She slid the journal in her pants pocket and used the space in the drawer for the mailer and the little ship in a bottle. She closed and locked it using her own spell to safeguard them.

Back up in her room, she locked the door and put a salve and bandages on her ear, chin, and hand wounds, which throbbed painfully. The exhaustion of spell work was also setting in, but she wasn't ready to rest.

# CHAPTER
# NINE

S he sat on her bed and opened the journal.

*Jekyll Clan. Our headquarters in Jekyll Island's tidal marshes is remote enough to be left alone by mundanes, and hopefully by the water mage enemies we fight, as they are at a disadvantage on our earthy turf. I am fond of this island because I was born here. Its beauty is under attack from all sides. We will not stand by and let it be overrun by Bastard Blade's evil shenanigans. He is the kingpin of the Demon Three Eyes operation, yet he sits in anonymity while others get blamed. We will not stand for this either. We must expose Vex Blade for the selfish, sadistic bastard that he is. This goes against everything we supernaturals stand for. The mundane world will never believe the trashing of the shoreline was done by an evil overlord who supernaturally controlled the mundane builders and destroyers. Must we prove it to the humans? Could we ever?*

*Or just invisibly, steadily, demolish the enemy.*

*We call for war on the seas that only supernaturals will see.*

"Good lord, Ray, why didn't you ever tell me any of this?" Celestine mumbled. "Why didn't you let me into your private world?"

After this, she flipped to a big gap, where a chunk of pages had been ripped out. *Did you tear all of these out, Ray? If not, who?* she wondered. In either case, why would some pages be spared?

Celestine read the next entry about Ray's Jekyll Clan shipmates. Some names were familiar. The hairs on the nape of her neck bristled.

*Harwood Port is the guts of the mission, always brave in the face of calamity, with nerves of steel and ironclad confidence. Peter Leger is the capable all-hands-on-deck man, sailing the craft, hauling up the sails, and rolling them down in a storm. Edge LeRoux, part Gaule, part French Creole, is the beating heart of our mission. He reminds us we are bound by love of the earth, the seas, and its creatures. We must be the stewards who protect it all. LeRoux lifts our spirits. He has an open, giving heart.*

Celestine's focus went back to the line about Peter Leger. "Hands on deck," she read, and repeated it slowly. "Hands. On. Deck. Holy crap! His hands! His fingers." Her stomach flipped in nauseous alarm. "Body parts," she muttered, reading the passage again. Harwood's guts, Peter's hands and fingers, Edge LeRoux's heart... Why did they want these body parts? For some blood magic ritual? A demonic spell? Peter Leger was murdered. Ray too, and they had gotten his eyes. Her belly clenched in revulsion.

"I have to find Harwood Port and Edge LeRoux, the sooner the better," she mumbled. "But how? Where?" If Irma Mae was telling an accurate version of this, the original destruction to the shoreline happened some thirty-five to forty years ago, and Ray was describing a similar sort of trashing of the coastal areas. *Damn, Ray, I can't research historical data and records on supes like I can with mundanes.*

*Was this destruction visible to mundanes? How do I find out what happened in your world?*

"Maybe I can look up street addresses and the schools Harwood and Edge went to, just not research their undercover work," she said to herself.

She leapt out of bed and groaned when her injured body objected. Logging onto her desktop, she searched local phone records for Harwood Port first.

There were two of them in the Savannah area, but she was able to eliminate one who was still a kid. The correct Harwood Port would be in his sixties. She jotted down his address. Next, she searched for an Edge LeRoux. This was harder, since she figured that Edge was probably a nickname. Who in hell would name their child Edge? On second thought, people were nuts and named their kids all kinds of weird—Phelony, Nutella, Chardonnay. Two Edward LeRouxs were too young. There was an Edgewood LeRoux about two hours west of the city limits who fit the age span, and an Edgar LeRoux just within the northern part of the city. She wrote down the last two.

Her stomach ached, not from injuries but from hunger. She was too weary to go downstairs and cook. Instead, she pawed around in her messenger bag and found a granola bar. Wolfed it down. After this, she must've drifted off, because the next thing she knew, her phone was dinging incessantly.

She rubbed at her eyes and read through the many texts.

Oryn: *You coming to the Seahorse? We're all there.*

Oryn: *You ok? We've been waiting an hour.*

Detective Wade: *Come into the precinct tomorrow morning for more questioning at 10 am sharp. Or we will come to you. Please confirm. Thanks.*

She confirmed. The last thing she wanted was trouble from Wade. She read on.

**Newsflash Savannah:** *Celestine LeBlanc, a person of interest in the murder of Ray Bartello, was released from Southeast Georgia Health, where she was treated for injuries sustained in a mysterious attack in the salt marshes on Jekyll Island. She claimed she was on the hunt for clues to Ray Bartello's murder. Her actions raise suspicion since she was told in no uncertain terms to stay in Savannah. Will there be consequences to her ignoring this request?*

Oryn: *Leaving the Seahorse. Officially worried about you.*

Her pulse shot up, reactivating the throbbing of her injuries. How long had she been out of it? She was studying her bedraggled appearance in her bathroom mirror and brushing a hand through her tangled black hair when the bell rang. She threw on a clean purple shirt and black jeans.

*Damn reporters*, she thought, heading into the bedroom and stashing Ray's journal in one of her boots. The bell rang again, and this time, whoever it was did not let up. Her phone dinged again.

Oryn: *here with Aline and Riley. you home? ringing your bell. you okay?*

Her heart pounded. She hurried downstairs. Peeked through the curtains on the glass partition. She needed someone to talk to, and she was beginning to trust this ragtag bunch. Better than the persistent group of reporters. She swung the door open, and Oryn gave her a nervous hug. She hugged him back. His arms were soothing, reassuring, warm, not cool or distant as she always imagined faes to be.

So much for assumptions.

He stared at her. Up close, his face vibrated with intensity. "When you never showed up to the bar or answered my texts, I had to make sure you were okay. Riley and Aline were worried too, so they wanted to come along." He stared at the bandages on her hands, her chin. "Celestine, what happened?" he whispered.

She needed to say *something* about it all, but Aline and Riley were mundanes. Granted, *artist* mundanes, and as such, naturally visionary and free-thinking. Yet how much experience they had with supes was a real question. Had they ever watched a spellcaster? A divining trance? It was an entirely different matter than trusting someone not to leak news to the press. Still... if Oryn trusted them...

"Sorry I didn't show up. I was repairing something in a crawl space and, uh..." She rolled her eyes. "It was an incredibly tight spot with jagged edges and zero wiggle room. I got kind of stuck."

"You're all cut up!" Aline said, stating the obvious. Her cats-in-sunglasses PJ set distracted in a good way.

Celestine nodded. "I know I look awful, but I put medicine on the cuts. They're not quite as bad as they seem." She gestured to the partially cleared-out front studio space, hoping to shift the focus off her. Oryn was still frowning at her chin bandage, likely gearing up to ask more questions. "This was my friend Ray's leather store. I've been clearing it out. I have an idea for it. I'm going to make it into an art gallery at some point."

"Great idea!" Aline whirled around, looking at all the walls, the remaining bags of leather, the narrow table Celestine had dragged in. "Wow! I love the paintings and drawings on the walls. Did you do them?"

Celestine nodded.

"This *would* make an amazing gallery. High ceilings, light from four windows..." Aline peered out of one. "That is, when you can open the curtains… when those annoying reporters are totally gone-zo."

"Yeah, the art rocks," Riley chimed in. He was staring at one drawing in particular. The one of Bonaventure Cemetery. "I feel serious vibes from that one. It's alive."

Celestine smiled. Apparently, some mundanes felt magic. Regular humans could be empaths, right? Maybe her new friends would understand her hidden world of magic better than she thought.

Another old assumption dashed.

After all, Aline and Riley hung out with a freaking fae. Oryn's sexy grin seemed to track her. His eyes had gone gold and silver, like liquid gemstones.

*Damn! They are pure art.*

She hauled over one of Ray's stools and opened a couple of folding chairs. "Sit, get comfy. Can I get you all some drinks? I have pomegranate seltzer or vodka."

"How 'bout a combo?" asked Riley.

"I'll second that," said Aline.

"Same," said Oryn. "Can I help?"

*No* was perched on the tip of Celestine's tongue. She was so used to being on her own, doing everything for herself. She needed people, though. It was another wrong assumption to think that everyone was out to get her. Boy, the universe was sure schooling her on the stupidity of making assumptions tonight.

Back with the drinks, they settled in, complimenting Celestine for the tasty mixes.

"So, what do you like to draw, Riley?" Celestine realized she'd never really had a conversation with him. She liked how his brown hair was shaggy, as if he had trimmed it himself, to resemble a jagged waterfall. She realized that not only did he have a crown tatt around his neck, but ones around each ankle too.

He drew out a small sketch pad from one of his many cargo pockets and flicked his hair from his face. "I do comics. Of supes." He presented pictures of dragon and wolf shifters and lots of angels flying above buff satyrs. His style was masterful and dynamic, as if the characters could gallop right off of the pages into the real world.

"How do you know supes so well?" she asked him.

He shrugged. "I study them, draw them." He turned to Oryn. "Hell, I hang out with them! I wish I wasn't a normal human. I'd like some magical powers."

Celestine was bowled over. Usually, so-called normal people wanted to get *away* from supes and found them scary. The prejudice against supes in Red River and how Nola Jaye was murdered for being a psychic was a trauma she'd never forget.

"Well, your drawings are magical," Oryn offered. Riley lit up at the compliment.

"I was going to say that, too," Celestine agreed. She turned to Aline. "What's your favorite thing to draw? I've been so busy keeping up with the lessons, I haven't spent time looking at other work."

"I draw lots of things. Botanicals that I sell to the tattoo parlors who always need designs. I'm obsessed with unique pottery and quirky dishware for still-life setups. Portraits, too—of willing street folks." She looked at Oryn. "We go out with Oryn and make the rounds, check in with the kids, the runaways, the struggling supes. I might be a mundane, but I vibe with supes." She wrapped her arm around Riley's, and he leaned over to kiss her. "Riley and I are weird that way."

"Aww, you guys are too cute." Celestine gestured to the

line of backpacks and the brimming bag of Ray's leather pouches near the front door. "I like to help the folks who struggle that way too. I have these ready to pass out. Let's join forces at some point."

"That would be great," said Oryn, sitting next to her, his muscular legs flexing below his long hiking shorts. He took a gulp of his drink. "You pour heavy. That's a good thing."

She giggled. Then she felt self-conscious. Was it too early in the mourning period for giggles? Especially a giggle that revealed her budding crush. *Dammit, I deserve some respite.* This logic sequencing raced through her in seconds. Man, she was weary. Oryn was next to her, and she drank in his evergreen energy. Well, the vodka, too. "Hey, Aline, if you like supes, art, and the unexpected, when I open my gallery, you could be one of the point people, the gallerist at the desk."

"I accept!" Aline was off her chair and dancing around in gleeful anticipation.

Riley snorted. A twirling woman in cat pajamas *was* rather amusing. "What position am *I* being offered?" he quipped.

"Sell your comics and drawings here. This place could be like a salon, you know, with an open mic night and dark espresso and art symposiums. Supes and mundanes alike will be welcome. No prejudices."

"Great idea," Oryn said.

Celestine rubbed at her chin bandage. "Who knows? It could also be an effective front for, you know, other activities..."

"Like what?" Oryn asked.

"Investigations. I'm thinking of calling it Shadow Salon for that reason. You know, two purposes, a PI operation protected and shrouded by the art biz."

"Clever name, clever idea," Oryn said. Aline and Riley nodded in agreement.

"You'd start a private investigation business on top of a gallery?" he asked. "That would be tons of work."

"I'm all in with trying to figure out what happened to Ray. If I can figure it out, if I can ace it, well... it'll be the most important thing I've done so far. I'd be up for more. That's exactly why it would be smart to have a mundane front for the gallery part," Celestine continued.

"Use me!" Aline joked. "I'm mundane as hell if you want me to be. A salon! I love it. I'll help you paint and decorate." She grimaced at Celestine's bandaged hands. "I mean, you can't do it all. You're a delicate soul who seems to injure yourself a lot."

Oryn cast Celestine a worried look. "Yeah, take care of yourself."

"I'll try. Here, Aline." Celestine tore a page from her vellum pad and got fat markers and tape from a container on the sill. "My hands are clumsy at the moment. Make me a sign for the window?"

"Sure, what should it say?" Aline took the supplies to the narrow table.

"Shadow Salon Art Gallery, Coming Soon."

Aline drew the letters in no-nonsense black, but she put a purple border around it, noting purple seemed to be Celestine's go-to power color, like the purple shirt she had on.

Aline taped the sign face-out on the right-side glass partition and closed the curtains behind it. "This should start some good buzz," she noted.

"Yep, thanks." Celestine's chest lilted as the idea settled inside of her. It would be the next level—in honoring the memory of Ray and Nola Jaye, while celebrating art and the creative community here.

They all sat in a moment of silent camaraderie, and then Aline and Riley finished their drinks and walked into her kitchen. Without asking Celestine, they washed their glasses and set them on the drainer. A pointed glance from Oryn seemed to be their cue. "Look, we're so glad to see your place and get to talk," said Riley. "But, um... we need to get some errands done before it gets too late."

"I won't forget your job offer." Aline gave Celestine a hug, and she and Riley took off, leaving Oryn sitting next to Celestine, and the atmosphere decidedly awkward.

He turned to her. "Are you in pain?"

"Yes," she admitted. Granted, the vodka was taking the edge off it, but her fatigue was again canceling out any major relief.

"What were you really doing if you don't mind me asking?"

"I found Ray's secret stash, a valuable journal." She sighed. "He'd given me the key to it, but I guess he didn't have time to tell me how to undo his ward spell, so I got clobbered—glass shards, rat bites, you name it."

"Holy shit, Celestine! Do you need a rabies shot?"

"They were phantom rats, but yeah, I'm going to get one tomorrow."

She gazed at him in the darkening space. He had helped her down in Jekyll Island, he had shown her his own air magic, revealed parts of his vulnerable self. "Can I trust you? I need allies in this fight."

He put his hand on her knee. The sudden touch was like gentle fire. "I'm here for you. Yes, you can trust me."

She described what was in the journal, all of it. She told him she would be on the search for the two men Ray had mentioned in his diary. That it seemed that time was running out and that whoever was behind this was probably building an evil blood magic spell with the body parts.

He took it all in. "I can help you look for the men. It could be dangerous for you to do on your own."

She nodded, so unused to relying on anyone else. This, in itself, felt dangerous. But the mystery was deep, with such winding roots...

"Will you let me try an air magic therapy on you?"

She flinched, and his face took on a clouded look of disappointment. "What is it? Can you describe it?"

"It's kind of like the mundanes' hyperbaric oxygen therapy. Compressed oxygen, but, um... less risky." His kind smile was the thing that tipped her to yes.

"Okay. Do I just sit here or what?"

"Well, you could stretch out on a bed, but I don't want you to think I'm putting the moves on you. So, do you have a yoga mat or..."

"The couch in Ray's den."

"Lead the way."

She spread out on it, and he sat on one end. He was so tall he was able to lean forward and reach her with his long arms. He held them over her as if he was doing a type of reiki. He began to chant. He kept his eyes open, and their gazes locked. As the air circulated faster and faster, she kept looking at him for grounding. He gently removed her hand bandage and the others. The air funneled into an intense pressure suit around her, pushing in on her, energizing and healing. He chanted under his breath and then shut his eyes. She looked at his hands. Violet light beamed out as he moved them, as if a search light was gliding back and forth over her. Her skin in the affected areas prickled like her nerves were on fire. As intense as the pressure and tingling became, it gradually eased and quieted. She looked up. His eyes were open, on her. Questioning.

"How do you feel?"

"Remarkably good."

He opened his phone's cover and had her look in its mirror. She drew in a surprised breath.

"Wow! I heal fast as a supe, but this is ridiculously fast! The bite marks are gone. My hands and chin are pink, and the gouges are gone."

"It's a rapid recovery process," he murmured.

He was close enough that she felt his warm breath on her, saw his nostrils flare and his eyes shift from silver to green. He moved closer, and she thought he would kiss her. She *wanted* him to kiss her. But he stopped moving, just kept on staring at her with what looked like curiosity, hunger. She was tempted to grab his shirt and pull him down. Something stopped her. She had told him she wasn't ready, that she was in a vulnerable place. And she realized that it would be best to wait just a little longer to see how things went. After all, he had promised to help her work on Ray's case. If they jumped into something hot, and it cooled or soured, it would screw up everything. Reluctantly, she turned on her side.

"Oh. My. God. You really do have magic hands," she whispered, remembering how amazing his massage had been that other night. "Thank you, thank you."

He rose and spread one of Ray's fleeces over her. "You good? You seem super tired. Best to get a long night's sleep after this procedure. Does the door lock automatically?"

"Yes, thanks, Oryn, really." She kept herself awake until she heard the click of the lock, and then she raised the wards to a high level. When that was done, the cost of all of her spellcasting set in, and she sank into a deep sleep.

# TEN

The next morning, Celestine snuck out the back door because a couple of the press still loitered in front. So she was a person of interest. Hadn't they realized by now she wasn't going to feed them any clues? She took a quick satisfied look at the Shadow Salon sign Aline had put up for her and then dashed to the downtown clinic for a rabies shot, just in case. Then she headed to the precinct, following Detective Wade's orders.

This time, he ferried her into one of those one-way-mirror rooms or whatever you called them. She knew she better parse her words carefully.

He leaned forward, elbows on the table, his face mottled pink with irritation. "What the heck were you thinking, heading down to Jekyll Island? You had clear orders to stay put. Not only does it look suspicious, but it gives me a mind to slap you in jail to keep you in town."

"No need for that, Detective. I'm sorry. I won't do it again. I cared for Ray. He was like a dad to me. Please believe me."

"Plenty of family members kill each other," he said in a hard monotone. "Your word holds no water with me. What did you go to the island for?"

"I told you. I feel an obligation to Ray to find out what happened." She held up a hand before Wade could blow his stack and continued. "I promise, though, that I'll check with you first before following clues outside the city limits."

He narrowed his owlish eyes at her. "If you have leads that tempt you to leave Savannah or any concrete intel *in* Savannah, you bring them to me. Understood?"

"Yeah." She clenched her hands. "Um, have you ever heard of a man named Vex Blade, also dubbed Bastard Blade? Might be a guy from back in the 1980s, 1990s. A bad troublemaker. Or a full-blown criminal." She held off going so far as to mention the Demon Three Eyes Clan Ray had written about in his journal or saying that Blade was a supernatural pirate with dangerous water magic. Mundanes like Wade didn't know what the heck was going on in the supe world. Only in the *interface*. She thought about the part in Ray's journal where he said Blade had conscripted the mundanes into servitude of some sort. Like an invisible kingpin moving the minion chess pieces around without them even really knowing.

Wade scrunched up his round, serious face. He jotted down the name on one of his lined memo pads he had on the desk. "Can't say it rings a bell. Tell me more. Where'd you hear the name from?"

Celestine was reluctant to tell Wade she heard the name from Irma Mae because the old woman wanted to be left alone and was suspicious of cops, of intruders on her turf. Instead, Celestine relayed tidbits she'd read in Ray's journal or heard from Irma Mae and reframed them as a distracting flurry of questions for Wade. "What was the situation on the Savannah coastline in the late 1980s, early nineties? Was there some type of problem? Some terrible accident... or even a battle?"

"Whoa. Hold up." Wade frowned at Celestine. "I'm the one who asks the questions. And I asked you one you haven't answered." She noticed he'd written down more notes. "Who told you all of this, huh?"

Celestine sighed. "I had a conversation out in the salt marsh with the old lady who lives near Peter Leger's cabin. But please don't go harassing her. She's in a delicate and fearful state, and I promised I wouldn't bother her."

"That's not up to you, is it?" Wade growled.

"Not entirely," Celestine admitted. "Though if you want me to feel safe to tell you stuff, it's to your advantage to pay at least some attention to what I say." She gave him a shady side-eye. All she could do was continue to forge an unlikely connection where they both fed each other clues. Because she wouldn't stop sleuthing. Nor would he. They locked eyes as if in an evenly matched duel, where they held out swords, each person ready to stab a vital organ.

To her surprise he snorted and said, "You're incorrigible." He rubbed at his chin. "Look, I'll do a little digging. Back in that era, I was a junior cop, busy learning how to become a detective, but I do remember various troubles along the coast."

Celestine's wolfish ears perked up. "Exactly what kind of trouble?"

"Well, you know, there's always *some* kind of trouble. There were hurricanes that tore things up."

"I'm wondering about man-made messes."

"There was a rash of robberies and murders on Bay Street, in the tourist areas."

"Okay, anything unusually bad? On a larger scale?"

"Let me see. Oh, a contractor who seemed to come out of nowhere had built condos up and down the coast that weren't up to code. Not even close! I mean, tons of 'em, densely packed. And they fell apart in no time. Badly. Concrete collapsing, electrical fires, sewage polluting the waters. People crushed and dying."

"Awful!"

"Yeah, many lawsuits over wrongful deaths. They also dumped pollutants from construction into the tide pools, the barrier reefs, the salt marshes. The company fought off lawsuits, rebelled by unloading unmarked truckloads of industrial waste in the middle of the night, and so on. It took many years to clean up." He shook his head. "Hell, it will probably never go back to what it was."

Celestine shuddered, thinking about Irma Mae's rant on greed and power. "Who owned that company, and what happened to it?"

"I'd have to look it up. Give me a few days." He made more notes.

"Okay, thanks. I'll do research too."

Wade's reply was gruff. "Just no leaving town."

She nodded, tempted to tell Wade about her blood magic suspicions, about how the water villains seemed to be collecting body parts. About Harwood Port and Edge LeRoux in Ray's Jekyll Clan. But for now, it was part of the shrouded world. They were Ray's people. She needed to proceed with care, even if the clock was ticking down. Careless, panicked moves, like when she walked too fast in the salt marsh and got sucked way down in the muck, could set her back badly.

They spoke for five more minutes, and then, in a tense truce, agreed to meet again in a week or so. Celestine was tired all over again. Mundane conversation was almost as exhausting as earth magic. Or maybe her injuries hadn't completely healed after all. She headed to Magic Hands.

"Male or female masseur?" asked the woman with the red lipstick.

"Male. I need a pummel. Sore as hell."

The woman chuckled. "The same guy, Oryn?" asked Red Lipstick as she studied Celestine's massage record card.

The sound of his name gave Celestine a sharp zing to her gut. "No," she decided. "Anyone else this time."

The woman frowned. "Was he that bad?"

"Not at all. I just like to change it up." Celestine had already relied so much on Oryn. They would do well to slow down. But when she was sprawled on the table and a guy named Sam started in on her back and shoulders, his style felt flat, lame-ass, vanilla. It had her yearning for Oryn's sizzling touch, and for his emerald gaze to focus only on he

She texted Oryn after the massage and conducting some research.

Celestine: *Come with me if you want to help question one of the men Ray wrote about. Rather than asking the guy's permission, gonna take my chances and show up. Leaving in half an hour if you want in. That detective yelled at me for skipping town, so it's good this guy is (barely) within the city limits. LOL*

Oryn: *I'm game. Glad to help keep you out of a mudbank or far from phantom rats.*

Celestine: *Thanks, but don't need your protection. Just your company.*

On one level, she knew that was bullpucky. She needed all the protection she could get, but she didn't want to fall into the role of damsel in distress with Oryn, or anyone, ever.

Her heart sped up weirdly. She wasn't used to any of this—a sleuthing partner, a sort of non-date date, whatever it was... Sure, she'd been with guys in Red River. Some hot ones, too. There was a sexy redheaded guy with muscles like Thor from her school who she smoked blunts with and made out with in his car. There was a sullen dude with movie-star looks who lived in her building. He played guitar and even wrote her a sad ballad. But there was something about Oryn. Something magical, elevated, sparkling, utterly charming—something *fae*—that drew her in like a cool, rushing brook on a sweltering afternoon.

She dashed around, filling her go-bag with spellcraft items like crystals and salt and a few of the divining poultices in a baggie. Then, she put on a tight lavender top and black skinny jeans with boots she'd painted wild lilies on. She wove purple ribbon through her long ebony hair and twisted it into an elaborate but practical style that would keep the hair off her face in case this trip required extreme action. She applied lip gloss and even some cat eyeliner.

When Oryn rang her doorbell and she opened it, her breath caught, and time seemed to slow. His tight jade T-shirt matched eyes that stared brazenly at her, clearly taking in every bit of pretty makeup and care she'd put into her look. He towered over her, and she liked that. Strength radiated from his broad shoulders and chest, his long arms, one encircled with the wide copper tribal bracelet. "Hi," he said simply, as if he, too, was temporarily at a loss for words.

Then things sped back up to regular time. "Hey, come on in before those darn reporters storm the gates." She looked past him and gave them a scowl as he shut the door. "We can take my car and go out the back way," she added.

She led him back to the kitchen and poured them each a thermos of coffee before slipping out the back door and raising the wards. They hopped into her beat-up Honda Civic. She dumped her loaded messenger bag on the back seat and gunned it out of the alley and through the old part of town. She put on a playlist of Southern blues and kept it low so they could talk.

"So, the detective gave you a hard time?" Oryn asked when they were on the highway.

She rolled her eyes in reply.

"How much did you tell him?" He looked at her as he took a slug of coffee.

"I didn't mention the stuff in Ray's journal. I did ask if he knew of any big trouble along the coast in the 1980s and nineties." She described what Wade had told her about the robberies and murders in the tourist areas, and the sudden construction of subpar condos and their subsequent collapse.

"You know, I was poking around online myself and I found articles about those condos," Oryn said. "If that's what the old woman you visited referred to, and that Ray referred to in his journal, why would a pirate captain with magic want to invest in such a disastrous mundane business venture? Aren't there better ways to rake in treasure and stay out of the news than to crush people in collapsing buildings?"

"You'd think so!" Celestine exclaimed. "Though maybe it was slim pickings back in the day? No more sailing black flags on the high seas and robbing from other ships. Maybe the pirate supes wanted to plant their cash in a land-based project, and they just hired really shady builders who cut corners. What was the name of the contracting firm?"

"There was more than one." Oryn scrunched up his face as he thought. "I wanna say... Titan and Mornay Corp."

"Titan and Mornay. Okay. I wonder if Detective Wade's heard of them? What happened after the companies were sued? Did you get to that?"

"Yeah, they just disappeared, went incognito, the way you described Peter Leger dropping off the face of the earth."

"Hmm, but Leger came back. And then got murdered. It's all very weird. People don't just vanish forever. Though maybe supes can." Celestine looked over at Oryn, and they locked eyes for an unsettling moment before she focused back on the road. She steered off the highway and followed Google Maps to the address she'd logged in. They were in a suburb, where the lawns were mowed and the bushes neatly landscaped. Where the cars were mostly the latest model Nissans and Volvos.

She parked, and they walked to the house in question. Up close, it was a bit rougher around the edges that the others on the block. The side yard was overgrown, and what she could see of the backyard was in even worse shape—tilting fence, a junked car with the back wheels missing.

She took a deep breath and looked up at Oryn. He gave her a quick, terse smile. She rang the bell.

It took two rings before they saw a hand pull the left curtain aside. It took another two rings for the person inside to answer them.

A man cracked the door open about ten inches and peered out. Glasses, thinning white hair, in jeans, a grubby T-shirt, and corduroy slippers. "May I help you?" he asked in a gravelly voice, as if he wasn't used to talking much.

"Are you Harwood Port?" Celestine inquired in her most gentle, friendly voice.

"Why do you want to know?"

*It isn't a no*, she thought. "We're trying to find a Harwood Port, who knew my friend Ray Bartello," she started to explain.

"I don't know any Ray Bartello," he replied and began to shut the door while muttering, "They always ask me that."

Oryn placed his palm on the door to stop this clearly frightened man from closing it. "*Who* asks you that? Look, we're friendly. We're just trying to get some answers to a mystery and—"

"I don't like mysteries," snapped the man.

"We don't either," Celestine chimed in. "We're just desperate for answers, and we'd love to just have a few minutes of your time if we could. Harwood Port may be in danger. We're only trying to help."

The man opened the door a bit more. "Who are you, exactly?"

"Friends of the Jekyll Clan, if that makes any sense to you."

The man shook his head but stayed at the door. Celestine explained to him in simple terms what she'd read in Ray's journal and that she had found two Harwood Ports in Savannah. She left off the grotesque details of Ray's demise, while playing up Ray's admiration for Harwood, his burning desire for her to find his old friend and shipmate. Though, if flattery didn't work, there was always option two: amp up the fear factor.

"You seem like nice enough folks," the man said after another moment's hesitation. "I can only talk for a few minutes, and I doubt I can help you. But I could stand a little distraction. Best to talk inside." He peered at his neighbor's house across the street and off to either side yard.

The guy seemed slightly paranoid. She was glad she hadn't scared the shit out of him from the get-go.

Inside, Celestine smelled sage, and Oryn was scrunching up his nose, too. Was the guy burning smudge sticks? If so, what was he trying to ward off? His furniture was covered in plastic and his Venetian blinds were all the way down. Although the lights were dimmed, she saw smoke wafting up from a few ashtrays on side tables around the room. To make the air less stinky or to discourage bad juju?

"The place is a mess," he said as they perched cautiously on the plastic slipcovers. "I never have guests."

Celestine smiled. "So, are you Harwood Port?"

"That's my name. What is it you want to find out?" Even in the low light, his unhealthy pallor and sickly thin torso was obvious. Ray's Jekyll Clan all had magic. She tried to sense if Harwood had any magic in him. None. Or was it undetectable because he was so physically weak?

Celestine glanced over at Oryn, sitting next to her. He gave her a subtle cock of his head as if to say *Carry on*. She turned to Harwood. "You sure you don't recall a man named Ray Bartello? If not, why would people have asked you that over and over?"

"I'd know if I met the man, wouldn't I? Yeah, they've asked me that."

"Who?" asked Oryn.

"Can't say." Harwood's eyes darted around his living room as if searching for ghosts. "I'm not who you're looking for, okay? They thought I was that guy. I'm not that guy. Years ago, they sent their hit guys to taunt me, to hurt me."

"Who?" Oryn persisted. "What did they say they wanted with you?"

"I told you, I'm not at liberty to say." The man struggled to his feet and reached for a stick of burning sage in a ceramic ashtray on a side table at the end of the couch. He swished it around, as if it could ward off monsters. "All I can say is they stopped, and then, a month ago they were back," he said. "They just want to give me hell now just because I have the same name." Harwood gave them a long, pained stare.

"What exactly are you saying?" asked Celestine. "Do you know anything about another Harwood Port?"

"Hey, do you people want to get me killed?" Harwood's tone abruptly went cold.

"No! We want to help Harwood Port. We want to warn him about—"

"Sorry, but inviting you in was a bad mistake," he cut in. "I'm going to pay for this. The conversation is over." He pointed the smoldering smudge stick at them. "Go now. I'm a very sick man. This is too much stress."

Celestine was ready to argue her point, but no matter what this Harwood was ill from, making a sick man worse through unwanted interrogation was not something she could do in good conscience. She and Oryn stood and headed to the door. Just before Harwood closed it in their faces, she tried one more tactic. "Look, we might be able to offer you protection. We're supernaturals. Whoever, *whatever* is after you, we have sufficient magic to ward them off."

A flash of interest sparked in Harwood's eyes, but he shook his head in defeat. "It won't do no good. I can't talk anymore," he mumbled, looking down at the smudge stick. He closed the door on them.

Celestine and Oryn walked reluctantly back to her car.

They got in, but Celestine didn't drive off. They sat there quietly while she studied the houses Harwood had peered at when they'd first arrived. She saw a woman's face in the window across the street, who quickly closed the curtains when she saw Celestine studying her. Looking to her left, she saw a man coming out of his house with a dog on a leash. The guy scowled as he strode past, and his German shepherd barked at them before taking a piss on the hydrant just in front of the car. "Friendly crowd, eh?" she grumbled at Oryn.

"Super friendly." They exchanged bemused glances.

Celestine could swear that they had the same thought at the exact same time. "Shall we—"

"Pay them a visit?" Oryn finished.

"The woman first?" Celestine suggested.

"Sounds like a plan."

They approached the house across from Harwood's and rang the bell. Celestine heard someone arguing inside, and then the door swung open. The same woman who had peered out the window was in full makeup, her brown hair freshly done up and the living room behind her a stark opposite of Harwood's—this one in cream colors with a luxe couch and a pastel painting of a sunny meadow over it. "May I help you?" she asked them.

"Hi," Celestine started. "We were just calling on Harwood Port, your neighbor across the way…"

"I saw that. He doesn't get many visitors."

"Yes, and well, we just wanted to make sure he was okay. It was kind of a wellness check." Celestine offered the woman a smile, while she quickly ascertained if this person had any magical energies. Nada, zip, a solid mundane.

"Are you relatives of his or what?" The woman looked

them up and down with a cynical air, surely calculating any physical similarity to Harwood.

"Distant," Oryn said, offering her his own dimpled grin.

"Very distant," added Celestine. And before the woman could ask more questions, Celestine beat her to it. "How has he been? I mean, the times you've seen him out on the street?"

The woman emitted a rude grunt. "He never comes out. He gets some food deliveries. Even then, he must tell them to leave it because I don't ever see the man open the door." She rolled her eyes. "Since you asked, though, I do hear him yelling—frightfully loud! There's no one else living with him, is there?"

"I don't think so... um, no." Celestine caught herself not playing the part. A family member would probably know this. "What does he yell about?"

"I don't hear everything, mind you. But if I'm walking by or out in my driveway, I do. He screams for killers to go away and leave him alone." She frowned, bringing out her jowls. "The man needs to be committed. He yells to himself about demons, about guts spilling."

*Guts spilling, ugh.* Celestine shook off her dread. "Anything about pirates?"

The woman arched a tweezed brow. "You're joking, right?"

"Have you tried to get him help?" Oryn asked.

"Well, no, it's his business," she scoffed.

"So, you prefer to eavesdrop on the man and spy on him out the window," Oryn grumbled. "Not sure how that helps a man in extreme distress."

Celestine's heart warmed. Oryn's natural inclination was always to help those in trouble. Though she was worried that this particular woman might lash out at being confronted. It could backfire on Harwood.

Already, the woman was red with huffy outrage. "Who the hell do you think you are, coming to my house and berating me? I have a mind to call the cops on you."

Oryn didn't argue. He gave her a sardonic grin, turned on his heels, and said, "Have a lovely day."

Celestine followed. They hopped back in her Honda. Just before she drove off, something wavy caught her eye. Harwood had actually hobbled outside and was gesturing to them.

"Guess that woman can't say she's never seen Harwood outside now," Celestine said with a snort. "Give me a minute, Oryn. Be right back." She was outside, hurrying up Harwood's front walkway and by his side in a flash. He ushered her to his side yard, beyond the prying stares of any neighbors.

Harwood was white as dry bone in the sunlight. Facing her, he said, "I saw you trying to question my neighbor."

"Sorry if it embarrassed you. I was only trying to—"

"It's okay," he cut in. "She's a nosy harridan. Seeing you try to get info from her made me change my mind about talking. It's best you hear anything from me. It's not her I'm scared of."

"Then who?"

"My death, but not in the way you might assume." He sighed. "I'm dying of cancer. They can't save me. I'm more scared of that than the supernatural freaks that have come back. They tortured me for years before they finally went away. But like I told you, they returned about a month ago. They appear at all hours. They fly inside, taunt me when I'm lying in my bedroom, sick and drenched in sweat. They turn my handful of days left into nightmares."

"I'm so sorry. We're trying to help by figuring out this case. Did they say what brought them back? Who they are?"

He barreled on, not answering her exact questions but still giving her other information. "Let them kill me if they want. I'm going to die anyway, so if it helps you, I might as well tell you what they warned me not to tell anyone."

"Okay." *Am I ready for this?* Celestine's heart rattled against her ribs.

Harwood's pale face became resolute. "You came too late to save your Harwood Port. The phantoms told me they scooped out his guts many years ago and threw him in the swamp."

"Huh? What swamp, where?" Cold sweat broke out on her back, in her armpits. "Are you sure they told you the truth?"

The man heaved out a pained laugh, which turned into a wheeze. "The truth! These evil brutes are as serious as a heart attack. They didn't say which swamp, but those shits like to brag about their crimes. Some sicko honor badge."

"But there *was* no other Harwood Port in Savannah except some teenager living here now, too young to be the guy. I did extensive research."

"Wrong. They picked a guy who lived off the grid. Some loner with no family and no regular job. Untraceable, they bragged. Off the birth charts." He paused to catch his wheezing breath. "You're right, it makes no goddamn sense, except I ain't lying to you." He stared at her with eyes as haunted as she felt.

"But why carve out his intestines?" she whispered in a tremble.

"They said they needed the guy's guts 'cause he was some magical pirate who would make their spellcraft unstoppably strong. Who knows why they told *me* of all people? And what the hell is a magical pirate?"

*I know very well what that is. Scooped out his intestines. Ray's entry was all about how Harwood had major guts, so it wasn't just a metaphor.* This was sick and it was making her stomach churn. She might puke out her own guts. *Holy crap! Hold it together, girl!*

Harwood barreled on. "I guess psychos and criminals can't keep their mouths shut any better than an average Joe. But why me? Why confess to me? I never wanted the burden of keeping their crimes top secret."

"That *is* a heavy, heavy burden." No wonder the guy's health had deteriorated. Talk about stress! Her concern for him was the only thing distracting her from heaving. She took a long breath and wondered, for a minute, why Harwood hadn't gone to the cops and reported the crime. But only for a minute because if the other Harwood really was never on the birth records, and his powers were as extraordinary as Ray had written, a mundane cop would never believe this man who thought phantom pirate hunters were torturing him. It was the same reason she'd held back with Detective Wade, and especially the clueless cops who had questioned her down at the hospital near Jekyll Island.

"Anyways, they're back," Harwood ranted, "and threatening to cut off *my* body parts to add me to a poisonous cannibal stew. Not because they need them, just for extra flavor!"

Celestine swallowed back bile.

Harwood added, "They said they torture me just because I have the same name. They have no reason. Proves they're pure evil."

She reached out and patted Harwood's shoulder, to

which he started, jumped back, and then, promptly apologized for. "Sorry, lady. I'm just so jumpy. I guess you was just trying to comfort me."

"I was. Sorry, I should have asked permission." They both let out an awkward chuckle. "My name's Celestine. I truly appreciate you telling me all of this. You're obviously under huge stress in addition to your illness."

At this, she felt a sudden cool breeze on her shoulders and neck, and her hair actually swirled up. Oryn had soundlessly gotten out of the car, walked along the path to the backyard, and whooshed over to Celestine's side. "What's doing?" he asked, looking from one to the other.

"I'll fill you in soon," she promised. "Harwood, this is Oryn. He's a supe like I am. Before we take off, we should put up some wards on your house."

"Wards?"

"Protective guards. Think of them as invisible walls that the phantom hitmen will, er, bang up against if they try to mess with you."

"Okay, but what if they stop my food delivery guy? I'm pretty stuck here."

"We'll take that into account. We'll make sure it applies to a narrow set of... individuals." She glanced over at Oryn, who nodded. "Can you describe the, um, bad phantoms in more detail? Did they tell you their names?"

"Let's go back inside. I need to lie down."

"Of course," said Celestine. "Be there in a sec. Have to get something from my car." She retrieved her messenger bag, and they followed Harwood inside, waiting while he painstakingly lowered himself on the couch.

Oryn got Harwood the glass of water and some crackers he asked for. Celestine handed him a pillow for his head. She settled into a chair alongside Oryn. The fae's kindness was palpable, like a comforting quilt he bestowed around everyone's sore shoulders. It dashed any preconceived notions of all men being selfish pricks or of human kindness being exclusively feminine. Oryn was as masculine as they came, with his assured strength, his rippling muscles, his unwavering, determined energy, square jaw, and lion's mane hair. Her heart fluttered. She willed it to calm the fuck down. Now was not the time to let her smoldering crush blaze. She waited until Harwood had swallowed a third of his water and set the glass back down with a shaky hand before offering him a gift.

"Do you like to read?"

"Sure. Why?"

"Ray willed his set of pirate books to Harwood, and well, since you're the surviving Harwood..." She pulled out the set of pirate books from her bag and put them on the tea table with the crackers. "You can learn more about pirates."

"What a nice surprise!" he said. "I'll look through them after my nap."

"So, I started to ask you outside, do you recall any specific names of the guys who tortured you? Names they called out that identified them?"

"Like I said, years ago, they kept asking me if I knew Ray Bartello. They despised the man. I was shocked to hear you say his name."

"He was murdered a couple of weeks ago."

Harwood grimaced. "Oh, no! So sorry."

"Thanks." She shrugged off the chills that came with saying it out loud. "Any other names come to mind?"

Harwood brought a hand to his forehead and rubbed it. He took so long to answer that Celestine almost thought he had dozed off, and his voice was so faint. "Vex. Vex Blade."

Celestine's blood ran cold. She'd lost count of how many times today that had happened. "According to Ray, Vex Blade was the captain of the Demon Three Eyes Clan. Oh my god. Anyone else?" But this time, Harwood really was asleep, for he began to snore.

Oryn and Celestine locked eyes. "Shall we let Harwood sleep?" he asked her.

"Sounds good." They rose and took some time putting air and earth wards on the door and around the perimeter of the house. These enemies of Ray's were water mages, and she couldn't match their strength in water magic. Nor could Oryn.

But by the time they left, Oryn had a significant hurricane trap set, and Celestine had set up pebble storms. Any supe foolish enough to crash the wards would get pierced with tiny rock shards as forceful as shrapnel and then lifted off the ground only to be thrown on his head by hurricane-force magic.

Still, while they drove back to Bay Street, the air was thick with Celestine's and Oryn's palpable worry.

"I hope he's safe," said Celestine.

Oryn nodded. "Me too." He reached over and momentarily curled his hand over hers on the steering wheel. Sweet heat flickered through her from his touch. It was just as well she had to drive because otherwise, she'd be all over Oryn. There were tangled mysteries yet to unravel, and she wanted to avoid distractions a little while longer.

That said, she didn't resist when she put the car in park to drop him off at his place, and he reached out and cupped her chin. His long fingers caressed her as if her face were royal silk. His green eyes in the lamplight changed to periwinkle twinkles. He moved closer until she could feel his breath on her.

"I'm glad you came today," she whispered. "I guard my space, my world, but it's a tired playbook of mine to reflexively reject company."

"I fall into my own ruts, so I get it. I like your company, Celestine. A lot." Oryn stroked her cheek, and it felt natural for him to lean closer and kiss her softly on her lips. It wasn't an open-mouthed kiss, but it was a lingering one. Not totally chaste. Just delicious—like ripe peaches and red grapes and syrup. With a zing of his evergreen. Then they wrapped their arms around each other and hugged for dear life. His hard muscles pressed against her eased from the day's tension. Hers, too. Skin on skin was a blessed lifeline.

"These last couple weeks have been so scary," she whispered into his hair.

"It's hard. But you can get through it. You're incredibly strong. And I'm here." He kissed her cheek.

"Thanks for going today. I'll need to do some of it on my own."

"I get it. Just text or call me when you want company," he whispered into her ear. "See you in our last art class soon."

"Yep."

When they pulled apart, Celestine was flying high. It hadn't seemed like the right time, but the kiss and the long embrace calmed her soul like nothing else could. She didn't want to get addicted to him. She needed to be able to sleuth on her own. But he damn sure made her less afraid.

BACK AT BAY STREET, every last member of the press had finally dispersed. Her wolfish senses sprang to life in the dusky light. She parked in the back alley and was careful on the walkway to suss out nasty water entities by sniffing in bursts of the cooling night air. It was free of fetid water phantoms. Maybe they'd followed the reporters' lead and had taken the night off. She lowered the wards, entered the house, and was careful to raise them immediately.

She settled into Ray's desk chair and opened her journal. Jotted down the day's new data.

*Vex Blade scooped out Harwood Port's intestines years ago, and then dumped him in a swamp. Which swamp was Harwood's final resting place?*

*In addition, Blade has tortured the wrong Harwood Port for years out of spite or sadistic delight. One helluva grudge-fest against Ray and his clan. What did Ray do to raise that much ire from the petulant pirate captain? More connections between these creeps and the disastrous condo oppo? If so, find them!*

*Sharpen focus on Demon Three Eyes reasons to chop off body parts. Who can I ask?*

*Locate the real Edge LeRoux before he gets hacked up!*

*Why did the Demon Three Eyes Clan disappear? What made them return?*

She shook off her boots and trudged upstairs to her old room. She hadn't yet taken over Ray's larger bedroom. It seemed disrespectful as long as his spirit still hovered nearby. Sometimes she sensed him trying to make sure she was okay, other times in his kitchen, she swore he was feeling nostalgic for times he could whip up barbequed ribs and greens. The dead couldn't cook on stoves. She lay on her bed and stared at her newest automatic drawing tacked up on the wall: the odd three-spouted vessel. What kind of sea critters were on its surface, and why exactly had she drawn it? Usually, she had a hunch. In this case, no idea.

Two other needs floated up in her mind. The first: *When I open a sleuthing business, I'll need a water mage.*

The second: *I need to commune with Nola Jaye. Now.*

She gathered up her spellcasting items and a new tarot deck, then she swallowed down a power poultice ball and packed two peaches. Lowering and raising the wards once again, she streaked out the back, this time with her pack on her back and a change of clothes rolled inside it. She transformed to wolf form, swiftly taking the alleyways and darkened city squares to Bonaventure.

# ELEVEN

B y the time Celestine entered the cemetery, the magic poultice had done its trick. It had roared through her veins, up to her synapses, and out through her eyes, which, in her wolf form, already saw the night clear as day. She snarled up at the ancient tangled tree forms, the Spanish Moss. It was a warning to any threatening water specters that might be hiding up there. She hadn't come to Bonaventure to be thrown under their crashing breakers tonight.

In her hyperaware state, she was able to see the newly dead as they rose from their graves and appeared as flickering blue lights. They trailed her like moths to a lamp's glow. *What do I look like to you, and what color am I? I hope ultraviolet.* She identified with shades of purple.

The resentful spirits who hadn't resolved their violent, tragic deaths had red auras and chattered in harsh, undecipherable gibberish. Some stuck to her fur in gluey blobs. She shook them off and trotted on until she saw Lionel and Lonetta, Nola Jaye's parents' twin gravestones under a sloping willow.

Celestine transformed to human form, her fur receding, her haunches smoothly changing to legs. She was used to it, yet sometimes it made her skin itch. She quickly pulled a jersey dress she'd packed over her head and smoothed it down over her hips. Then she sat cross-legged and presented the peaches and the new tarot deck with her favorite art—black outlined figures filled in with jewel-toned colors, like fine stained-glass windows.

"Nola Jaye," she crooned, "it's Celestine. I come with treats. A pretty new deck and some fruit."

The willow branches shuddered, and a cool breeze wrapped around her shoulders. She shivered. A soft chewing and slurps sounded. Looking down, she saw one of the peaches was half eaten. Celestine grinned at the sight. "I'm glad you like them. Can I ask for your counsel?"

The wind whooshed, blowing the tall grass almost side-ways, and then Celestine felt Nola Jaye's trademark tap on her shoulder.

*The deck is colorful. I hope you still have my Oracle deck. What does my favorite lady ask me tonight?*

Amazing how Nola Jaye could speak inside Celestine's mind without uttering one word out loud, and vice versa. Her inner hearing was amplified by the poultice.

*Did Ray's second mate, Harwood Port, really get his guts scooped out? Or was that other Harwood telling us lies?* Celestine asked Nola Jaye silently.

*The sick man tells truths on his deathbed.*

Celestine's heart pinched. *Is he dying so soon? Hopefully not from the hand of Demon Three Eyes. What did he think of us?*

*No frivolous questions, witchling! Your purpose here? You know how quickly magical energy evaporates... raindrops in noonday sun.*

*Okay, Nola Jaye. Sorry.* Celestine watched as the rest of the peach disappeared with more juicy chewing sounds until only a fuzzy pit remained on the grass. Magic made one weary but also hungry. Celestine was careful to ask a very important question next.

*Where is Edge LeRoux? Is he dead or alive? I need to warn him!* She couldn't help slipping in two more quick questions. *Which swamp is Harwood in? And why did the Demon Three Eyes Clan come back?*

Nola Jaye didn't answer in Celestine's head. Instead, three cards began to simultaneously slip from the deck and hover in the air. They landed in a neat line in front of Celestine's crossed legs. The Empress, the Devil, and the Reversed World card. The angry spirits stopped their jabbering and crowded around her like buzzing mosquitoes. She swiped at them until they dispersed. Looking up, she saw the dark pierced by silent lightning flashes. *Nola Jaye, I don't understand the cards.*

Nola Jaye intoned directly into Celestine's mind: *The Empress is the artist who finds answers in pictures. The Devil, a demon's swamp, the topsy-turvy world is in crisis.* With that, the second peach rolled swiftly into the darkness. *Do not forget the troubled woman from before. Stir all pots. Sew all stitches, witch.*

As Nola Jaye's energy diffused, Celestine felt terribly off-kilter. Was she going to faint? Or was malicious magic gathering in the air?

More thunder exploded. Jagged white lightning divided the sky into crooked sections. An abrupt roar was followed by driving rain. Celestine leapt up just as a wide bolt of lightning hit the old willow and split its wide trunk. With a sharp crash, the top half of the tree toppled onto Lonetta's gravestone, smashing it into the grass.

Celestine's rage boiled as she looked up, holding an arm over her eyes to shield them from the storm. "You just had to follow me here! You couldn't leave me be, huh? And destroying an old woman's grave. Shame!" The digested juice from the magic poultice had Celestine seeing things even her wolf self could not. Above her, a towering phantom with a full beard, wild blue hair, and a dreadful scar cutting across his face hovered over the broken willow.

"You continue to meddle in our affairs!" he shouted, gravel in his throat.

She transformed back to wolfish form, tearing the jersey dress in the process. Lunging upward on preternaturally strong haunches, her fangs descended and bit a hefty chunk out of the half-formed pirate's leg. He howled. Apparently, half-formed flesh could be flayed, and half-formed nerves could ring out in agony. Black blood poured from the gash. She snarled loudly and pushed out gravelly English words through her muzzle. "Stay away from me, Blade. Your phantom breakers can't catch me unaware anymore. I have my own magical weaponry. I'll work on Ray's or any case I damn well choose!"

Another deafening thunderbolt shot through the old cemetery trees. Half a dozen broke and fell, toppling grave-stones in their wake.

"Demon Three Eyes is back!" bellowed Blade. "You are nothing to us."

"What do you want with me, then?" she asked, her heart bleeding from the sight of ancient fallen graves and trees.

"For you to mind your own business."

"What do you *really* want?" she persisted.

"You'll see—wolf woman or witch woman, or whoever you are—but when you do, it will be too late." Blade fell into a fit of chortling and then gurgled clear away in the rain, which slowed as fast as it had come.

Celestine huffed out an outraged sigh. She thought of Nola Jaye's line about how quickly magical energy evaporated, of needing to act decisively before one's supernatural arrows dulled. Blade's magic had dulled in no time. Duly noted. That didn't mean he couldn't inflict severe damage. She stared out at his malevolent handiwork and then struggled in vain to lift the fallen willow trunk off of Lonetta's bent gravestone. Worse, the thick granite had cracked in three places under the great weight of the tree.

So, Bastard Blade could bring on a flash flood, thunderbolts like Thor. He could fell a tree. Hell, fell a dozen trees with his sinister water magic.

*But he can't break my spirit. And Nola Jaye is sprinkled all over this special graveyard, energizing the grass, the stones, the rotting flowers folks place on the graves, the towering mausoleums, the night guardians—bats and mice and snakes. Nola Jaye isn't stuck under anyone's foot at all.*

Celestine raced home still in wolf form, her pack strapped to her back. She was newly determined to stop Bastard Blade, whatever it took. She was grateful for her fine black fur, her sharp fangs, her fleet paws and limbs. Her muzzle that could smell thunder and her fine, fine mind, enhanced by magic or not.

*Blade might be the captain of a deadly clan, but he has nothing on a badass bitch like me.*

~

Back home, she shifted to human form in the kitchen, pulling on a robe and assessing the damage to the things in her pack. Her new stained-glass—style tarot deck was ruined, warped with the inks running. Her jersey dress was ripped to shreds. Just *things*, she decided, and tossed them. She was damp and shivering. Yet her pride was buoyed by her sheer nerve during the back-and-forth with Blade. He had not managed to mangle her. She had stuck to her guns this time.

Though upstairs, soaking in a hot tub to warm up, her nerves and her confidence began to unravel. He would surely wreak revenge. *How can I possibly anticipate his every move to protect myself and the ones I care about?*

Nola Jaye would tell her to carry on. She'd say, "Witchling, use your skills. You were born for this. Defeat this sickening demon and his mad plans!"

Her father and mother would be scared for her, yet they'd give her a pep talk, not beg her to stop. She would not consult with them this time. She would stand in her power no matter what it took.

Ray would tell her to be more careful. She already sensed him hovering like a helicopter parent. But she was an adult, and he wasn't her dad. And was "more careful" the answer? Back in his day, Ray and his Jekyll Clan had waged a supernatural battle royale. Irma Mae had hinted at it when she relayed what Harwood had told her years ago. Somehow, Celestine needed to find out much more about it. Whatever they'd done, they had totally riled up Bastard Vex Blade. So Ray hadn't exactly followed the "careful" path.

Shuddering, she stepped out of the tub and wrapped herself in a downy towel. What if she performed another divining ritual? Visualized the battle with the help of more poultice balls? The idea of chewing those foul weedy things right now made her gag. Plus, she was dog tired. Nola Jaye had said that magic evaporated rapidly. Celestine hadn't used much in that cemetery. But she might want to have Oryn by her if she went into a serious divining trance since it wasn't her specialty. Oryn would be her rock, her ever-green, her grounded mage.

She got out her drawing pad and a soft graphite and slipped into bed, the vellum balanced on her legs. Her last art class was tomorrow, and maybe if she satisfied the automatic impulse tonight, she could finally draw something normal in class.

She closed her eyes and took slow, deep breaths. Thought of the first card Nola Jaye had pulled. *The Empress is the artist who finds answers in pictures... the Empress is the artist who...* Celestine's fingers began to twitch this way and that. She was along for the ride, her preternatural mind the conduit between the ether and concrete, visual clues. "Pull them in, pull them in," she intoned as her hands warmed and their movements sped up. Finally, when the pulsing energy seeped out of them and her heart slowed, she opened her eyes.

A jail cell!

She had drawn ten distinct bars, a dim interior with a metal cot affixed to the wall. She squinted her eyes. No one. Not a soul in that cell.

"What the hell, Nola Jaye? How am I supposed to inter-pret this?" she grumbled.

She heard a pop and looked down. One of Ray's tiny ships in a bottle had careened off the wall shelf, and its glass had cracked in two. The wooden boat looked forlorn, exposed on the plank floor. Was that a display of Nola Jaye's hair-trigger temper, like when she rolled the peaches into the dark? Next, the old card reader would be tossing peach pits at Celestine's head.

"Okay, Nola Jaye, I won't complain. I'll figure it out. Promise."

Staring at the jail drawing left her blank. Celestine was beyond exhausted. Her magic was truly drained now. She rested the vellum pad on the rug, switched off her lamp, and slid further under the covers. "I'll sleep on it," she murmured.

CHAPTER

# TWELVE

The class had assembled, and Prof Gray, up on the risers, was explaining how watercolor pencils worked. "Use them dry, and they function as normal colored pencils, but..." Celestine had used regular colored pencils but never these watercolor deals. He dipped two pencils of varying hues of blue in a cup of water and began to run them across a paper clipped to an upright easel. Nice! He squiggled and swerved and smeared them until the image looked like a flowing stream.

Oryn looked over at her with a Cheshire grin and a knowing nod. Celestine was shy having him next to her after their kiss the other night. Ridiculous, as this wasn't exactly her first rodeo. She'd had pretty decent sex with the depressive musician, albeit on an uncomfortable concealed balcony with only a threadbare quilt between their butts and the deck floor's sharp iron lattice.

Oryn's kiss, and now his sensual grin, unlocked the padlocked Pandora's box of heartthrobby daydreams she normally avoided. A messy rush of invisible virtual hearts floated all around her, mixed in with some of his sparkly will-o'-the wisps. Shit! She might as well be in some kind of sappy Hallmark made-for-TV movie. She snorted and turned back to the Prof.

He had set up two still lifes: one with a wide bowl filled with water and floating toy boats, the other an aquarium filled with all stripes of tropical fish. Impressive.

The tiny boats reminded her of the one that had tumbled out of her cracked jar last night. A wave of anxious sadness wafted through her. She needed to tell Oryn about what happened in the cemetery with Vex, about her prison cell drawing. But she also needed to get through this last class. One thing at a time.

She decided to focus on the fish. The last thing she wanted to do was a freaky prophetic drawing, and no doubt the tiny boats would set off an emotional burst.

"You okay?" Oryn whispered.

*Gawd.* She couldn't hide anything from him—he was already so synced with her in some way. She almost hugged him in relief that someone saw past her guarded façade. Instead, she delivered a little smile and stroked his arm. "I'm okay for now," she whispered back. "We can talk later."

That was enough to put on pause the spell they were beginning to weave together.

Celestine dipped her pencils in the cup of water she and Oryn shared on the floor between them, and she rendered the fish outlines with liquid strokes, making it seem like they were really swimming. It was cool how, unlike with gouache or markers, she could easily do water current swishes as well as the harder lines of the fins and scales. Though if she carried these pencils with her on an investigative trek, she'd need access to water to use them to their full potential. It was freeing to get lost in the wonder of colors and shapes. She forgot, for at least a blissful forty-five minutes, about all of her troubles and responsibilities. Artists called it being in the zone, a sort of REM dream state without actually being asleep.

When she took a break to assess the image, she was also pleased it was actually of *fish*, that it hadn't turned into an inscrutable automatic drawing that warned of another calamity. Glancing over at the Prof, she was also grateful he'd taken her request to heart. He was leaning over the easel of a student across the room and hadn't stepped foot near her once.

Oryn had done a bright-hued pencil painting of the toy boats. "It's beautiful," she whispered.

"Not as beautiful as you," he whispered back.

"Aww, that's nice." She heated up in a blush from her chest to her forehead while stuffing her pencils in a cloth sack and then into her messenger bag.

Aline and Riley joined them. Riley was talking about a Bonaventure Cemetery article.

"What happened?" Celestine's heart hurt. She knew.

Riley grunted. "They said marauders went into the cemetery during that storm and cut a bunch of trees down, smashed a bunch of historic gravestones."

"So it wasn't just from lightning?" Aline asked. "What kind of assholes would do such a malicious thing?"

"No," said Riley, "they said one was from lightning, but others looked cut."

"How demented," Celestine grumbled. "Those trees are so old. Living history destroyed."

Oryn looked long and hard at Celestine, as if his attuned senses detected an absolute connection, but he wasn't going to open his mouth here. For this, Celestine was grateful. She would tell him soon enough.

They all compared drawings. Riley had done a comic-book-sized image of the fish with lots of graphic bubbles. Aline had rendered the little boats with more subtle, realistic colors than Oryn had. It was clear to Celestine that while Oryn was a mystical stylist, Aline was a meticulous realist.

"Impressive," she said to Aline, who was already studying Celestine's drawing.

Aline didn't seem to hear the compliment. Instead, she pointed to something in Celestine's art. "Hey, is that a letter in the water, just behind the fish? I see a V..."

"Huh?" Celestine squinted her eyes at her own work. "Wow, I hadn't noticed."

"And these, over here." Aline pointed to two more giant letters, seeming to undulate behind the fish. "An E and an X."

"Vex," Oryn read, worry in his tone.

"Vex," Riley echoed. "What's that?"

"Holy crap," Celestine hissed. "I thought for once I could take a tiny break from this nightmare."

"Sorry I pointed it out. Who or what is Vex?" asked Aline.

Other students started to look their way to see what the commotion was about. Oryn turned his back on them to block their view.

Celestine patted Aline's arm. In a hushed tone, she said, "No worries, it has nothing to do with you. I promise I'll clue you both in soon." She leveled her gaze at Aline and Riley. "Right now, I have pressing business." She flipped the front of her drawing pad over the image and stuck the thing under her arm. "We can walk out together. Maybe we can meet tomorrow? Talk more about the gallery? Distribute the leather goods?"

Aline and Riley nodded and took the lead out of the room and down the hall. Celestine and Oryn followed.

"You need company?" he asked quietly.

"Yeah. Thanks." Celestine was shaking, and her knees wobbled.

"Where to?" he asked.

"Your place for a change?"

"Sure. I can give you a lift. I parked around the corner."

They said their goodbyes to Aline and Riley and made tentative plans to meet at Celestine's studio the next day if the timing worked out.

In Oryn's car, she relayed last night's scary events in Bonaventure and described the automatic drawing of the jail cell she'd done afterward. He took it all in without interjecting, just nodding. She appreciated what a good listener he was. It was comforting.

"What do you make of the prison cell drawing?" he asked finally.

"Honestly, no clue. Something that hasn't happened yet. But what?"

He shrugged. "You're better at interpreting your drawings than I am."

"Thanks. Well, it doesn't feel like someone being *convicted* of anything," she mused. "It feels really different than that, though I can't say why."

"You'll know when you need to," he assured her.

"I hope so."

At his house, she took out the LeRoux list and proceeded to call to try and make appointments.

Her rap was basically: "I'm a distant relative of the LeRoux family, and I wanted to make contact to ask some important family heritage questions... No, I can't describe them on the phone... They're kind of, um, delicate."

A white lie, but one that might make them curious enough to meet. People couldn't resist juicy secrets, and she couldn't exactly tell them the truth—that their time left on this earth might be only a matter of weeks or days, that a bloodthirsty supernatural was after their heart.

But at the end of it all, Edgar LeRoux agreed to see them that afternoon. And she wouldn't have to report her trip to Detective Wade unless it became a solid lead, since the guy was within the city limits. She also contacted Edgewood LeRoux, who agreed to see them tomorrow. He was a two hour's drive west, outside the city limits, so she'd have to get Wade to approve that trip.

THEY TOOK ORYN'S FORESTER. No time to hang out in his lush garden or get involved in a heavy make-out session. One drama at a time was all she could handle for now. Though Celestine *had* imagined a lot more than just kissing: sex on the massage table, in Oryn's garden on a chaise, up in her own lair on Bay Street in her comfy double bed with all of her woo-woo drawings around them.

It was enough right now to just enjoy his presence, his sexy pine cologne, how he owned the road as they drove north and west. The address said Spring Street, but when they arrived, they realized it was a cemetery—Laurel Grove North.

"Someone lives here? Or did we get the address wrong?" Oryn asked her.

Celestine checked the listing in her phone again. "This is it. Maybe there's a house on the grounds. Let's pull in and ask."

They drove past an area marked infant section, another

marked unknown section and one marked war fallen. Celestine shuddered at the sadness of what these meant— people buried without being identified, tiny babies never making it to adulthood, much less childhood. Finally, after a winding drive around the inner roads, they came to a wide gray barn and a small building next to it marked office. They parked and hopped out. Despite the somber vibe, the lawns were impeccably groomed, and the air smelled of freshly cut grass.

They rang the doorbell. A bulked-up man with thick brown hair answered. He wasn't quite as tall as Oryn but had wrestler's muscles under a T-shirt and baggy overalls. "Y'all part of the LeRoux clan?" he asked with a wide grin that showed a missing bottom tooth.

"You're *Edgar*?" Celestine blurted with an almost rude astonishment.

"That's me!"

Right away, she was skeptical. *He's too young to be Ray's contemporary. The online data said he was in his sixties. This man is twenty-eight at best.*

She figured she'd play along, though. Find out what she could. She didn't look over at Oryn. He'd probably heard the cynicism in her voice, and if they locked eyes, he'd know this was all wrong.

"Why yes, I'm a distant relative," she professed. "I'm Celestine, and my friend here is Oryn."

Oryn nodded and gave the guy the requisite smile.

"Do you mind if we ask you some—"

"'Course not," Edgar cut in. "Y'all come in." With a sweep of his arm, he ushered them into a small office and then to a side room filled with chairs that looked like a doctor's waiting room, though instead of health magazines, there were two copies of *Municipal Cemetery Report* on a side table. A framed photo of a mausoleum with a wreath of white lilies was the only art. "Cold drink? All I have is chilled Gingerade. Will that do?"

Celestine and Oryn nodded. He distributed cans of the cold soda, settled into a chair across from them, and took a draw of his own Gingerade while wiggling his booted feet clotted with mud.

Celestine's animal senses weren't as attuned in the daytime, but she tried to smell him for any whiff of water magic or mystical mage vibes. Not only was this guy way too young, but she was sure he was a mundane—no whiff of magic. Glancing over at Oryn, she knew he was conducting his own energy search because his eyes rapidly shifted from gray to green to amber. When he did this, it reminded her of a literal scanner.

"So, Edgar, you work here?" asked Celestine.

"I'm a caretaker. I mow the lawns. Gardener by trade. I worked a lot of the, um... graveyards around these parts." He shrugged. "Woodville, Lincoln Memorial, hell, even over at the pet cemetery."

"Oh! That's a noble profession," Celestine said.

Oryn grinned, and she shot him a warning look not to blow their cover.

"It ain't exactly noble, but someone's got to do it." Edgar squinted at her. "Say, what did you say you was looking for a LeRoux for? Who's your daddy and maw? Your granny and grandpaw?"

Celestine's face heated up. She sucked at lying, and she wasn't sure how to string the conversation along until she was able to improvise her next line of bullshit. "Well, um... I have a good friend, actually *had* a good friend, who was very fond of Edgar LeRoux."

"Oh? And who was that?"

She heard tension in his tone. "Uh, you don't know him," she hedged, holding off the mention of Ray. Instead, she asked if anyone ever called him Edge.

"Edge? That's a mighty odd name." Edgar gritted his teeth. A look of confusion clouded his face.

*It isn't a yes, but it isn't a no.* Celestine was about to tell Oryn they should mosey on, when Oryn threw in a puzzling request.

"Hey, it's kind of breezy today, not too hot," Oryn said in a cheery voice. "I'd love to have you take us on a walking tour before we get into a longer discussion. I've always been fascinated with cemeteries. Would you indulge us?"

Edgar's jaw unclenched, and he fairly bounced out of his chair. He seemed relieved by the distraction. "Heck, I'll do you one better! How's about I take you for a spin in my golf cart?"

Celestine gave Oryn a frown, but he winked, signaling he had a plan. "Sure!" she ad-libbed. "I'd enjoy a quick tour as well."

Edgar took them outside. He propped open the barn's double doors, and they followed him in, where he seemed much more at home, clomping around in his muddy boots and overalls. The spacious barn had an impressive array of lawn mowers, rakes, and other landscaping tools like electric weed whackers hanging from hooks.

"Nice space!" Oryn remarked. "Looks like you put a lot of energy into it."

"I do keep up the machines, oiling and cleaning them. You could call them my babies." Edgar huffed out a laugh.

"Do you ever mow Bonaventure?" asked Celestine.

"Can't say I do, ma'am. Why do you ask?"

"Just curious. It's such a famous cemetery." She ran her hand along the edge of his shiny blue golf cart. "Do you ever sail, or go boating? My, er... relatives loved to go boating."

"Why, um, that's a very particular thing." Edgar glanced at her. "Can't say that I love to take a boat out. Had me a bad time or two out on the waves." He ushered them into the back seats of the cart and started the motor.

"Oh?" Celestine's ears perked up. "What kind of bad experience?"

"Mile-high whitecaps. Savage undertow. Let's just say we almost capsized one windy day." His uneasy chortles and sudden acceleration of the golf cart implied he was done with this conversation.

Celestine and Oryn exchanged inquiring glances, and Oryn put a finger over his lips to signal he was onto something and to have patience. Or at least, that was how she read it. She wished they could at least whisper plans to each other, but she wanted to trust Oryn. Because her own senses were off. This guy's youth had messed with her surety, and his apparent wavering between brain fog and clarity confused her, almost as if he had a split personality. They barreled off in the cart.

Edgar drove them around an area lined with flowering trees and oaks. The graves here were tall, thin slabs of granite whose angles had smoothed out from many years of heat, wind, and hurricane floods. "This here is the old section," Edgar said proudly. He slowed the cart so they could study some of the gravestones.

Celestine read a few surnames out loud. "Iverson, Hunnicutt, Peevy, Slappey—that's a memorable one."

"Good old stock from colonial times, I reckon," said Edgar.

"Can you take us to one of the marked sections?" Oryn asked. "I remember passing some on the way in."

Celestine raised her brows at him.

"Which one do you have a hankering for?" Edgar looked over his broad shoulder at Oryn.

"When we drove in, we passed a section called Infants, and another called Unknowns. How about the Unknowns? What are they, orphans or street people or foreigners with no citizenship?"

"Could be all of that... and more," Edgar replied. He made a U-turn and veered onto a smaller roadway branching off the main one.

Under the rumble of the engine, Oryn leaned close to Celestine and whispered, "I'm following a strong hunch."

She nodded, glad to have invited him. Once in a while, two heads *were* better than one when working on a mystery. If she were to start a PI service, she'd keep this in mind, though if Oryn ever became more than just a friend, it might be unwise to combine work and romance. She shook off the whole line of thought. She was getting *waaay* ahead of her skis, as the saying went.

They rolled along, and the sun kept slipping behind clouds and the next moment peeking out—from poignant to cheery, from dim to vivid brightness. This matched Celestine's mood, of not knowing if this was fruitless or if Oryn's intuition would pay off.

*Or if my own supe senses will finally perk up. Uncertainty makes me anxious.*

After about five minutes, Edgar parked the cart and ushered them out. The sign up ahead said unknown. Celestine's skin crawled.

Oryn began circling around a cluster of gravestones, his eyes changing color at a rapid rate again. Celestine could see this even from ten yards away.

Edgar trooped over to a thick oak tree and leaned his

weight on it as he watched Oryn pace around the granite slabs of the Unknown.

Celestine didn't want to break his concentration. She kept quiet as she, too, approached the gravestones and read them. unknown number eleven, unknown number ten, unknown number nine… a meditative act that brought out her wolf senses, though it was still day. She scented the rich earth, the gamey smell of the squirrels peeking down at them from the trees, and the locations of the savory nuts they'd buried all around the graves. Unknowns reminded her of the street supes who Ray had helped, who Oryn counseled, who Celestine wanted to give the remaining leather goods to. How many anonymous beings had lived and died without getting much love, much comfort, even one lucky break? Sadness and a longing to help filled her, and tears pricked her eyes.

By the time she looked up and realized Oryn was in a full trance, his air magic had already stirred up air tornadoes around each grave. Swirls of leaves, loose twigs, and something else more startling…

*Wide-eyed, tousled, half-materialized, half-translucent human torsos!*

Four of them spun around Oryn. They looked to be ten or eleven. Two boys, two girls. Unknowns.

"What do you see in him?" Oryn asked them, cocking his head toward Edgar.

It was only then that Celestine turned toward Edgar. He was in suspended animation, still leaning against the tree. His wide face and husky body were frozen, his eyes fixed in a flat, unseeing stare. It made her insides churn. What in the hell was going on?

"What do you see when you look at that man?" Oryn asked the spirits again.

"A costume," chanted the Unknowns, swirling faster, like a gigantic blur of frothy egg whites, which drew twigs and grass into its wake. "We see a hidden soul. A timid man."

"What does he hide from?" Celestine couldn't help asking. They looked from her to Oryn, as if they could only be loyal to one human. They kept talking though they didn't answer her question—at least directly.

"Skirting death and cheating life," wailed an Unknown.

"Planning a second life," shouted another.

"Distortion," they chanted, in a tone between a nursery rhyme and a bully's taunt. "Distortion, distortion!"

Celestine turned her attention again to Edgar. Her mouth gaped as she watched him stretch and crack open from the center of his meaty torso like an overripe piece of fruit. There was a soft tearing noise, not unlike the chewing sounds that Nola Jaye made when Celestine brought her peaches. From the cavity of his center, Celestine gasped as a very different Edgar emerged.

An older and skinnier man than the bulked-up groundskeeper riding the golf cart appeared, wearing an almost embarrassed expression. He was slightly hunched, still with a barrel chest, but with a wider, darker face and thin gray hair in two braids, Native American style. She rubbed her eyes and shot a glance at Oryn. Oryn gave her a knowing look and they both went back to staring at the shocking sight unfolding in front of them. Was this yet another mirage? A mirage within a mirage? Magic could get very complicated. Celestine only had expertise in a few lanes so far. Though it dawned on her what the Unknowns meant, why Oryn was doing this magic right here, right now.

"A distortion spell!" she exclaimed to both Edgars. "You

did this to yourself!" He was still frozen, but the magic she felt seeping out of his open center told her he had.

"Is your real name Edge?" Oryn asked the Edgars with a controlled, steely calm.

"He seems deaf," Celestine said to Oryn, still ten yards away. "No wonder he's confused. He's two distinct people. Each one in a sort of brain fog."

"Unaware, yeah, probably for his own safety," Oryn replied under his breath.

"The hiding man *is* Edge!" insisted the Unknowns. "We see through the distorted man! We had no choice to hide when we lived. No two names, no two bodies, no two lives. We were always out in the open, in the cold." They swirled faster around Oryn. One yanked his hair over and over, each time harder. He swatted them away.

"Enough!" Oryn warned. "Calm down. You don't know what this is."

"You brought us out! You asked for our help! How dare you make us leave!" they accused, all rushing over to the broken versions of Edgar, still immobile and wordless against the oak tree. They swarmed around him, chanting, "You have no right! No right to hide in a costume!"

"Leave him be," Celestine growled. Her earth and wolfish magic senses powered up all at once. She sensed her fangs lowering, her ears and muzzle pushing to transform. Everything in her screamed to defend Oryn and not expose this poor man Edgar in real time. This old ally of Ray's. Exposure in the open would put him in worse danger. There was a reason he was unhearing, unresponsive, frozen.

"Go back to your resting spots, Unknowns!" she snarled, not quite changed to wolfish form but with all feral senses on fire. "Go back. You have been a huge help. We thank you with these..." She pulled out a bag of apples from her go-bag, and Oryn, whose face was uncharacteristically gray, grinned for the first time.

She placed the apples on the graves and, when she saw the phantasms still circling, roared at them with wolfish ferocity. "Eat up. Be proud. Accept our thanks. Leave us be! Go now."

The air swirled slower and the Unknowns began to fade into the mineral atmosphere and down to the earth. Celestine rushed over to Oryn and gave him a hug. He hugged her back, and they watched, hearts pounding, as unseen entities took bites from the apples with juicy gusto.

"Edgar needs our protection," Celestine whispered to Oryn, who nodded. "It's too dangerous to tell him what happened. The fog of the spell is keeping him from freaking in terror over the Demon Three Eyes Clan who wants his heart. Thanks for running with your hunch. I owe you one. Is your head okay?" She brushed a hand through his blond mane. "They pulled your hair awfully hard."

"My head will heal."

Just then, Edgar let out a pained groan.

"Tell me later," Oryn murmured.

Amazingly, Edgar had morphed back into the husky twenty-something groundskeeper. They watched him lurch away from the tree with another bellow of discomfort. His legs must've fallen asleep leaning against the trunk for so long.

"What the devil?" he groused as he rubbed and shook them. He stumbled toward the golf cart. "Have you found what you were looking for?" he asked Oryn.

"Yes, thanks. Quite illuminating."

Celestine rubbed her head and grimaced. "Edgar, I'm afraid I have a sudden migraine. I need immediate bedrest in a dark room unless I want it to go on and on. Rain check on the LeRoux connections?"

"Fine by me. Phew-ee!" Edgar huffed. "I feel like I've mowed a hundred lawns and need a long nap." Clearly, he was suffering the aftereffects of being dragged out of his distortion spell, only to be yanked back into it. Celestine wondered how that would feel. Worse than a migraine, no doubt, judging by his continual cursing and fumbling. They climbed into the blue golf cart. Edgar gunned the motor and they sped away.

SHE AND ORYN said their goodbyes and exchanged numbers with Edgar.

Then they didn't talk until Oryn had steered the Forester onto the highway. He glanced over at her. "I have to say, your ferocious side is sexy."

"Your heroic side is sexier." She squeezed his hand on the wheel. "By the way, I have an idea."

Oryn grinned. "I knew you would."

"Before I tell you the idea, I have to say that under that distortion, it's clearly Edge. The age, the Guale genes in his wide, ruddy face, the way he wears his hair in braids. His fear of boats from a traumatic event on the ocean. The fact that he knew he was in danger enough to hide behind the cipher of a young man in overalls. That the accompanying brain fog magic would help keep him calm. Hide his magic from detection by enemies. Genius, really. It totally fooled me." She put a hand on Oryn's shoulder. "How did you know he was under a distortion spell?"

"Faes often see the invisible, sense beings in space, almost like a blind man knows a person is walking by or whether a door is opening by its breeze. I've witnessed a distortion spell or two. It can be confusing at first because these spells shroud an entity's magic as well as change his or her appearance."

She nodded. "What gave you the idea to use the Unknowns?"

"Most fae have lines of communication to the dead, the same way you have a connection to your Nola Jaye. Except you have that bond because you *know* her, right? The fae straddle the membrane of the world that connects the living to the dead. In fact, we cross from one to the other all the time. We have family on the other side."

"You do? You never told me about your line."

The light in his face dimmed. His eyes went dull again. "It's long, and complicated. Can I take a rain check on that too? I'm sorry." They were stopped at a traffic light, but he kept staring straight ahead.

"It's okay. I just hope you'll trust me enough to tell me sometime."

"Fair enough." His deep sigh was rife with exhaustion. The magic had clearly taken its toll. He had helped pierce the hidden shell of the distortion spell and eked out the Unknowns and directed them, all in the span of an hour. Anyone would be tired. And she heard pain in his voice. Some profound wound that hadn't healed, even though he was a supe. She wanted to tread lightly. People didn't jump through others' hoops unless forced to. Besides, that was no way to get information out of... someone she was starting to care a lot for.

She got out her phone and sent some texts. Pinging text sounds shot back and forth. "Canceling the trip to see the other Edge," she explained to Oryn. "And I made an appointment with Wade for later today."

"That detective? What are you talking to him about? You found your man Edge, so you don't need to ask permission to check the out-of-town man."

"Right, but... I want to show him one of my drawings."

"Oh? Which one? Have I seen it?"

"Ooh, I don't think I've shown it to you yet."

"Showing it to Wade before me, eh?" Oryn's tease was innocent enough, but it irritated her.

Pressure, guilting, and petty jealousy were up there on her pet peeve list. "Look, I don't want to jinx it. I'm superstitious that way. I'm sorry I jumped the gun. If all goes well with Wade, I'll be super relieved. I promise I'll show you the drawing. It's of a ja—"

"Shh." He put a finger lightly over her lips. "Tell me later. It's okay. You didn't pressure me to tell you all about my strange family."

Relief flooded through her. No wonder people avoided relationships. They were fraught with emotional peril, even over the small stuff. "Thanks, Oryn. Afterward, we can finally deliver some leather goods to the street supes. Talk about the gallery with Aline and Riley. Have some actual fun."

"Sounds good. I'll await word." He turned into the area of Savannah with the old town squares and let her out near the police precinct. She was tempted to give him a peck on the cheek but held back. They waved instead.

"WHAT BRINGS you here on such short notice?" Wade ushered her into a small office, took a seat at the desk across from her, and studied her through his owlish glasses.

It was time to reveal more. Celestine had brought documents—show-and-tell items—so she was glad that Wade honored her request to sit in a private room. She produced a folded paper from her bag, opened it, and brushed it flat it on his desk. "As you know, I do drawings that prophesize."

Wade's face was skeptical, unsmiling. "I'm aware. What is this, exactly? A picture of the Savannah prison?" He looked closer. "There's nobody in the cell. What am I supposed to make of it?"

Celestine took a clearing breath. She and Wade weren't professional partners, and definitely not friends. She was still a "person of interest" in the case, and she needed to tread lightly and parse her words, yet somehow convince him of the need to act. "Look, I know you don't believe in the supernatural, but you need to understand that there's a whole other world right here in Savannah that you can't see."

"Yeah, I'm aware. But I've also seen unexplainable things," he groused. "I've been around the block a few times. Look, I know that this town is full of ghosts or whatever you want to call them..."

She frowned at him. "More than ghosts. If I tell you things, I need for you to keep an open mind. Because if we don't work together at least a little bit, this mess is going to take us all down."

"Fire away." He slid his coffee mug off to his left and got out a pen and a pad of yellow lined paper.

*Good sign.* "The body parts," she started. "There's a rhyme and reason to them. We just haven't figured out what it is, exactly. The clock is running down fast, though. All of the victims are dead—Ray Bartello, Peter Leger, Harwood Port. All except one man. His heart will be cut out if we don't take immediate action. And I know where he is." She stared at Wade.

"Where? You were supposed to run anything by me first."

"I am. Right now. His name is Edgar LeRoux. *Edge* LeRoux. The name Edge ring a bell?"

Wade shook his head.

"He lives within the city limits, at Laurel Hill North Cemetery, to be exact. So I went to figure out if he was legit first before I bothered you with it." She described Edgar's job and location but held back on the weirder stuff.

Wade jotted down notes and set the pen on the desk. "Who exactly is going to cut the man's heart out? And what do you want me to do about it? Set up a stakeout at the cemetery? No crime has been committed—"

"Yet." She tapped on her sketch. "Put Edge in jail. Protective custody. That's what my drawing means."

Wade didn't say no, he just grunted.

"There's more."

"Oh yeah?"

"Edge doesn't look like himself. He's so scared that he's in a form of disguise."

"Huh?" Wade took his glasses off and rubbed his eyes. She saw they were bloodshot, and a pang of empathy ran through her, realizing he seemed almost as stressed as she was.

It was time to talk about Ray's journal. Relay the stuff that was bizarre, even to her. God knew if Wade would believe a word of it, but she had to try. Edge's life was in extreme danger. She took out Ray's raggedy leatherbound book and flipped to the relevant page. "Look, I know this might sound like something out of a freaking *Alien* film, but bear with me."

Wade shrugged but picked up his pen. Celestine went on. "Ray, my murdered friend who had his eyes gouged out, wrote in this journal years ago, and he left me clues to find it."

"Okay, go on…"

"Ray wrote that he was a supernatural pirate captain of the Jekyll crew, and his arch enemy was the Demon Three Eyes Clan. Remember I asked if you'd heard the name Vex Blade or Bastard Blade, as they called him?"

"Rings a bell. Supernatural, huh?" Wade grimaced. "Still listening."

"Anyway, Demon Three Eyes committed criminal deeds around Savannah's coast. Not sure exactly what. You mentioned the trashing of the coastal waters and the collapse of a series of crappily built condos that killed people, but I have no idea yet if that has anything to do with it. I'm still patching clues together. Jekyll Clan fought Demon Three Eyes in some epic sea battle and somehow took the Demon Three Eyes's power away—at least for a long time. Not sure how."

Wade slid his glasses back on. "But us mere mortals heard nothing of fantastical pirate battles off Savannah," he grumbled.

"That's the part I'm asking you to trust—take a leap of faith or whatever. The supe world is not always visible to the human one."

Wade's eyes narrowed under his glasses. "Are you a supernatural?"

"Yeah. Part shifter, part witch. Earth magic."

"Oh, *really?*" He huffed in disbelief. "Well, *you're* visible." He pushed his cold coffee back in front of him. "Can you turn my coffee cup into a pile of gemstones? Or even worthless pebbles?"

Celestine rolled her eyes. "Look, I know it's not easy, Detective Wade, but try to keep an open mind. Do you ever look up in the stars and wonder what's out there? Like if there's tons more to the universe than you assumed. Other beings?"

He snorted. "You made your point. Go on."

"Demon Three Eyes is back out. Don't know how, but they escaped Ray's magic. This clan that Ray knew was dangerous enough to banish. It's body parts they're collecting. I don't know why, but I swear they're going to make something with them—concoct dark, evil magic. Once they do, it'll be too late to stop them. You may not believe I'm a supe, but at least believe I have very, *very* strong powers of intuition. And what I've been sensing recently keeps me up at night, sweating and shaking. Not just for myself but for all of Savannah. I'm not kidding. We may all die. This city may burn to the ground. We have to do something to stop them!"

"Melodramatic, but I'm still listening."

She barreled on, reading Ray's description of his clan, of Pete being all hands on deck, of Harwood being the guts of the mission, of Ray himself being the visionary—the eyes. And then of Edge being the beating heart. "They're harnessing the magic in Ray's clan."

When she looked up at Wade, he was gaping at her with a new glint of fear in his eyes. There was a dawning horror in the clench of his jaw, in the way he white-knuckled his pen.

He cleared his throat. "How the hell can we just drag this guy in? Under what pretext?"

Celestine's chest pinched in a nervous hope. Wade was going to help. "I'm not sure. The thing is, well... there's a bit more to the story."

Wade groaned. "What now?"

"I'm not sure how much Edge remembers of his trauma.

He put himself in a distortion guise... spell. I think he was so terrified that they'd come after him, he changed his whole body, his whole identity."

"Hell's bells, what is it with you people!" Wade smacked his fist on his metal desk.

"I know it sounds nuts. But don't give up, Detective Wade."

"Did I say I was?"

"Not exactly," she said in a small voice.

He sighed. "I can likely haul this guy Edge in on a trumped-up charge related to a lapsed cemetery grounds permit. If he's posing as an office assistant and caretaker at Laurel Grove North, he may not have the right papers. I'll look into it."

"Now you're talking!"

"Or you could use your supposed earth magic on him. Send along a sandstorm to blow him into the prison."

They shared a rare laugh.

"I'll do some quick research. I'll bring him in. You stay clear of the cemetery. We don't need complications. Understood?" He popped open his laptop and was already typing.

She was flooded with relief. "Thank you, Detective Wade. You'll let me visit once he's in there, right? I may need to break his spell. He'll need to know what's really going on." He nodded. "Thanks for believing me."

"Who said I believe you?" Wade groaned and took a slug of cold coffee. "It can't hurt to play it safe is all."

"You're right. It's worth protecting a life," she said as she rose, folded the drawing, and stuffed it in her bag. "Or protecting all of Savannah," she added as she walked out.

# THIRTEEN

Wade called Celestine the next morning with good news. At dawn, he and two of his strong-arms had personally hauled Edge into jail incognito. Indeed, Edge had no official certificate or contract to oversee a cemetery database, or even a permit to be a groundskeeper and bury bodies. Celestine figured he must have glamoured the owners of Laurel Grove North.

Wade had instructed her to please steer clear of the jail for a day or two. And then, to visit only before or after office hours. Wade said he would personally let her in. "The guy is agitated and confused. He needs you to explain why he's really in there. That said, the less people to ask questions the better."

"Thank you so much!"

"Just trying to keep folks alive," he said. "Take the day off, do some art or... witchcraft," he joked.

"Very funny," she replied, deadpan. Her body went strangely limp. Until that moment, she hadn't realized how incredibly much tension she was holding in every muscle.

She thought of heading over to Magic Hands and called

the tattooed receptionist to ask about who was on shift. "Oryn's here until one p.m.," the woman said. "He has an open slot at ten a.m. if that's not too ear—"

"I'll take it. Tell him it's the witch with the wolfish howl."

The desk woman chuckled. "Will do."

~

THE LIGHTS WERE DIMMED, and she was under the sheet on her belly when Oryn walked in. "Eucalyptus or unscented oil?" he asked her, and even with her eyes closed, she sensed his secret smile, the flush of excitement between them.

"Eucalyptus," she murmured, sending him a virtual dart of lust.

She shivered as he drew down the sheet and began to knead her shoulders and back with the oil, already warmed in his capable hands.

"Any areas I should pay special attention to, Madame Wolf?" he whispered.

"All of it. I've been so tense lately. Under so much pressure."

He leaned close to her head and whispered into her ear, "I can help you with that." His breath fueled her, was everything good in the world.

Let him *earn* his pay. Because man, she was tense and needed the massage for real. The ambient music spun around the air like glazed honey, and his hands—oh, Lord, what magnificent hands—pummeled her knotted muscles, her racing brain, her troubled heart, her bruised soul.

He raised the sheet to her neck and moved the bottom of the cloth up to just under her butt. Tucked it naughtily in a crisp parallel line. With a new splosh of heated oil, he stroked her right leg from ankle to thigh, moving his arms up and down in a seesaw motion. She moaned yet still said nothing. Nor did he. He migrated from one leg to the other and gave the second one equal and ample languid attention.

She roused out of a sort of sugar coma as he whispered, "Time to turn on your back."

When she did, their eyes met, and the room turned electric, charges zinging everywhere and back, into her heart, her head, his mysterious, ever-changing eyes, his hard-bodied chest and inspired hands. She slowly reached up and took hold of the long strands of his hair that had escaped his loose ponytail. Drew his face down to hers. He took her cue and moved in for an epic kiss. Open-mouthed, tongue-flicking, hungry, and hot.

When they stopped to take a breath, he murmured, "You're going to get me in trouble."

"So much trouble."

They went in for a second, longer, deeper kiss.

He kneaded her shoulders and then slid his hands down to her breasts, just under the sheet. Teased her nipples until they were rock hard. She moaned, low in her throat. "No fair, I can't do you," she joked as she snuck a hand behind her and cupped his hard length.

"Yeah, not here," he agreed, though she distinctly felt him lean into her hand and the counter-pressure she was offering.

"Where, then?" she rasped. "My place? Tonight? After we meet with Aline and Riley?"

"Yes," he said. "If you're sure."

"No strings attached. I'm sure."

CELESTINE WAS CLEARING out her studio and setting up display areas when the bell rang. She glanced up at the wall clock. Odd, it was only one p.m. Oryn and Aline and Riley had all agreed to meet at 3:30 p.m. to talk about the gallery and then hit the streets to pass out leather goods to the street kids.

She didn't get many visitors. The reporters had finally left, and Wade wouldn't stop by without calling or texting her first. In fact, he'd never come to her place; she had always gone to the precinct. She thought of the earth magic wards. Anyone the wards deemed dark-intentioned or violent would suffer a blast of dirt and sharp-edged pebbles.

When the bell rang a second time, she ventured forward and peered out of the curtains on the left side window.

Celestine's breath caught. The woman, in about her midtwenties, looked so familiar. From where, exactly? She had intense green eyes, flowing light auburn hair with glimmers of coral pink that curled around angular cheekbones, and her slightly opened mouth, as if she was endlessly curious yet held many secrets. Answers, too. She cradled a large satchel like a baby or something quite valuable. Her long denim jacket made it hard to glean more clues from her clothes, her posture, or body shape. Celestine *knew* her somehow. This sense permeated her, like a forgotten phrase on the tip of her tongue or an old childhood friend seen in passing. The young woman saw her staring out the window. She grinned and waved. Celestine, suddenly embarrassed that she was shamelessly gawking, quickly drew the curtain back over the window.

She smoothed down her clothes and hair and opened

the door with the strange breathlessness of a teenager fangirling. "May I help you? Who are you looking for?"

"I saw the sign." The woman pointed to the Shadow Salon Gallery announcement that Aline had taped up. Celestine nodded dumbly. "Mind if I come in? This thing's kind of heavy." She held out the satchel like an unwieldy bowling ball. "Are you Celestine LeBlanc?"

"Yes, welcome! Sorry, you caught me at an odd moment."

"Is it a bad time?"

Celestine shrugged as she led the way inside. "No, not really. Here, you can put your package over here." She gestured to one of the empty tables pushed against the wall.

"Thanks." The woman grinned. "I'm Luna. Luna Finley. I came here from up north. I heard you were opening a gallery." She glanced at the paintings, her eyes lingering on the Bonaventure one. "Beautiful work! I love how the moon peeks out from between two graves."

"Thanks, these are mine. I haven't opened the gallery quite yet. So, where up north are you located?"

"Massachusetts. Um, a... glamoured town called Pyreshore."

Oh?" Celestine's mind wrapped around the glamoured part, decoded layers of unspoken information—Luna was a supe, protected from mundanes in a secret city, unlike Savannah, where supes and mundanes all shared the real estate. Luna Finley was stunning—or more accurately charismatic—a gathering force, like unsettled wind in a tropical squall.

Images of the ocean with whitecapped waves flitted through Celestine's mind. *That's where this person calls home.*

*Like Ray and the Jekyll Clan. Or Demon Three Eyes. She spends time on and in the turbulent water.*

She ushered Luna to a set of chairs arranged in a corner of the studio. Offered her iced tea. Luna accepted the offer and settled into one of the black chairs with leaf-pattered fabric cushions that Celestine had sewn for the gallery. "What brings you all the way down to Savannah? Are you on vacation? Gallery-hopping?"

"No. I moved here last week. I needed to get out of Pyreshore quickly. It was untenable."

They regarded each other. "How so?" asked Celestine.

"I was being stalked—a constant curiosity. Some folks blamed my parents for my birth, my celebrity. It got bad, really bad."

"Yikes!" Celestine shuddered, thinking of how awful it had been for the reporters to hang around Bay Street, weaseling out salacious bits of gossip about Ray, about who she was in relation to Ray, and what business she had staying there after he was brutally murdered. "What kind of celebrity?"

"I'm a different type of supe. A variant. You'd think that supes of all beings would be open-minded, right? Nope. They were only tolerant of the same old kind of supe. First they wanted to use me for ads, for gossip rags, second-rate action films. As a freak curiosity, and all of this in a para-normal community that was supposedly tolerant of all kinds. When my parents shut the media circus down, people figured if they couldn't get to me, they'd kill my parents. And that's eventually what they did. Surprised them in their sleep with foul, criminal magic."

The air left the room. "No," Celestine gasped. "I'm so sorry."

"Thanks. It is what it is." Luna shook her head. "That

was last year. I'm coping. I just had to get out of there. Start a new life."

"I hear you. I knew someone dear to me from a small town called Red River that was killed for her magic." Celestine nodded to the Bonaventure painting. "Her ashes are scattered in this cemetery. I visit her often. Talk to her."

Luna's face brightened into a wistful smile. "That's sweet. I talk to my parents whenever I'm in the ocean. Their spirits live there."

Celestine wanted to ask what kind of supe Luna was—a seelie? A siren? She figured she'd wait a bit longer, see if Luna volunteered the information. "Why did you choose Savannah?"

"Savannah's known for its supernaturals, its ghosts. It's tolerance for hybrids." Her green eyes misted with fear and relief jumbled together. "I can be safer, near the warmer salt water, where I feel alive, and..." She looked deeply into Celestine's eyes, sending shivers through her. "Hopefully I can exhibit my artwork."

"What kind do you do?"

Luna got up and walked to the table where her satchel lay. From it, she withdrew a glittering cone-shaped thing that caught the light in twinkles of aquamarine, violet, and green.

"Wow," Celestine whispered, wandering over.

"It's made of sea glass," Luna explained. "I learned how to build them from my mother, Indigo. She had them all over the house. We used to go on undersea forays together to collect the glass." Her voice took on a sadness mixed with pride. "My sculptures are a way to honor my mom, to always remember her."

"Spectacular." Celestine was bowled over by another wave of déjà vu. Of an image she herself had drawn. What was it, exactly? It clawed at her. And then, Luna took her denim jacket off, and everything flooded in. A wing tip appeared over Luna's shoulders, released by the removal of the coat. *The mermaid leaning over Ray!*

"You're... Oh my god! You're the woman in the first prophetic drawing I did here. I had no idea why, what it meant, what it means... You're a mermaid with wings, aren't you?"

Luna nodded. "I am. I hail partly from the New England waters, and partly from a sky tribe—from the water star Emiya." She turned slightly and rustled her wings, freeing up the feathers that sprang from slits on her tailored shirt.

"Holy shit! From another star? That's so incredible!"

"Yep." Luna laughed. "You *drew* me?"

Celestine nodded, suddenly holding back tears. "It was when I first moved here and a family friend Ray, who used to own this house, let me stay here. Um..." She stopped to wipe tears away that had spilled over her lids.

"Are you okay?" Luna asked. "You don't have to tell me the story if it upsets you."

Celestine smiled through her tears. "I think yours is even sadder, and I need to tell you everything."

"Okay." Luna looked understandably confused.

"Shall we sit again?" The women settled back into the chairs across from each other. "I signed up for a few classes at the art school here," Celestine explained. "During the very first one, I drew *you,* leaning over Ray... His eyes were gouged out." Celestine said in a choked whisper, "I apologize in advance, but, um... you didn't have anything to do with it, did you?"

Luna gasped. "God, no! I could never harm a thing. After all I've seen, everything I've been through." Her horror, her innocence, was palpable.

"So sorry, I just had to ask."

"I understand," Luna replied. "It's only logical if I was in the picture with your Ray. Fact is, I was hundreds of miles away, dealing with my own nightmare. I'm so sorry too—for your pain. Will you tell me more? Only if you want to."

"I had no idea who you were or why in hell I had drawn what I did. Though back in my hometown, I'd drawn a few prophetic images, so I had a sinking feeling about it. By the time I ran home, Ray was splayed on the pavement. Dead, no eyes, blood running down his face. They thought I might be the murderer because he willed the house to me, and my drawing got leaked to the press. Talk about piling on the pain." She stared at Luna to see if she could take this more detailed horror in. Luna paled, yet she seemed resolute about hearing more of Celestine's story.

"In a nutshell, I found out through Ray's hidden journal he was the captain of a pirate clan, that he fought against a deadly group called Demon Three Eyes. That he had stopped them for a while, but after years went by, they had escaped his magic."

The rest of the saga poured freely out of Celestine, because deep in her soul, she was convinced that Luna was fated to hear it. "My pictures were speaking truths. I just had to figure out who you were. How you fit in. If you knew Ray Bartello—"

"No."

"No? Well, I wonder exactly why you were in that scene. You see, I'm putting together clues, interviewing folks. I'm in touch with Wade, the local detective on the case. But he's a mundane, so he can only know so much. He doesn't have access to all of the puzzle pieces." Celestine took out a rolled-up drawing from a wide side table and opened it up.

Handed it to Luna. The drawing of Ray and Luna bending over him, her wings upturned.

Luna examined it closely. "Incredible. I'm shaking." Her deep green eyes moved slowly from the paper to meet Celestine's. She rolled the drawing up and handed it back. After this, she sat motionless except for the gentle rustle of her wings.

"What do you think?"

"Maybe I was in that scene to watch over your friend, observe the situation, the mystery," Luna mused. "Could it be that I'm meant to help you? I have strong water magic."

*A water mage! That's exactly what I need.* "That would be asking too much. You don't even know me. You owe me nothing, and I'd hate for you to be tangled up in this dangerous mess."

"Yet... maybe it's why I found you from so many miles away." Luna's intense gaze certainly blurred the lines between a random stranger and a recognizable realm traveler.

"I... I don't know. I'm overwhelmed, so confused. Let me think on it all." Celestine nodded toward the sea-glass sculpture. "I'd love to show your work, though. I can feature it at my very first Shadow Salon show."

Luna's pretty face lit up. "I'd be honored. Are you sure?"

"Positive. I've never seen such a radiant sculpture. A room full of them will be truly magical."

"Thank you!" Luna said. "Sea glass helps bring good luck. That's why mermaids like to fill their homes with them."

The two women hugged. When they made contact, Celestine could sense Luna's magic; it had the force of rolling breakers, the elegance of pastel coral gardens, the ease of water lapping at an island shore.

They exchanged numbers and other information. "Let's talk again soon," said Celestine. "I can visit your studio and see the rest of the work."

"Wonderful. Yes! I'm in a studio sublet on West Alice Street off Chatham Square." Luna started to pack up her sea-glass art, but Celestine stopped her. "Can this one stay here? I'd love to have it around me. I need the luck."

"Of course."

Celestine watched Luna almost skip down the sidewalk leading to the street. Her wings were tucked safely inside her denim coat.

*A water mage. Oh my!*

CELESTINE WENT UPSTAIRS TO SHOWER. She put on fresh clothes —a black jersey and artfully torn skinny jeans. Pinning part of her hair back, she freed side wisps to silhouette her face. Around her neck, she fastened a silver chain with a wolf's head carved into a black gemstone her mother had given her.

She rested on her bed and stared at the one drawing of hers she had not yet figured out: the three-spouted ceramic container with engraved images of undersea creatures she'd never seen before. It occurred to her that Luna might recognize them. She sent Luna a photo of it with a question. In the meantime, she scrolled through her phone, doing another fruitless round of research on the pot itself and its engraved creatures—in museums, on the Smithsonian site, on niche pottery sites.

She must've fallen asleep because the next thing she knew, she was startled awake by a determined series of doorbell rings. One of her arms hung over the bed's edge, and her phone had fallen on the rug. Luna had texted her back.

*Nope, never seen any sea creatures like this!*

Celestine thrust her phone in her back pocket, then ran downstairs to get the door.

Aline, in a silk PJ set featuring floating cat and dog heads, greeted Celestine with a hug. Riley stood there grinning with a sketch pad under his arm.

"Come on in," Celestine said, ushering them to the clutch of black studio chairs. "I'll bring out the leather goods. We have to wait to give them out. Oryn's not here yet."

"Okay, let's chill." Aline leaned back, hands behind her head, and looked around the studio, her eyes landing on Luna's sculpture. "What is this? So spectacular!" Aline leapt up and scurried to Luna's glittering work. She gazed at it from a few distinct angles, making her purple earrings clink. "It's made all of sea glass. Brilliant! Where'd you get it? Did *you* make it?" Her eyes darted from the sculpture to Celestine.

"No. Someone who stopped in. An artist named Luna Finley from Massachusetts who just moved here and saw your sign."

"That old magic marker rag?" Aline laughed. "Cheap advertising works, I guess."

"The sea-glass thing is good," Riley agreed. "*Really* good."

"Yep. It blew me away. I told Luna she could be in my first show... along with some work from both of you." Celestine nodded to her friends. "Aline, you can have the director role if you want it, be hired for the front desk and some curating."

"You're the best! I'll take it," Aline exclaimed. "What

about a piece of your art?"

Celestine thought of the one drawing even she couldn't figure out, at how she'd studied the strange sort of teapot contraption before her impromptu nap. The pressure of Ray's case weighed heavily on her; time was sifting away. LeRoux was in protective custody. But how long could he be kept there? Unsettling specters were closing in. She was the guardian of monsters she didn't understand, couldn't see.

"What's on your mind, Celestine? You look miles away," Riley said boldly.

He was normally the cute, thoughtful introvert. It caught her off guard. "I do have one drawing that I... I wouldn't put it in a show, but it's bothering me that I can't figure out what it means."

"Let's have a look!" said Aline brightly. "There's power in numbers."

Celestine nodded vaguely. "Yeah. You did say something about being a pottery enthusiast. A collector of sorts."

Aline nodded. "Officially obsessed."

"Well, come have a look. Riley too." Celestine waved them upstairs. In her room, she pointed to the drawing of the three-spouted teapot she'd tacked to her wall. "I've looked on every freaking website, on historical sites, on the Smithsonian database..."

"That's a super-odd specimen," Riley blurted, his mouth agape. "Fantasy fish."

"Hmm. I can't say it rings a bell," Aline noted, "and that's saying a lot for me." She chuckled. "Because I kind of know everything about crockery, porcelain, historic, and unique ceramic collectibles."

Riley moved closer to it. "The fish have three eyes. Is that normal for fish?"

"No." Aline huffed. "Nothing normal about any of these.

I've never seen a fish with a snake neck, with paws like a wombat, a nose as big as a ketchup bottle." They chuckled together. "But if anyone knows, it might be Ardenia."

"Who?" asked Celestine.

"Ardenia Culpepper is a curio dealer who travels the globe for one-of-a-kinds. She's got a fancy mansion called Ardenia's Antiques over on Lafayette Square by appointment only. She trots around in khaki safari pants with high leather boots as if she's traveling to the Sahara. Quite the character."

Riley gave Aline a playful elbowing. "Coming from you, Ms. Cat and Dog PJs, that's saying a lot."

She elbowed him back. "Thanks, friend."

Celestine's pulse jumped. "Can we go over in the morning?"

"I'll have to set up an appointment," Aline declared. "Make sure the old bird is in town. She's always traveling."

"Thanks, keep me posted."

Just then, the bell rang, and they all clattered downstairs. Celestine's chest did a giddy flip when she saw Oryn, knowing they'd agreed to be together later and finish what they'd started at Magic Hands. God, he looked hot. His blond mane flew free in waves. Its gold tones contrasted nicely with his tight black jersey and amplified the gold gleams in his large amber gemstone set on a leather necklace. His grin seemed to say, *Hey, sexy one, we're going to have hella fun later. May relieve some stress, too.*

They didn't kiss. Instead, they went in for a long, greedy hug, and every part of Celestine's body sang. She caught Aline smirking congenially and knew that Aline knew. Women, mundanes or not, had an innate radar.

Oryn had brought a stuffed backpack with supplies for the street supes. "There's a few down there we should talk to about the case," he said. "They have a second sense about things."

"We could draw with them," Riley suggested.

"Smart idea," Celestine said. "Who knows, there may be another art intuitive there. It'll also be good to clear out these bags to make room for the gallery." She hauled over her bags of leather goods. They each took a load and set out.

Bay Street was bustling. The sun beamed down, and it was one of those sparkling September afternoons where the sky was a teal blue, and the air was tinged with the lingering scent of flowers mixed with caramel popcorn and fried cashews from the vendors. Pops of color from the store displays flashed in Celestine's periphery as they hurried down Bay Street, and things seemed momentarily peaceful with the protection of her crew. They were on a noteworthy mission, and for once it wasn't fraught with peril. Only the warm memory of Ray's generosity and the pleasure of paying it forward.

They walked about three quarters of a mile, and then Oryn led the way down a hilly side road to an underpass where Celestine saw a large huddle of twenty-somethings. Some had large box constructions set up with clotheslines, others sat in chairs, no doubt scavenged from the historic district on trash night. Two people gobbled down what looked like baked beans from cans. One woman tended a small bonfire. Not exactly glamping, but Celestine sensed a cohesive geniality.

"Hey, guys!" Oryn called. "Hi, Helen. How's it going, Blackfire?"

The supes turned toward him with wide grins. "Oryn!" cried the woman tending the bonfire, probably Helen, and hurried toward them. Her wild brown hair was pinned haphazardly, and though her clothes were clearly dumpster finds—ragged with rips in the hem—they were scrubbed clean. She had on scuffed combat boots and a raspberry-hued shift. When she held out her arms to hug Oryn, Celestine's curiosity grew. How well did she know Oryn? Had she known Ray? If so, what tips might she have on Ray's case? These questions were followed by alarm when she saw Helen's arms were covered in tattoos and *cuts*—from living outdoors or what?

"I brought my art crew," Oryn explained, waving his hand in their direction. Introductions followed as more people milled over. Riley, as if punctuating this, held up his sketch pad like a banner. "These tunnel guys like to draw too," Oryn added. "Check out the mural they did."

Indeed, the group had painted the inside arch of the curving concrete tunnel: angels and birds and spirits flew above, and a colorful cityscape below was filled with dragons and werewolves, strange ramblers in bowler hats and trench coats and women with long gowns dancing in the clouds above the harbor.

"Welcome to Supe Tunnel," Helen said with a gentle smile.

The young man named Blackfire, wiry and raven-haired in a dark oversized hoodie, invited them to sit. Aline, Riley, and Celestine settled on scavenged footstools. Oryn sat next to Celestine on a swivel chair that had seen better days. More folks crowded in, whether they had a chair, a stool, a mat, or simply sat on the concrete cross-legged.

"Oryn's told us so much about you all," Celestine said.

"Good things, I hope," said a guy next to Blackfire with ice-pale eyes.

"Only good things," she echoed. She dug into her bag of

leather goods and handed Helen a backpack. "An old friend made these. Could you use one?"

"Could I ever!" Helen smoothed the luxe leather surface as if it were a kitten. "Thank you so much! I've been carting everything around in grocery bags full of holes."

Celestine handed out dozens more fanny packs and backpacks to the sound of grateful *oohs* and *ahhs*. She sensed Ray's supportive spirit watching over the scene.

Oryn doled out his bags, full of water, clean socks, toothbrushes, shampoos, T-shirts, and combs.

"Did you know Ray Bartello?" Celestine asked Helen.

"Sure, most of us knew him," she said. "Is this his leathercraft? It looks familiar."

Celestine nodded.

"I'm so sorry he died," Helen said. "We heard about it. Blackfire and I had a bad feeling the last time we saw him." She looked at Blackfire, who nodded in silent agreement.

"Exactly what kind of bad feeling?" asked Celestine.

"Doom. Darkness falling. I had a dream someone hurt him. Nothing specific, just messed him up." Helen glanced down at her arms. "When I woke up, I had cut my arms."

"Oh no!" said Celestine. "Are you okay now?"

"Yeah." Helen sighed. "It's something I do once in a while when I have bad premonitions. By the time I had the dream, he was dead."

"I get it," said Celestine. "I do drawings that foretell stuff, yet I don't always understand what they mean. Can I show you one? See if you get a sense from it?"

"Sure." Helen studied the teapot image that Celestine unrolled. She rubbed at her eyes. "This clay pot was buried. Your Ray touched it, but it wasn't his. That's all I get. Blackfire?" She handed it to the hunched guy in the hoodie.

He ran his spindly fingers over the paper. "Energy was trapped in there," he murmured after a weighted silence.

"What kind? Anything else?" asked Oryn.

"Rotten energy is all I get." Blackfire handed the drawing back to Celestine.

"Thanks for your input. Much appreciated." Celestine rolled up the paper and stuck it in her messenger bag.

"Anyone hungry?" asked Aline. There were lots of eager takers for the protein bars and bananas she began to pass out.

Riley asked Blackfire if he could sketch him, to which Blackfire agreed. Helen went back to feeding her fire with twigs, her face a miasma of flickering lights and shadows.

"Everyone here has a special talent," Oryn said. "Not everyone understands it, though. Even here in Savannah, people get freaked out by supes. I have to be careful as a fae, what I say, what I do."

Helen stirred the fire with a knobby branch. "Yeah, I scared my parents. I had an unruly power from around eight. I had no idea what it was. Neither did they. All we knew was it destroyed things—household things. Dishes flying out of cabinets and smashing, rugs lifting up from the hardwood floors, my kid brother's toys crashing all around. I remember him running from me and hiding in the closet. I learned later that my extreme emotions brought it on. But by then, they were ready to kick me out. They were frightened of me. Hell, I was frightened of myself. I ran before they could throw me in juvie." Her milky face seemed to sag. "Blackfire found me wandering the streets." She smiled wistfully at him.

"Yeah, I kind of took Helen under my wing," he murmured in a tone contrasting his tough look. "She became like the Wendy from Peter Pan over here. You know, everyone needs a mother."

This made Helen laugh, and the life returned to her face. "It made me happy to be needed, not that I want to play den mom to all of these grown-ass hardheads," she joked.

"What brought you to the tunnel, Blackfire?" Riley asked as he penciled in an amazing likeness of Blackfire's soulful eyes and shadowed brow under the hoodie.

He sighed. "Trouble. Family trouble, but not the kind most people think of. My dad was killed defending my mom, a shifter. She worked nights at a bar and I guess got pissed off by some creep putting relentless moves on her, who wouldn't take no for an answer. She turned full wolf and fanged the guy." Blackfire's chuckle was low and raspy, fitting with his thuggish hoodie but not with his kindness to Helen.

"The creepster didn't run," Blackfire went on. "Instead, he pulled a firearm. My dad arrived to pick her up, stepped in between them, and *boom*, he got the slug instead."

"Oh no! But your mom..." Aline started.

"Yeah, my mom," he muttered. "The guy finished the job a few days later. Stabbed her to death with an iron cross and poured holy water all over her before stomping on her. Good Christian and all that." He gazed up at the mural with a haunted stare.

"You have her magic," Oryn reminded him. "You have her power inside you."

"True, but I'm really careful not to shift around the wrong people. I don't trust no one. I stay here, with my own."

The guy next to Blackfire with the ice-blue eyes patted his shoulder. Celestine wondered if they were lovers. She was pulled toward Oryn, sitting so close to her, and found it hard to resist snuggling against his broad shoulder, his sexy body. He must've felt it too because he glanced at her and settled his hand atop hers.

"Shall we all draw?" she asked. It seemed right for the moment.

"Yes!" said Helen, followed by a chorus of at least six of the supes. Riley finished his sketch, tore it out, and gave it to Blackfire, who gazed admiringly at it.

"You made me look good, man."

"The least I could do." Riley began to dole out paper and pencils to the crowd.

People settled in, and a meditative vibe shimmered through the air, punctuated by the crackle of the fire, and the scratching of pencil on paper. To Celestine, it was like the art class but more spiritual, more organic somehow.

Celestine and Oryn released their hands to join the group drawing session. She started out doing a sketch of a pastoral stream. Uplifting, like the mood here. But after five minutes or so, she realized she was drawing a swamp with jutting cypress trunks like crooked canines. Her heart jumped. She tried to smooth it out, cover up the sharp cypress roots, to no avail. Her hand automatically penciled in a rendition of the blue-bearded pirate, shrouded high in a tangled swamp tree.

*Vex.* He glared down at something in the fetid, bubbling water. A freaking foot, no, *an entire leg*, breaching the surface of the soupy liquid. Celestine startled and threw down her pencil.

"What's the matter?" whispered Helen, putting down her own drawing and hurrying over to where Celestine sat. The moment she touched Celestine's shoulder Helen went into a frozen state. Celestine whipped around for a closer look and saw Helen's eyes roll in her head as if she was seizing. Had some energy in her transferred to Helen? Helen's motionless torso and fluttering stare reminded her of Edge LeRoux, stuck inside Edgar, and how they both stiffened after their core cracked in two. Celestine jumped up. "Helen? Can you hear me? Snap out of it."

Blackfire scrambled over. "She does this sometimes. Helen?" He put a hand on each of her shoulders and shook her lightly. "Helen?"

All around the tunnel, sketches in various supes' hands began to rattle, rip, and fly in the air, whooshing over to the bonfire like rudderless kites in a tornado. Then, they swooped into the flames and burned to black sooty bits that raced off into the sky. Seeing this, Celestine quickly rolled her own drawing and clutched it with both hands.

"Golem!" cried the man with the ice-blue eyes, which were shut hard now. "Golem!" he repeated in a loud hiccupping bark.

Helen snapped out of her frozen state and stared at Celestine in horror, as if she could see a whole other landscape invisible to the outside world.

"What?" whispered Celestine. "Tell me!"

"Death, fires," Helen mumbled to herself.

"Waters running with blood and fire," intoned the supes sitting at Riley's feet.

"The golem is in my head," repeated Ice Eyes, his head buried in his arms.

"What the actual fuck?" shouted Aline, fear and panic colliding in her tone. "Have you all gone mad?"

As Helen approached the fire, Celestine saw a shadowy figure flicker above it and an odious liquid dribble down. It smelled like tar and caused the flames to rage up toward the tunnel ceiling and scorch the mural black. A group of supes rushed to control the fire, beating it down with cushions and water and dirt, and Celestine could swear she heard a man cackling.

The fire was doused as fast as it had flared, yet the black detritus of the burned drawings still twirled like hellish confetti—a reminder of fearful magic.

"What evil did you bring here?" Ice Eyes accused, now staring at Celestine.

"Leave us be," said another in a trembling voice.

"Life is hard enough already," said a third.

"It's not Celestine's fault," Oryn insisted. "It's bigger than that, and if push comes to shove, we will defend you."

Aline and Riley were already halfway back up the hill path, clutching each other.

Celestine was gutted, waves of guilt and bafflement rolled through her. "Helen, I'm sorry you got scared," she called out. "Are you okay now?"

Helen gave a stunned nod. Her dress was crooked. Her hair had escaped its clips. She scratched at the cuts on her arm.

"It's not us. I need for you supes to know that!" Oryn said to Blackfire, who had no retort but had pulled the ragged hoodie almost completely over his eyes. "I'm sorry that you got spooked, and I'll make sure you're all safe."

"We're all just desperately trying to figure things out," said Celestine. "Bye for now. I'm sorry you got scared and your pretty mural got damaged."

"Stay safe. We'll make sure you do," Oryn promised them. He swung a protective arm around Celestine, and they walked slowly up the hill toward Riley and Aline.

Celestine suspected deep in her gut that they *had*, in fact, brought this nightmare to the Tunnel Supes, who'd never asked for trouble, and in fact, had run hundreds of miles to escape it. Vex was in her swamp drawing. It was Vex who had cackled in her head. He was tracking her. He was onto them.

"Beware the golem," Ice Eyes yelled after them.

BACK IN CELESTINE'S PLACE, after they said their uneasy goodbyes to Aline and Riley, Oryn and Celestine put double wards on the house. Then they ran upstairs, threw off their clothes and desperately fell into each other's arms. She had imagined it would be languid and sexy and teasing for their first time. Like at the Magic Hands but with finishing flourishes—clever, elegant, naughty.

But as it turned out, being thrown without warning into the nucleus of terror made them fast and hungry and clingy. As if they were literally sucking the life-force from each other's kisses, trying to merge into one being in their feverish, sweating embraces, trying to fuck each other back off a cliff's edge in their pounding, bucking thrusts. In the violent releases accompanied by screams.

She quite liked Oryn's driving side, because some part of her had worried that his gentle, caring kindness might translate to ineffective sex. No need to add that worry onto the burdens of trying to save the world from Vex and trying to convince the Tunnel Supes she and Oryn weren't double-crossing them.

For Oryn was quite the primitive Viking in bed.

They slept for a spell, and when they woke, they launched into a second lovemaking session. For this one, he eased her onto her back and straddled her, dangling his impressive cock in her face. "Ooh, I wanted to do this on the massage table," he confessed. "My mind was completely in the gutter."

She would have laughed at the humor of it if he wasn't so very well-endowed. If it wasn't so tantalizingly close to her mouth, within sucking distance.

"The Witch with the Wolfish Howl, was it?" he parried, dangling his hard cock above her like some ripe exotic vegetable.

When her hand went up to stroke it, he shifted his hips back, just out of reach. "Would Madame Wolf like a bite of it?" he teased.

Just as she reached up to pull him down by his hair, he moved quicksilver fast and rammed the entire shaft straight into her, which made her yowl with exquisite pleasure.

Then she did haul him down by his hair and bite him squarely on his upper lip with her canines, tasting blood. Her wolfish senses awakened, every part of her vibrating with energy.

They were off for round two, just as passionate, but with a more athletic charge, like the alpha fae Oberon and his magical queen, Titania.

Afterward, they dropped, breathless and dripping, onto the wrinkled, sex-scented sheets. They slept for hours and woke at night, famished and thirsty.

Downstairs, she fixed them turkey sandwiches, and they sat in their underwear in Ray's old den with tea trays. The conversation got serious again after she brought over Ray's earmarked dictionary and read the definition of the word Blackfire had blurted out.

*"The Golem, according to Czech legend, was first made from clay and brought to life by a rabbi to protect Prague's 16th-century ghetto from persecution. It's said to be called forth in*

*times of crisis. The golem, in this globally diverse twenty-first century, has been transformed by public imagination into a monster, independent of its origins as protector."*

"From a protector into a monster," she muttered. Goosebumps broke out along her arms. "Monsters. Is Vex spawning a monster? Is that what this is?"

Oryn stopped chewing and put down his sandwich. He screwed up his face in a cringe. "Oh, Lord, what a disaster that would be."

"Where is Vex? Who is he with, exactly, and what in blazing hell do they want with us? With the Tunnel Supes? With Savannah?" Desperation gripped Celestine, to find the missing pieces that remained elusive. Impossible to assemble otherwise.

"Have you found out more about the Demon Three Eyes Clan? Did you find any more writings from Ray?" Oryn had pulled on his shirt. No doubt these questions chilled him. Her own appetite fading, she wrapped a fleece throw around herself.

"Not more of Ray's writing, but I did draw Vex Blade when we were in the supe tunnel. I heard his cackle inside my head. It scared the crap of me, Oryn," she confessed.

"Why didn't you tell me?" He pushed his tea tray away and went over to her. Sat down and pulled her close.

"I'm telling you now. I also drew a swamp. I wasn't *trying* to draw a swamp," she emphasized. "I was trying to draw a lake. Or a stream."

"What's your theory about the drawing?"

She shook her head, miserable, baffled. "I saw a foot floating in the water. So damn gross." She sighed and went on. "I also saw a severed leg."

"Ugh, what's your take on it?"

"Hell if I know." She chewed on a ragged fingernail for a

minute. And then a few of Harwood's lines filtered back to her. She mumbled them aloud. "You came too late to save the real Harwood Port. The phantoms told me they scooped out his guts many years ago and threw him in the swamp." She cringed and looked at Oryn. His eyes shifted from amber to gray in apparent confusion. "Harwood said that, remember? I drew severed legs, not guts, but it *was* a swamp." She sighed. "And the last time I went to Bonaventure, my old card reader friend who passed on, Nola Jaye, spoke to me from the grave."

Oryn raised his brows. "Oh?" She hadn't told him a lot about Nola Jaye, but he didn't press her on it now.

She went on. "Nola Jaye showed me the Devil card from my deck, and she said it represented a demon swamp, the topsy-turvy world in crisis." Celestine yelled up at nothing, "Where exactly is this godforsaken swamp located, Vex, you vile creep?"

"What do you think is in there?" Oryn asked her.

"Who knows, maybe lots of severed corpses under the bog. Maybe Vex himself. I'm afraid to find out, but fear is not an option if you're on the hunt for the truth, is it?"

"I pray for your safety, but no." He pulled her in and kissed her.

# FOURTEEN

At ten in the morning, Aline came to escort Celestine to Ardenia's. She gave a knowing grin when Oryn answered the door with his rumpled black jersey on inside out, the tag and seams showing.

Celestine was beyond hiding their coupling. She kissed Oryn and promised she would text him with any news. "No need to hurry. Finish your coffee and lounge a bit. Just put up the wards on your way out. I'm off to Ardenia's, then Luna's, then back to the house," she told Oryn. "Texting you Luna's address and number, just in case..."

"In case of what?" He sounded alarmed. "I'll go with you," he whispered in her ear.

*Fear is not an option, right? My mantra today for the both of us.*

"No," she whispered back. "You shouldn't be my bodyguard. I'll be okay at an antique store." Out loud, she said overly brightly, "We should all be in the loop, and you may have news for me, too. You never know."

～

ARDENIA'S ANTIQUES was housed in a stately building off the corner of Lafayette Square. Its gray limestone façade was detailed with gargoyles and laughing cherubs, and the period wrought-iron gates and balconies were freshly polished to where the circular leaf patterns gleamed in the morning light. The wooden door was painted a crimson red. Aline gave the brass knocker three loud clangs.

Ardenia peeked out, then swung the door open with panache. Her white hair was piled in studied whorls atop her head and held with spray and turquoise barrettes. She did have on the jodhpurs Aline had described, these in tailor-made crimson, with high boots of gray snakeskin. She wore a crisp white fitted cotton shirt festooned with a gold alligator brooch with red ruby eyes at her throat. She ushered them into an imposing dining room, filled to the brim with object d'art and porcelain on the central mahogany table, china cabinets stuffed with pitchers, urns, goblets, and candlesticks. Every buffet held statuettes, one-of-a-kind curios—too many things for the eye to take in at once.

They followed her into a smaller, cozier sitting room with a jade-hued Oriental rug and luxe paisley throws. A three-foot-tall exotic blue heron lamp glowing from the inside sat on a gold-leafed table. Again, there were vignettes of story in each corner, clues to a traveler's life well lived. Ardenia whirled around with a wave of her arm. "Please, have a seat. What can we get you?"

Seamlessly, a distinguished gentleman of a certain age sailed in, with the classic white linen towel draped over an arm that held a tray. He was clearly not her husband or partner, but hired help who'd been working for her forever. Drink orders taken, he returned in a flash and then left them alone.

"So good to see you again, Ms. Aline," Ardenia declared. "Who is your friend? Have we met?" She turned to Celestine with curiosity and eyed her up and down the way she might assess a unique floor lamp or credenza.

"This is Celestine LeBlanc," Aline said. "We met in a continuing ed art class at SCAD. She's quite talented."

"Do tell. And what is your specialty, Ms. LeBlanc?"

Celestine wondered if she should launch right into her real talent—prophetic drawings. She wasn't sure how much Aline had told her, so she opted for a simplified vague version just to be safe. "I can work with colored pencils and charcoal, though I used to only do computer art. That's why this class was valuable. It helped me diversify."

"Celestine's too modest," Aline declared. "Sometimes her drawings reveal untold truths, things that haven't even happened yet."

"Oh?" A note of alarm was evident in Ardenia's response.

Celestine sent Aline a warning frown. Who knew how open-minded this woman really was? They needed to see if she could provide information before they scared her off. Celestine should play to Ardenia's interests, distracting her off this thread of conversation. "Aline tells me you've traveled the globe in search of precious pottery and the like. So fascinating! I'd love to hear about your adventures and what you found."

Ardenia took a sip of her cocktail and smoothed down her jodhpurs. "Well, I've been to Borneo for a rare set of rhinoceros hornbill porcelain pitchers, and to the lower valley of the Himalayas to bid for Gobind Singh's golden tea set. In 1676, he became the tenth Sikh guru and helped hold off the Mughal invaders." She looked positively gleeful that she had rendered the women speechless. She shrugged with faux modesty. "It's a learning experience. The world is chock full of rich history, and we, in our conscribed lives, know so little."

She took another sip of her drink and sucked daintily on the lemon rind. "Well, then there was my Arctic jaunt, hunting down Stone Age dinnerware. I got to buy sub-zero designer long underwear and a head-to-toe Arctic thermal-tech snowsuit for that one." She giggled. "But dammit, I lost that rare find to the Museum of Fairbanks. You win some, you lose some. All part of the chase." She peered over at Aline. "I forget what you said you were after... something about a drawing?"

Aline jumped in. "Yes, Celestine did a drawing of a strange sort of teapot that she hasn't been able to find on any database. And we figured if anyone could—"

"Oh, I love mysteries almost as much as I love teapots. One gives you anxiety and the other gives you hot chai." Ardenia giggled, tickled pink by her own non-joke. "Let's have a look, shall we?"

Celestine's chest pounded as she pulled the drawing from her pack, rolled off the rubber band, and stretched out the paper. She walked it over to where Ardenia was seated and placed it on the wide coffee table.

As Ardenia studied it, Celestine noticed her neck and cheeks flush a dark rose, her position tense, and her mouth clench as if she was closed to any further conversation.

"What?" nudged Aline, who clearly noted Ardenia's stiffened posture.

"So, have you seen this kettle design?" asked Celestine.

Finally, Ardenia spoke. "Why did you draw this?"

"I don't know. I told you, I sometimes draw things for reasons I can't say at the time."

"Where and when did you draw this?" Ardenia persisted.

"In art class. Um... maybe the third class? I can't recall exactly. Why does it matter?"

Ardenia didn't answer. Instead, she bolted upright.

"What's wrong?" Now Aline was alarmed. "So you've seen this thing before? You act like you've seen it. Why are you so upset?"

Ardenia snapped out of her unease enough to look down at Aline and try to answer her. "I hauled one up during an airboat expedition."

"Okay. In what country?" asked Celestine.

"Here. Right here," she intoned in a husky whisper, as if someone might overhear. As if she could be harmed if they heard her.

"Like here in the city?" asked Celestine. Ardenia was beginning to piss her off, but she needed to appease the woman, who was clearly spooked.

"Yes, not far from the city. I think it was south of here. Or southwest. The guide took us all around the salt marshes and tide pools." Ardenia sat back down and wrung her hands. "He called it mud larking, and I thought it sounded like fun. I put on a wetsuit in case of messy splashes, and I was all in. I had the pole with the net. The last stop was in a bog, a stinking, foul swamp, really, and I was scraping around its murky bottom, dreaming I'd find the best treasure there. And..."

"And what?" asked Celestine.

"I pulled it out of the mud and cleaned it off. I thought it was the most exotic, unusual teapot I'd ever seen."

"Where was this swamp? Any identifying factors? Visuals?" Celestine persisted.

"Well, I don't know... Oh, wait, the guide said the area

was rumored to be a cemetery, of all things, before it sank and became a swamp. I just thought he was spinning a tall tale. Like one of those melodramatic ghost tour barkers." She emitted a nervous chuckle. "It had jutting cypress roots, like swamps all do. I thought I saw a shoe caught in one." She groaned.

"Did he mention a name?" asked Celestine.

"Demon Swamp or something like that? But again, I thought he was play-acting for the tourists. Making up a Halloween-style name." She flinched. "It was revolting, though. The rotten stench."

*Demon Swamp.* That's what Harwood and Nola Jaye had called it. Celestine's gut clenched. "Tell me about the images on the teapot, Ms. Culpepper."

"Such unusual fish, their trios of beady yellow eyes. I took it around to the experts, you know. No one could tell me what era it was from, where it really originated. And..." She stopped again as completely as if she'd hit an invisible concrete wall.

"Why stop now?" Celestine asked. "Did you sell the teapot, or do you have it here?"

Ardenia flinched. She shook her head maniacally. "I hid it. It gave me nightmares. Bad juju. I cleaned the damn thing off with a special rag. I polished it to a fine sheen. And then a Pandora's box of trouble happened. Shadows flitted from the spouts and whizzed around every corner, away from the clear line of sight. Drawers opened and slammed shut. Sharp cutlery flew around as easily as smoke. Rugs began to trip me in the middle of the night. I broke my hip over one, and I suffered a long recovery in the rehab only to get deep gashes from antique glassware that just wouldn't stay put on the credenzas when I returned." She shook her head. "I just can't."

"Can't what?" asked Aline.

"I can't get the teapot. I put it in a metal box and locked it. I was afraid to throw it out, but it couldn't stay in here, so I took it out back and put it in a shed. I thought that would help keep it contained."

"Can your, um… personal assistant go get it?" asked Aline.

"No, I don't want him touching it!" she shrilled.

"Okay, calm down," Celestine urged. I'll get it. Just tell me where the shed is."

"Take it away from here, then, you hear?" ordered Ardenia. "I'll give you the padlock key to the shed out back and the box. Just take the damn thing."

Celestine promised.

Ardenia handed over the keys. "Just push the shed key under the back door and keep the box key," she instructed.

Celestine and Aline thanked her and said their good-byes while Ardenia led them through her kitchen. She was quick to shut the door after them, as if the box might fly through it otherwise. They hurried down the cement stairs to the yard and made their way along a bluestone path to the shed.

Opening the creaky door, Celestine pulled a twine cord to an overhead light that flickered from neglect. The metal box had been pushed into a far corner past the garden brooms and rakes. Celestine unlocked it and stared at the teapot, touching one of the fish images on its surface before closing and locking the box top once more. She held the box at arm's length as if it contained a bomb. It might as well have, being such an object of terror for Ardenia.

*Fear is not an option.*

"Such odd fish," remarked Aline.

"For sure," Celestine agreed, carrying the box with her

arms stretched forward like some wooden soldier on their way out to the public sidewalk.

As they hurried down the block, farther and farther from Ardenia's Antiques, Aline said, "Sorry, I had no idea she was so superstitious."

"It's not your fault." Celestine's heart clattered against her ribs, and her hands sweated so profusely she was afraid the slippery box would slide out of her hands. "She sure was flipped out." Inside, Celestine was forming a stark picture, and it scared the pants off of her. Indeed, Ardenia had dredged this thing up from Demon Swamp. Ray must've trapped the Demon Three Eyes Clan in this very teapot with his strongest magic and thrown it there, hoping they'd rot forever, along with the corpses of the folks in that graveyard, already under the swamp... and unbeknownst to him, the guts of the real Harwood Port.

The puzzle pieces were coming together faster now. *Fear is not an option,* she repeated to herself. "Hey, I have to stop by Luna's studio."

"Can I come along?" Aline asked when they were a block from Ardenia's Antiques.

"If you want. Sure." Celestine tried to keep the hesitation from her voice, though her gut clenched in sudden worry.

"I feel protective of you... of us both," Aline said. So she sensed the same thing in reverse. "Let me get us an Uber."

"Kind offer, but you already helped me get the box. And Luna's only about twelve blocks away on West Alice Street. I'd hate to mix you up in more messes. This case could blow up in my face, and I don't want you hurt."

"I insist." Aline eyed the metal box. "That thing is unwieldy."

Aline ordered the Uber. One came almost immediately.

The driver was a friendly looking sixty-something-year-old guy with faded-jean eyes, receding gray hair under a white golf hat, and driving a midnight-blue Cadillac. He started off and then slowed for a red light at the next corner. Celestine and Aline looked at each other and let out relieved sighs at the same time.

Aline tapped the box sitting between them. "Do you agree with what Ardenia said? Do you really believe all of the woo-woo stuff about that teapot releasing like, bad spirits?"

Celestine shrugged, unsure of whether to talk about it even in the relative privacy of an enclosed car. "Let's talk later," she whispered. When the light turned green, the driver lurched forward and sped up. Vertigo overtook Celestine with an unexpected pinch of fear in her chest. Battling dizziness, she heard the door locks snap shut.

"Well, I believe it," the driver crowed, catching her eye in the rearview mirror.

"Excuse me?" Celestine said.

"When you opened the box, the teapot alerted me to your whereabouts. Kind of a magical GPS." In the rearview mirror, the guy's eyes heated to scalding blue flames, and his genial grin was replaced by a hateful smirk. "A few months ago, when that uppity bitch rubbed that teapot, I flew up and out faster than a hawk in a tornado. Your so-called sweet uncle Ray stole my own damn teapot from under me and trapped me and Vex inside it for years. He'd already killed Sharker Titan, our second mate. So I was thrilled when Vex scooped Bartello's damn eyeballs out. The murderous jackass deserved it!"

"Who the hell are you, you sick fuck?" Celestine blurted, her heart sinking to her gut. "Let us out of this car!" She and Aline struggled to open the car doors, to no avail. The vehicle was suddenly riding on a whitewater turbulence of magic, tossing them violently in all directions. Celestine's head bashed against the overhead light, the window, the headrest.

"Open the doors!" Aline yelled as the metal box flew up and one of its sharp corners gashed her in the temple. "Ack!" she yelled harder, her hand flying to her bleeding head wound.

With a gush of water magic, the man fountained the metal box into the front seat. "It's mine. It stays with me," he declared and launched into high-pitched *heh-hehs* to the sound of water splashing down to the floor well.

"Who *are* you?" Celestine yelled again.

"Mornay Dred! Demon Three Eyes Clan. Don't you forget it." He steered the car-boat through more towering, arcing waves. "I'm your worst fuckin' nightmare," he bragged and cackled again with a sociopathic laugh that made the hairs stand up on her neck.

*Mornay. Vex. In Ray's journal. And the third—Sharker Titan, already dead.* "Look, it's me you want!" she screamed. "Let my friend out, she has nothing to do with this."

"Let us both out!" screeched Aline. "We can't help you! You have your damn teapot, your precious freedom. What more do you want?"

"Oh, more, a lot more," he seethed.

Despite this, Aline's door flew open, and an invisible hand shoved her out of the car. Celestine's messenger bag strap was twisted up in Aline's arm, and it tumbled out as well. Celestine leaned out to grab it when Mornay slammed the door with the tip of her finger caught in it. Celestine howled and managed to pry her finger out. She pressed the crushed tip hard with her other hand to staunch the bleeding.

Mornay Dred's water illusion faded just long enough for her to watch in horror as Aline crashed onto the sidewalk and rolled to a deadly stop, tangled in Celestine's go-bag. She uttered a silent earth charm to help the soil's minerals resuscitate her friend from injury.

Then, Mornay steered them into a nightmarish storm surge. His corny golf hat was gone. His receding gray hair was stringy and long in the back. In the rearview, she saw his bulbous forehead gleam over downturned brows and thin, tight lips. Celestine now understood the full horror of what Ardenia had wrought when she shined up that bewitched piece of crockery. The opposite of Aladdin's three wishes, this deadly polish released some hellish villains. Before Celestine's very eyes, the streets and sights of Savannah dissolved into roiling tsunami-sized waves that plunged them abruptly, violently under its surface.

"Girl, when do you intend to wake up?" More a demand than a question.

Celestine tried to open her eyes. They might as well have been glued together. She brought a shaky hand up to them and rubbed. Crusty bits rolled under her fingers. At least whatever had happened, her hands and arms were free, because she knew in her heart that horrendous things *had* happened. Her brain was fogged. She could only hope this was temporary because she needed to remember.

She made a second attempt to open her eyes, slowly this time, for she didn't want the lashes to rip. Vertigo roiled through her when they opened, making her body and mind lurch as if they'd forgotten how to function as one. The view before her was blurry...

In a room. Crowded with objects. An empty chair. Boxes and computers with blinking lights, an aquarium with fish or... what the hell? Eyeballs! Eyeballs swimming in the fish tank. And another tank with severed fingers. She swallowed down bile. Deep mauve shadows lurked on the periphery, a figure leaning forward in a second chair. Stringy gray hair like rat tails. Mornay. *Ugh*. She rubbed her eyes again and blinked hard.

"It's about time," he said and launched into his heh-heh-heh cackle.

With an impulsive streak of energy, she bolted to her feet, but something dug into her ankles, preventing her from moving forward. She stumbled back into the chair and looked down. Her ankles were cuffed and chained to heavy D-rings set into the floor.

"What do you want with me?" she asked, trying to stifle the tremor in her voice.

"Where is Edge LeRoux?" Mornay's affable grin was gone. His eyes burned blue flames. His smirk between pale simian jawbones made her skin crawl. "Where? I asked you a question, girl."

"Grown woman. Name's Celestine. And it's none of your damn business."

Another figure stepped forward from the purple shadows. Vex Blade himself, towering over the diminutive Mornay, who stood beside him. Blade's unkempt shoulder-length blue hair and bristled beard framed a glower that would make even the boldest thief flee. A scabbard was attached to his left side belt. "He's *my* business," Vex roared as he swaggered in front of her in hobnailed boots.

"How was LeRoux ever your business?" she asked boldly. "He wasn't a Demon Three Eyes supe. He was in Ray's Jekyll Clan."

"*Was*?" Confusion lurked in Vex's tone, though he quickly recovered. "Yeah, was, because Bartello's clan is gone. LeRoux is out of living allies. You and your trumped-up false hero, Ray Bar-tell-o screwed up big when you messed with me." He drew out each part of Ray's name as if it were a curse then he spat on the floor. "Now your dear old Ray is dead, the nasty trap spell is broken, and you're in *my* territory. You have no say here in Demon Swamp, know-it-all witch." With the speed of a glamoured supe, he flew so close to her that hate radiated from his coal-hot eyes into hers, burning them.

"Where is he?" Vex screamed. Her eardrums pinged with pain.

So they *were* in the notorious Demon Swamp. Vex couldn't be that smart to reveal this. Just then, as she turned her head to avoid his glare, she noticed half-rotted legs and arms floating behind the heavy glass of the back wall. How did they keep them from disintegrating? Were they in a vat of formaldehyde or what? Good god, were they all under the freaking swamp in some sort of glass cubicle?

"I'll never tell," she muttered.

Vex backhanded her so viciously she and the chair fell sideways.

THE NEXT TIME SHE AWOKE, her cheek throbbed. Raising a hand to assess the damage, she found her flesh was swollen. A hard, hot lump from Blade's vicious slap after her ballsy reply. She remembered the sickening chain of events starting with Mornay's cackling, which she'd under-estimated as all for show.

She opened her eyes and realized she was on a thin

cotton pallet spread out on the concrete. Her legs were still chained to the floor, but she was in a different space. This room had no furniture, just a heavy wooden door that contained a small window, and it stank of mildew and swamp rot. She sat up. Drawing tablets and pencils were arranged on the floor beside her.

Mornay's leering mug appeared at the door's small window. The lock clicked and he entered carrying a folding canvas chair. He opened it and sat a few feet away from her. "Ready to tell us where Edge LeRoux is?"

"Hell no." She was risking her life, but Mornay Dred pissed her off.

"You ain't gettin' out 'til you spill the beans, so make yourself at home, girlie."

"Woman."

"Ugly witch."

"Whatever, Ratty Dreds." They could call each other names all day, and it wouldn't make her tell them shit.

"Want some grit?" He leaned forward, causing his rattail strands to droop over his sunken-in chest. He had on a grubby metal-gray shirt with poufy sleeves, reminiscent of a foppish Victorian. His ill-fitting bellbottom jeans looked thrifted. She suppressed a cynical giggle, though she had to admit, her stomach rumbled. "What kind of food?"

"Fried catfish. Fried eel. Alligator." He cracked a grin, as if this fare was guaranteed to make her talk.

She needed something for her parched mouth. "You have water?"

"I got some, yeah. But first, how's about telling me where Edge went? I know you know, witch."

"N—"

He foisted the buck knife faster than she could get the *no* out and pressed it to her throat. This guy might look like a clown show, but even a court jester could slit a throat. He dug in the sharp tip just enough to nick her. A dribble of warm blood slid down her front.

It woke up her wolfish rage, and she let her fangs descend. Her pointed ears sprang up, and fur followed in a prickly rush. She heard the rip of her clothes as her torso shifted and she snarled and lunged at Mornay. Even though he moved fast, she was able to sink a deep bite in his bony wrist. The knife fell from his hand and clattered onto the concrete as he clutched at his wound. With her half-shifted claw, she attempted to grab it. Biting was one thing, but grabbing a knife with a wolfish paw was a clumsy proposition.

Her legs just above her paws were narrower than human ankles, so they slipped easily, joyously from the metal cuffs. She kicked the knife out of Mornay's reach with her powerful back haunch and lunged for him, fangs slavering, as he reached desperately for his blade. She tore into his shoulder, his wide cheeks, his exposed forehead. Blood spurted from his flesh, but what she normally would've lapped up disgusted her to the point of gagging. She spit the thick, sour liquid onto the concrete and kept up the attack. If she could kill him, she could figure out how to escape this prison. Get his key, find a tunnel grating to the outside. Or some dirt with which she could wield earth magic.

The door swung open. Vex erupted in a fierce bellow, and a gunshot followed. Her back haunch burned, and she collapsed on the pallet.

~

WHEN SHE AWOKE, she was back in human form. They had dressed her in a denim jumpsuit. Her left leg was throbbing —the bullet. Her ankles were back in cuffs, double ones this time.

Instead of Mornay Dred, Vex Blade sat in the canvas chair, tapping his hobnail boot impatiently on the blood-stained floor. A sickening dread rolled through her. This glaring, enraged water mage was not here to play. "You said you were thirsty, so drink this, bitch!" he snapped, and handed her what looked to be a plastic bottle of Coca-Cola. The cap was on crooked. What had he added?

Poison? No, he wouldn't want to kill her. He needed her for information. Some foul mix to keep her compliant? He wasn't exactly a pharmacist.

"Sit up," he roared. "I said drink this! Or do I have to shoot your other leg? Maybe one of your kidneys? Eh?" He held the bottle closer to her.

She took it reluctantly. "What do you want out of me?" she asked, stalling for time. Because something bad was going to happen. She could feel it like an arthritic person knew when rain was coming.

"You know where Edge LeRoux is. Our boy tracked you to him out in that Laurel Grove North Cemetery."

"Then you already knew. Why didn't you get him then?"

Vex didn't answer. Clearly, he screwed up but wasn't going to admit fault.

"Tell me," Celestine added, "what did you do that was so heinous Ray would seal you guys up for years? Was it something about building shitty condos that collapsed and killed hundreds of people? Pouring sewage and garbage into the tide pools? I remember the condo corporation's name now—your men, Mornay and Titan. Clever, clever."

Vex snickered and sat back in the chair. "Yeah. Mornay Dred and Sharker Titan. We killed the coral reefs so tourists wouldn't flock here anymore. So, we could rule Savannah." He shrugged. "That was a side hustle. We had much bigger coals in the fire."

"Like what?" She was praying that his overweening pride would keep egging him on. Let her find out as much as she could before he knocked her out again. "And what are you building with all of those eyes and fingers and body parts?"

"Wouldn't you like to know!" He broke out in guffaws.

She was burning, she was so enraged. "I would *love* to know. It sounds awesome. Wildly creative." She grinned at him, as if she was impressed, even tempted to switch to the dark side. "Is it a golem? A monster?" His jaw clenched. "What exactly do you want to do with the monster? With Ray gone, you're already the most powerful mage in Savannah, so why not stop while you're ahead?" Pouring on the charm, she almost choked on her own toadying words.

"No one will stop me, ever. Not you, you ugly witch. You are nothing. I could kill you now," he roared, triggered by something she'd said back into his former rage. "Quit playing coy and get drinking." He pulled out a shiny revolver from inside his jacket pocket and stuck it against her temple.

With a trembling hand, she tipped the bottle into her mouth and drank a few gulps. It tasted like cola, but God only knew what he'd added to it. Parched as a dry boot but not daring to finish it off, she capped the bottle. "Now what?"

"Draw." He kicked the drawing pad and some pencils her way.

Her gut twisted. This was bad. They were onto her. Her

prophetic art. If she could play dumb a little longer... "Why do you want to see my drawings? I'm not a good artist, and you don't seem like the collector type anyway, so—"

"I said get drawing. Show me where Edge went. Draw where he went. Now!"

"Okay, okay. I told you, he's dead, but I can do a drawing." She started to sketch in a pond, some random cutesy decoy with cattails and wild irises. "Why do you want to find his ashes, anyway?" Another misleading statement. If she made enough of them in a row, could she fool even a supe as wily as Vex? One never knew until they tried.

"Dead. Liar! My boy said you were chatting him up a week ago at that cemetery. So, tell me, were you chatting up a corpse?" Vex laughed despite himself. It sounded like a rusty blade scraping a frozen pine.

"Well, cemeteries are full of dead folk. Spirits flying 'round. You of all people should know this. Edge is dead. They cremated him. I was talking to his ghost is all."

"Keep drawing, witch."

"LeRoux was deader than a doornail, and all of his guts were burned to charcoal," she babbled. If Vex thought he couldn't harvest Edge's organs, he might give up. Her eyes grew a little blurry. Whatever Vex had laced that damn cola with was heating up her insides, making her woozy. "So he's useless for your monster-making, I'm *jusss* saying," she slurred.

"Shut up about monsters." Vex leaned forward and slapped her but not hard. Just enough to let her know there would be worse where that came from if she strung him along.

Her hand slid across the paper—an awkward mark that proved how woozy she was. Then another messy curve in the opposite direction that meant nothing to her, had no purpose. A third that connected the two random marks diagonally and covered the light sketch she had started of the pond. She giggled.

"What's so funny?" he asked, twirling his revolver.

"Whatever the hell you poured in my drink is defeating your purpose because it's making me so ham-fisted, I can't control the pencil at all." She burst into a giddy laughing fit until tears rolled down her face, stinging where she'd received slaps and punches.

Though moments later, her traitorous fingers seemed to take charge again, in an up-down sawing motion on the page. Her blurry eyes cleared just long enough to see with utter horror that the curving lines that had looked so clumsy, formed a heart with its valves. And now, it was situated behind heavy bars.

Vex let out a war whoop and leapt to his feet. He kicked her hard with his hobnail boots, releasing dirt stuck to the cleats that made her wince and cough. As she faded once again, she saw him race out of the room and heard him bolt the heavy wooden door behind him.

# FIFTEEN

W hen Celestine came to, it was dark, cold, and she was thirstier than ever. Her elbow and knee throbbed from sleeping on one side for so long. The bullet, still lodged in that calf, didn't help. She was feverish and sweaty on top of shivering from cold. The leg needed treatment to save it from infection, or worse: sepsis.

The lineup of calamitous events ticked down in her mind—her attack on Mornay, the conversation with Vex, him drugging her, demanding she draw. And that drawing was like a chilling road map if one knew how to read it. She had to escape fast to have any chance in hell of getting to LeRoux in time. But how?

She looked around for the cola bottle. There it was on its side. Regardless of what it was laced with, she needed liquids. No, she could not afford to pass out again. She rolled it away. Instead, she drew up as much spit as her parched mouth could and held it there. Pawing around, her fingers ran through the dirt Vex had kicked off his bootheels. Hopefully, there was enough to conjure some earth magic. She gathered up a mound of it and scooped it into her jumpsuit pocket. Then she groped around to find any other bits and pieces that could be used for elemental spellcasting. Along the crevices where wall met floor, she scraped off moldy deposits and some swamp sedge. Sometimes mold made powerful visioning fuel; other times it could make a witch sick. She would take her chances.

Her legs were still in the double irons, but she might be able to escape with narrower legs. She shifted into wolf form, every muscle prickling with the effort in her weakened state. Finally, her back haunches were free. She shucked off the bulky denim jumpsuit. With her wolfish sight primed for the dark, she spied the folding chair. Yes! They had left it there like idiots. Its metal legs could possibly be used to smash out the small glass in the door.

She must be smart about this. Her energy was already badly depleted, and magic-making used a ton. Vex and his cronies might still be in the other parts of what she was calling the cubicle, so she would either have to sneak past them or fight them directly. The latter was a bad option, as hand-to-hand combat would double the energy needed for spellcasting.

She thought of Nola Jaye. When Celestine needed counsel, she'd often gone to Bonaventure. Any help was key. To practice witchcraft, it was best to shift out of wolfish form, since the two didn't quite mesh. Yet to have a chance in hell of getting out through that small window, she'd need to be in wolf form. Maybe Nola Jaye would still sense her in wolfish form and from far away?

To ready for her next moves, first Celestine rolled up the jumpsuit so the pocket wouldn't spill its contents. This was difficult using her muzzle instead of nimble fingers, but she managed.

Next, she gathered more mold and sedge, a mound of the last precious dirt, and lapped up the foul mixture, chewing it into paste with her spit as best she could. Even for a wolf, its flavor was foul. Swallowing, she shook her muzzle in distaste.

Then she crawled back onto the pallet and circled to a comfortable position, her tail wrapped around her haunches to keep her warm. She uttered the affirmations for a vision quest with low growls and yips, and then waited. Beasts experienced mental pictures too, yet she'd only connected to Nola Jaye outside of Bonaventure once, so there was no guarantee this would work at all. Her mind floated on clouds fueled by virtual winds. And then she could hear the words of her mentor!

*Wolf Woman, I see you. Wolf Woman, the messenger has spread word,* Nola Jaye said in Celestine's head. More than a wolf, more than a witch, more than a mundane, Celestine had elements of all. Pictures flashed in her mind as Nola Jaye presented two cards. Temperance and the Ace of Swords. Pictures full of color—the winged woman in the flowing gown and a man's muscled arm gripping an upright sword with plant matter on it. Yet Celestine's wolfish mind could not comprehend them clearly after all.

*Why must I always struggle to interpret your words and cards, even in my own drawings, Nola Jaye?*

*Wolf Woman, nothing worthy is easy. Hurry! The lights move toward you, but not for long.*

With that, Nola Jaye's images and words floated off in the dark. Celestine felt badly that she had no fruit to offer. *The lights move toward me?* No time to figure it all out because time was scarce. She grabbed the folded chair in her muzzle and gripped it firmly between her fangs, its metal feet pointing forward. She leapt and charged with all her weight, banged over and over on the glass. Praying the racket wasn't heard throughout the cubicle, she feared for the worst. When the thick glass finally shattered, she grabbed the rolled jumpsuit in her maw and leapt a final time, shooting through the opening. She landed in a narrow hallway and pricked her ears for sounds.

Surprisingly, no one was coming to inspect the loud racket from the broken glass. Shifting back to human, she examined the few bloody cuts she'd suffered from the jutting shards. Her fur had been good protection, though she needed a minute to staunch the bleeding from shards in her side, and to ease the throbbing bullet wound in her leg. She used the time to don the jumpsuit and reach in her pocket and collect a handful of her prized dirt mixed with swamp moss. Rubbing it in her palms, she infused it with intentional earth magic.

*Crone, Keeper of the Cauldron of Knowledge,*
*Mix this earthen dirt and swamp sedge.*
*Send it forward as a magical scout*
*To find me the way up and out.*

At least this hall was dimly lit. She opened her hands palms up and coaxed the dirt mixture to rise, adding a drop of her own blood and spit to ground her to its journey. Like a tiny tornado, the dirt began to rise and swirl as it tore forward. As exhausted and injured as she was, she worked hard to keep up. She passed a door that said lab and one that said utilities. Swiftly, the earthen funnel approached the end of the hallway where there was a wide picture window, and it swerved to the right.

She ducked to one side of the window when she realized it led to the first space she'd been in, with the aquariums of floating eyeballs and fingers and the labyrinth of computers and beeping instruments. She gave a desperate peek, scanning for Demon Three Eyes Clan members. The only supe she saw was Mornay, eyes shut, splayed out on a stretcher, a swaddle of bandages around his head, his shoulder. His skin was blue, and his eyes were in a fixed stare. He sure looked dead! Perhaps Vex intended to use his body parts.

Her chest lilted. It might be easier than she thought to escape with no one here to guard the lab. This relief was short-lived when she realized it might mean that the demon clan had a huge head start on her.

She darted to the right to catch up to the dirt funnel, which was already at the end of the next hallway. Yes. The swirling soil was rising! Looking up, she witnessed it funnel up through grating that most likely covered an air vault.

She crooned another charm to push aside the grate and rise up with the dirt funnel, using the last of her strength. Gliding on its magic, it bore her up and up. The stink of the swamp hit her nose, and just as she was about to pass out, she saw sky. The dirt funnel spit her out on a cluster of wiry cypress roots, reinjuring her side. Staring up into the night sky, she saw thousands of tiny winking lights, too low to be stars. Where had she seen those fantastic lights before?

*The will-o'-the-wisps! Am I dead? Is this what Nola Jaye tried to explain when she said 'The lights move toward you, but not for long'?*

"There she is!" called Oryn, freewheeling down on what looked to be a boat made from the fairy lights.

*What a sweet, sweet voice he has.*

"Oh my god!" called Luna, leaping from the light vessel, soaring down on her fully spread wings and helping Oryn scoop up her new friend.

CELESTINE SANK into Oryn's arms, and he did his healing magic on her, steadying his hands above her face, palms down and intoning charms. Her facial wounds were glaring —deep cuts, bruises, and the swollen red cheek where Vex had backhanded her—they needed no explanation. Oryn's electric energy made her prickle and itch as it healed her. She moaned with relief.

Unable to talk much, she was able to point to the bullet wound on the back of her leg. Luna helped by carefully rolling Celestine on her side and raising that leg so Oryn could coax the bullet out with his masterful air magic. Luna let Celestine grip her hand during his procedure, and again when Oryn did his hands-on healing and sealed up the leg wound. Afterward, Luna helped sit Celestine up and gave her a bottle of water, which Celestine drank greedily.

As Oryn steered the vessel toward Savannah, Celestine slept for a spell, her head in his lap. When she awoke, she thanked them. "I can't describe how grateful I am you're both here. I thought for sure I was dead."

He leaned down and kissed her hand. "I couldn't let that happen."

When they were close to the city, she began to relay what had happened. Luna and Oryn were stunned. "How did you know where I was?" Celestine asked.

Luna spoke first. "Aline had my number and called me. She told me Mornay had taken you. She told me what Ardenia had said about Demon Swamp, about its location. We got in touch with Oryn. He knew about Mornay." Luna held up a phone. "You dropped your messenger bag when Mornay took off. Aline found it and rescued your phone. We didn't have the password, so we didn't try to unlock it, but she knew Oryn's number." She smiled.

"Oh my god, thanks!" Celestine took it and checked her messages. There were many from Wade.

*Ready to visit LeRoux? Worked out some times with the warden. We could get in tonight,* said one from yesterday.

*Answer your texts!* That was from this morning.

She knew better than to spill all her news on a phone text. She simply texted him back saying, *I'm on my way!*

"What are you up to?" asked Oryn when she clicked off her phone and gave him a serious look.

"I have to go to the prison. Now."

"You can hardly walk," Oryn replied with a groan.

"There's no other option."

"Then at least let me go with you."

She nodded. "I can do that."

"How can I help?" asked Luna, her wings fluttering and auburn hair flying in the night wind.

"God, you've already helped so much. I don't expect you to help anymore."

"But what if I want to?" Luna's eyes were deep and unwavering. "I have strong water magic. It looks like you might need a water mage. From what you say, these crazy bastards are still on the loose, trying to conjure a waterborne monster."

"I... I don't know what to say." Celestine glanced from Luna to Oryn. His mouth was open, about to add his opinion, but he closed it, clearly choosing to let the women come to their own decisions.

"Say yes," Luna urged. "I came to Savannah for a reason. More than the art pulled me here."

Celestine was convinced of this, too. Why else would she draw Luna kneeling over Ray? But what if Luna's involvement injured her, or worse, caused her death? Celestine would never forgive herself.

"Let me know. You have my number." Luna gave Celestine a gentle hug, and then, perching on the edge of the twinkling vessel, she leapt out into the sky, her wings bursting open like an enchanted parachute, and she flew off in the moon's glow. The will-o'-the-wisps seemed to sigh and brighten too, as if to wish her good night.

And then, cloaked in the glamour of Oryn's air magic, they descended to northern Savannah, and to the parking lot of Coastal State Prison.

"Do you never read your texts? Where the heck have you been?" Wade asked her as he observed the now-pink scars on Celestine's face and her disheveled look in the dirt-smudged jumpsuit. "And who is this?" He side-eyed Oryn. "I thought we had an understanding that no one else would be informed of the location or nature of the, er... client's detainment."

"I know, I know, but Detective Wade, today this man—Oryn Forest—helped me escape death."

Wade's eyes widened further. She gave him a Don't Second Guess Me on This staredown. "The Demon Three Eyes Clan had me in chains in their lair under Demon Swamp. I saw the freaking body parts they've collected, floating around in chemical-filled aquariums. It's real, Detective, way too real. So I'd be grateful if Oryn can join us. Their clan leader, Vex Blade, is onto us. Last week at that cemetery, his flunky saw me talking to the... man in protective custody. They're after Edge. They drugged me and made me do a drawing... of a heart behind bars. They *know!* We have no more time."

Wade gaped at her but didn't argue. "Let's go." He took

a key card from the warden out of his jacket pocket and waved them on as he opened one high-security door after another.

Celestine stuffed down her anxiety over entering another confined space so soon after being captive underwater. She winced at her still painful leg as they traversed through multiple barred areas whose doors clanged shut after them.

They rode down an interior elevator and entered through two more barred sections—truly in the belly of the beast. Each section had a guard who stared blankly at them. It was eerily quiet, unlike the upper areas, where prisoners shouted as they passed and gave Celestine catcalls she ignored though was flattered by in a politically incorrect way. Now, her heart raced for entirely different reasons.

"Just up here," grunted Wade.

They got to the cell at the same time and pressed their faces against the small window. Celestine screamed, "Nooo!"

Wade unlocked the heavy door. Inside was the corpse of Edge LeRoux, ripped literally in half—a raw, gaping cavity where his heart had been. His guts were spilling out on the floor in a swelling lake of dark blood. A bloody guard's uniform was floating in the red liquid. "Nooo!" she screamed again, leaning against Oryn for the strength to stay conscious. She rasped one last time, "Nooo."

ORYN HELPED her out of the cell, and they followed Wade to a small office down the hall. She slumped in an old-school wooden desk chair with Oryn next to her and Wade across.

"How the hell did anyone get in there?" Wade asked. "The warden was silent. Those guards said nothing. No alarm sounded. It makes no sense."

"Vex must've used a powerful spell to hypnotize the guards," Celestine explained.

"Yeah. He obviously stole a key card and uniform off someone and used it to blend in," said Oryn, a hand resting protectively on Celestine's knee. "For that matter, supernaturals with expert magic can coax a warden, the guards to open doors, silence alarms."

Celestine sighed deeply and sat up straighter in the chair. Time, once again, to gather her energy and act—no choice in the matter. "Detective Wade, we need to mobilize all units. They have the final body part—Edge's heart—all that was needed to animate the golem. No doubt, Vex is speeding back to Demon Swamp to sew it in, or however he does the deed." Her guts rolled as if she'd eaten rotting meat. Everything was flawed, perilous.

"You know what a golem is, right?" Oryn asked Wade.

Wade gave a simplistic answer: that he'd heard about it as a kid in Sunday school but thought it was some type of fairytale creature that protected the ancient world.

"On the right track, yet too optimistic," Oryn replied. "In modern times, the golem can also be a monster with supernatural powers. In this case, a water monster."

"Extremely dangerous," Celestine added. "Vex Blade never got over Ray trapping him and Mornay for so many years. Never got over Ray killing Sharker Titan, his second-in-command. Blade's rage is out of control. He wants to destroy Savannah. If he can obliterate it, he can rebuild it in his own image and rule it uncontested. It will involve many, many deaths."

She paused to see if Wade was getting it. His jaw was

clenched, and his forehead was etched with worry lines. She went on. "Vex boasted about his big plans when I was chained in his lab. You should evacuate citizens ASAP."

"Under what pretext? I can't exactly say there's a monster loose," Wade scoffed. "That sounds crazy, even for Savannah."

"This thing is most powerful in water. No doubt it will wreak havoc on the rivers, the tidal pools, the coastal waters. It may stir up a hurricane, a tsunami. Water disasters," Celestine said. "It won't be just in the glamoured, unseen world. Guaranteed, it will break through into the mundane, the actual city. Flood the streets, damage buildings, monuments, drown folks." She shuddered. "Can you get on TV, radio, streaming services and announce there's a deadly force weather system of the likes no one's ever seen before? Tell the people to evacuate. Tell mayors in surrounding cities to set up shelters in their coliseums."

"There won't be visible evidence on any meteorologists' systems. No weather patterns." Wade fisted the firearm in his holster. "Can you shoot a golem? I could have the National Guard on standby. Can we kill it with lead bullets, grenades?"

"Who knows?" Oryn shook his head. "It's a waterborne monster, yet it has body parts from the most powerful mages in Savannah." Oryn studied Wade. "Look, one thing I could do... I have a fae friend who's a newscaster. I can ask her to figure out a way to word the danger on air, spread the news to storm-chasers. Maybe even glamour some if need be. One thing's for sure... people need to get far from harm's way."

Wade nodded. "Okay, yeah, whatever you can do."

"Also, the beast's magic is strongest in water," Celestine

reasoned, "so it could weaken, even perish, if we block it from its element. Maybe try this first to slow it down."

"Good point," Oryn said. "Also, from what I researched, golems take orders from their creators, so if we capture or kill Vex, we could stop the thing. Not sure how much it thinks on its own. I'm an air mage, so I only know so much about how to kill a water mage."

"I'm texting Luna," Celestine decided. "She's joining the team. She's a powerful water mage. We need her badly." She got out her phone, and her fingers flew over its keyboard.

# CHAPTER
# SIXTEEN

The moment the water monster received the heart, it shuddered to life. Its many eyes, set in its translucent blubber, tracked its creator: Vex in the swamp's underwater cubicle. The truly magical eyes from Ray sat in the center of its face, while the others collected by Vex and Mornay lined up like blue and green and golden tribal tattoos around the beast's entire head to give it 360-degree vision. Its body, at first, stood at around ten feet high, but soon swelled from extreme water consumption, ballooning to twenty feet in height and a girth of over nine feet around. Vex had set eyeballs inside its blubbery body as well—in its gut, its chest, in its legs—peering here and there, stupidly.

In addition to sawing off live legs and scooping out live guts of unlucky lesser mages around Savannah, Vex and Mornay had scavenged for core bones—ribs and pelvises—deep in the muck of Demon Swamp. The monster's maw was lined with eight sets of teeth from the corpses of men hauled up from the sunken graveyard. They had dragged up mandibles, deformed skulls, and long bones from legs.

Mornay had even dug up penises that had amazingly petrified instead of rotting. He'd strung them up around its neck as talismans. Power. Potency, even, to coax the hope of a second-born golem.

Vex knew from studying how-to guides on monster creations that the golem's understanding of emotions and commands would be rudimentary. That Vex needed to keep his directives short—like crush, walk, follow, destroy—and that the golem would be driven more by magical force than complex sentences. So Vex shouted simple orders inside the monster's head: *Destroy men's water toys! Trash the river! Hurry, brute, do it now!*

The monster sloshed through Demon Swamp and then through Blackbeard Creek and then the Ogeechee River toward the Savannah coast, shoveling enormous handfuls of brackish water and fish into its open maw and gulping it all down.

*So thirsty*, it moaned. *So angry, want to tear things up.* With its magical fingers, it plucked up boats docked on either side of the waterway and hurled them violently onshore. The crash of broken wood had folks along the river screaming and racing for cover.

*Head toward the biggest river*, came Vex's order.

*The biggest river*, the brute echoed.

Seeing the monster forge the river, terrified people scooped up children and pets while hastily abandoning cases of liquor and soda, bags of chips and hot dogs—picnic supplies. For until now, today was a day where the sun beamed with the promise of fun, at odds with this panicked shock of seeing the water giant approach, blocking out the sky.

*Destroy the docks, whip up storm waves,* Vex ordered.

The monster writhed and danced and kicked up his

enormous feet, causing eddies and whip-fast currents to bash piers and yachts and fish hatcheries, and for waves to roll ashore in mini tsunamis. The monster heard the high-pitched screams of humans, some of whom were sucked under in the melee, yet it didn't understand what their rolling bodies were. For it was dumb and practically mindless and had never seen a human before, except in the inkling of insight that pricked through Ray's old eyes.

*Never mind who they are, never mind what they are*, ordered Vex, sensing the hesitancy of the brute. *Send the waves higher, toward the city. Then go up on the banks and run with them. Now!*

The water monster wasn't sure what a city was. All it knew was that it was loathe to step from the water, for its simple instinct was in self-preservation. It wobbled as it walked to the shallow, stony edge and up on the hard, soil-packed bank. As it walked inland, its blubbery legs weakened, its eyes dimmed slightly. Its translucent body sagged.

Yet it worked hard to blast floodwater inland. It couldn't see over the tree line, but the clamor of destruction rang out, combining with hundreds of human screams. Buildings, a supermarket, and a Walmart toppled in the unnatural water surges. A car dealership too. Cars bobbed on the waves and caught in trees, historic gravestones whirled in the watery stew.

*Good job, brute, keep heading toward the center of the city. Destroy the old town squares. You will get to the biggest river soon enough*, Vex ordered.

The water monster groaned. It craved water. Traveling away from it made it angry. It kicked things and howled, sending up eddies of airborne water, sending up houses and trees and mailboxes.

≈

LUNA JETTISONED her long denim jacket in favor of a blue jumpsuit with cutouts for her wings. She hadn't expected Celestine's call, but when it came, Luna immediately said yes to joining the team. She'd already been reviewing her best spells, practicing her water magic on a tiny scale in her bathtub, examining the map of Savannah with a special concentration on the waterways.

Celestine's text provided the details:

*Vex got the heart; we got to Edge too late. The water monster is already rampaging. Oryn's research on golems taught him it cannot think much for itself. It takes orders from Vex. First we need to slow the monster down before it kills people and destroys Savannah, and then stop Vex. Can a water mage be weakened? Be killed?*

Luna's reply: *I'm on it. All of it.*

≈

CELESTINE AND ORYN whizzed toward the water monster in Oryn's low-flying glamoured vessel, invisible to mundanes. They could sense its movements through Oryn's special GPS.

"Oh god, I see the monster!" Celestine exclaimed, pointing in the direction of Forest Park. "It's way too close to the old part of Savannah for comfort," she lamented. "We have to fight it before it destroys people and buildings."

Oryn nodded and guided the vessel closer.

The monster seemed to sense them, or maybe Vex sensed them *through* it, for it raised its bloated head and rolled its many glittering, juddering marble eyes at them. It let out a dreadful, grinding roar, like an industrial street cleaner with something clogging its gears.

Arms straining up for them, it lurched forward, knocking over two telephone poles. Celestine went to work, conjuring a dirt storm that battered the monster's pliable torso and spattered dirt into its many eyes and shovel-like maw. It spit out dirt as it howled but kept stumbling forward.

Below, at the street level, they gaped at the bumper-to-bumper traffic already snaking out of Savannah. Some folks were halfway out their car windows, screeching with terror as they stared at the towering beast. Luckily, the telephone poles had missed any cars, instead crashing onto the grassy yard of a public building.

"Thanks for spreading word to the weather fae," Celestine said breathlessly.

"Not a moment too soon," Oryn said as he steered the light vessel around again to the beast. "Let's hope it doesn't start throwing cars like baseballs."

"Oh, hell no!" Celestine shuddered.

Oryn shot up to about twenty feet above the monster, who now lumbered down a wide boulevard. Cars frantically veered out of its way, not risking a second to rubberneck the outrageous sight. Oryn aimed his arms and palms at a downward slant and detonated intense air pressure, sandblaster style, onto the crown of the beast's head. Lowering the vessel, Oryn aimed another hard beam at the beast's huge back.

"It'll feel this heat," he said as he kept the pressure going.

Then Oryn swooped to the front of the beast and directed a third unforgiving burst of concentrated air pressure at its barrel chest. The beast stopped in its tracks and shook its head and torso like a dog with fleas.

Celestine sent another barrage of soil mixed with jagged stones. In tandem with the air pressure, it detonated rocks into the beast's maw and down into its blubbery body.

It choked loudly and crouched down on all fours, crawling under the vessel and away, this time smashing parked cars in its wake.

*Attack them, Brute!* Vex ordered. *Get on your feet. Stop crawling like a dog!*

*Like a dog,* echoed the water monster, stumbling upright. *Attack!*

In her mind, Celestine could hear the water monster and Vex talking back and forth. A side effect of her magical entanglement. It would be an advantage for sure.

The water monster took off running. A bizarre sight, because even with its many eyes, it appeared to run blindly. It tripped over single-story buildings and young saplings as it ran. Clearly, it suffered from being on dry land, because it kept opening its shovel maw to gasp like a water-starved fish.

But it was a supernatural, and as such, it bumbled in fast motion.

"At that pace, the damn thing will get to the historic district in no time." Celestine groaned.

"Did you text Luna?" asked Oryn, speeding the light vessel the beast's way.

*Luna! We need you here ASAP!* Celestine texted her the coordinates.

"Oryn, I have an idea," Celestine exclaimed. "Can you steer near the monster's eyes?"

He nodded and accelerated to what felt like warp speed.

In moments, they were staring into the monster's line of glassy eyes as Oryn flew the vessel backward to keep up with the beast's forward pace. It roared at them, its maw opening to reveal lines of brown teeth. Bursts of foul swamp gas wafted their way.

Celestine gagged, blew out a cleansing breath, and then stared at the thing, trying to find Ray's eyes in the middle of its head. It wasn't hard. Ray's eyes, even post-mortem and set in the translucent head, shone with hints of his old compassion and sass. Celestine's heart bled for him. She yelled, "Ray, can you still see through your eyes? Can you see me, Celestine? I'm right here, Ray!"

The water monster slowed down as if transfixed. It rolled its eyes and swayed from side to side as it studied her.

"Ray!" she called louder. "Do you see what you *are*, Ray? Your enemy, Vex Blade, stole your eyes and put them in a water monster so he can usurp your magical sight. He intends to use this beast to hurt Savannah. To destroy the coastal waters as before. Kill people. Seize the city for his own. We can't let him do this. Ray, look down at your hands, *Pete Leger's* hands. The beast's heart is Edge LeRoux's. Vex is a filthy thief, a parasite who steals powers from other mages. Can you see?"

The water monster swiped at his own eyes and took a feeble swipe at Oryn's light vessel, but when Celestine spoke forcefully again, it cocked its ears as if listening to her.

"Ray!" she yelled. "This monster takes orders from Vex, but your eyes are sharp and have a magical mind of their own! Right?"

The water monster swayed and almost lost its balance but caught itself.

"Ray! See through Vex's evil. See through his monstrous plan! Don't follow his orders. Refuse to show him the way through your eyes. Your eyes can chart their own path. March this beast to dry land and lay it down. Weaken this monster who needs water to survive. Deny it liquid."

The water monster plunked onto the asphalt and shook its giant head as if an insect was caught in its ear.

*Brute, get up!* Vex ordered. *Ignore this witch! Grab their light vessel. Hurl it down!*

*Hurl it down*, parroted the monster. Faster than Celestine could see it coming, the beast bolted upright. With its massive arm and much smaller attached gray fingers stolen from Pete Leger, it batted at their ship.

Oryn and Celestine crashed violently onto a church, the twinkling ship catching on its sharp spire. They fell with a hard thud on the church lawn dotted with gravestones.

Groaning from the impact, Celestine clambered up and checked to see if Oryn was injured. She took his hand and helped him up, and they scurried for cover behind a granite mausoleum. The beast's arm reached down for them just as something fast and ivory colored swept through the sky.

*Luna!*

Her beating wings formed a mystical blur as she flew to the monster and caught its attention. "Beast!" she exclaimed. "Stop your violence or I'll harm you."

It raised its bulbous head and glared at her with its dozens of glittering eyeballs, each angry, each, irritated beyond belief.

*Kill her!* roared Vex. *Rip off her wings! What are you waiting for, stupid brute?*

It swatted at her, but she flew out of reach. "If you stop damaging things, I will show you to the water," she promised. "Ignore that man's voice. I will end your suffering. You need to drink and soak in healing liquid. I under-stand. I'm a water mage too."

*Water,* repeated the beast. It shambled after her like a huge bear.

*Answer only to me!* roared Vex. *Idiot brute, I gave you an order!*

But the monster was so very thirsty. It needed water down its gullet.

Celestine and Oryn peered out from behind the mausoleum. "What on earth is Luna doing?" whispered Celestine. "She must know that water will only strengthen the monster." She began to send Luna a frantic text.

"Wait." Oryn put a hand on Celestine's arm to stop her. "Trust her plan, Celestine. You can't do it all by yourself. She's a water mage. She's aware of this."

"Okay, you're right, she must be." Celestine clicked off her phone and stuck it in her pants pocket. She was so *not* used to letting others help her.

"Let's follow them," Oryn urged.

"Yes, from a safe distance." Celestine was worried about how tired she already was, beaten down by Vex, by crafting earth magic. And this fight had just started.

Oryn had already conjured a sort of light skateboard that whirred a few feet off the ground. "Hop on. Let's go before they're out of sight."

She climbed on and wrapped her arms around Oryn, indulging for a fleeting moment the sweetness of pressing close to him. Then they were off.

When they caught up to the monster clambering after Luna, she'd led him to a man-made reservoir with high concrete walls and hilly banks of tall southern pines around the perimeter of the dark-blue water.

"You see?" Luna said, whirling around. Was Luna trying

to convince the monster she was talking to it and not just mumbling at random? "A whole pool for you to drink!"

*Don't follow this silly woman!* Vex growled at the monster. *She's leading you into a trap. Get past her. Follow the road to Savannah and the town squares. Now!*

*The silly woman. A trap,* echoed the monster with a flicker of worry about a trap. Yet the hope of drinking water drove him on. *Need water!* It said as it bumbled into the deep reservoir. With a rasping moan of relief, the golem plunked down into it, scooped up great handfuls of the cool water, and gulped it down.

"I wonder what Luna's doing?" whispered Celestine, peering out from where they hid in a pine thicket about a half a ballfield's distance away.

"She must have a plan," Oryn replied. "We just don't know what it is yet."

Luna turned for a moment and peered in their direction. Could she overhear their whispered conversation? She whirred back to the monster still lapping up water and visibly bluing and swelling as he did.

*Brute!* Vex roared. *I gave you an order! Get out of that water and go to the old town squares. Kill people. Kill the lady with wings first.*

"Ray!" Celestine hissed, trying to send her message through the ether. "Use your inner sight to fight Vex. To refute what he says to the monster."

*Drink first,* the beast retorted. It paused from its guzzling and scowled at Luna. Still soaking, it punched at her. She was too far away to touch.

Luna began to intone a high-pitched song unintelligible to Celestine. As Luna circled her arms, she blew vast, gusty breaths at the monster, the water. Her wings beat so rapidly that Celestine could hear them whir through the pines.

The air grew cold, and intense winds whistled through the forest from where Luna was circling her arms. The draughts she blew out were frozen clouds of vapor.

By the time the monster was cold enough to notice, thick slabs of ice had formed on the reservoir's surface. The beast startled but couldn't get to its feet. Luna worked her freezing magic until, not only was the reservoir solid ice, but the monster's legs and all the way to its belly had frozen stiff. It reared its massive head and launched a monstrous roar of frustration and anger. Struggling in vain to escape, it was like a bear in a hunter's trap: the fight was useless. Its dozen eyes glared accusingly at Luna as it emitted a louder roar. Luna flew quickly toward Celestine and Oryn's hideaway in the pines.

Landing in a heap, Luna struggled to catch her breath. She shook water drops off her wings before folding them. Magic of this intensity was exhausting no matter how talented the mage. Looking earnestly from Oryn to Celestine, she said, "The ice won't kill the beast, but it will incapacitate it for a while and buy us time."

"Thanks. I mean it." Celestine squeezed Luna's arm.

"Has Vex been here?" Luna asked. "Or is he still holed up in his water sanctuary, giving commands from afar?"

"We haven't seen him, though I hear his voice in my head, yelling at the monster," Celestine replied.

Oryn huffed out a laugh. "His water minion is rather disobedient."

"Yeah, I spoke to Ray through his revivified eyes," Celestine explained. "I described where his eyes were and how he could defeat Vex by making the monster rebel. By seeing a different plan of action than Vex wants. Maybe it helped."

"Brilliant." Luna spread her wings as cover, for it had

started to rain. "I'd better get to Demon Swamp. Get Vex before he leaves his lair and reanimates his Frankenstein."

Suddenly, it was pouring, and not any normal rain. This rain was boiling hot as it pounded down through the pine thicket, sending up steam clouds and scalding them.

"You stupid bastards!" Vex appeared from above, crouched on a top pine branch. His blue hair was soaked and stuck to his bony jawline. His black eyes blazed, the long scar across his face stark in the eerie storm lighting. "You thought you could stop my golem, and I'd just be a sitting duck in my lab while you all saved Savannah. I curse you all!" His threat was sharp as driven nails. "You forgot I'm the most powerful water mage around. Surely in the entire world."

"Delusional," Luna dared mutter under her breath.

With that, Vex raised his head to the sky and bellowed a manic, garbled chant. Boiling rainwater tore down at an alarming rate, raising the floodwater level, forcing Oryn and Celestine up to higher branches. Luna flew alongside them, but the water's heat seared the edges of her wings, causing her to yelp, grab at the blistering injuries, and tumble into the scalding water.

Vex erupted in gruff laughter as he leapt from tree to tree. "Take that, arrogant water mage."

Celestine began an earth spell to tamp down the turgid storm surge with cool, absorbent soil, and Oryn sent out blasts of cold wind. The minute Vex leapt from his tree and streaked to the golem with supernatural speed, Celestine and Oryn scrambled down the tree branches and pulled Luna up from the scalding storm water, burning their own hands in the process.

"Thanks." Luna rested for a moment on a branch to assess the damage to her wings and reset her strength.

Oryn began to reform the small light vessel into a larger ship that could carry all three of them if need be, while Celestine kept a close eye on Vex.

"He's trying to thaw the beast by shifting the ice to hot water," she whispered.

Indeed, in the span of three or four minutes, Vex had melted the reservoir's thick ice coating and the monster's frozen torso. It was freed up enough to flail in an enraged fit and sent up gigantic waves that poured over the reservoir walls and onto the land, the streets no doubt drowning anyone in its wake. Then the beast struggled its way up and over the lip of the wall.

*I have a better idea, brute,* shouted Vex. *Go to the oil tanks toward the big river. Stomp on the tanks. Explode them. Hurry! I will meet you there.*

*Oil tanks. Stomp! Explode!* said the monster, wading through the floodwater and picking up speed. Despite its unwieldy body, it had gained magical strength, soaking in the reservoir. It practically flew to the oil drums.

Oryn waved for Celestine and Luna to climb into his larger light vessel. As they charged ahead in it, Celestine noticed his face was pale and his jaw grimly clamped. Luna appeared to be holding back tears of pain as she gingerly touched her damaged wings. They brainstormed various plans as they tracked the golem.

"To ace this, it'll take all of our skills," Celestine said. "Luna's water magic, my earth magic, and Oryn's aeromancy."

Luna nodded. "My magic is strong, but I'm injured, plus we don't exactly know the limit of Vex's water magic."

Oryn snickered. "He was no match for Ray, but I hear you. What's Vex's weakness?"

"Something that dries him, burns him," Celestine said.

"We need to do everything to stop the monster from sparking a dangerous oil fire that would burn thousands of innocent people.

"Let's keep brainstorming," Luna said. "Maybe something at the oil field will be useful." They raced after the golem as it flung cars in the air and squashed people underfoot. Swerving around a series of tall warehouses, they lost sight of the behemoth.

To Celestine's horror, by the time they caught up, the golem had breached the outer perimeter of the oil field. The beast was enormous now, maybe twenty-five feet high and bloated from glugging reservoir water. Celestine counted over a dozen oil drums. If even one was breached, the resultant fire would destroy neighborhoods, and the toxic oil would poison the rivers.

With dark relish, the monster clambered up an oil tank's ladder. It tore off sheets of metal and threw them in all directions as it climbed. Finally, at the top, it leaned over the railing and ripped it off its hinges. Again and again, it bashed the top of the drum with it. Then, with a sickening sound of shredded metal, it hooked the ladder onto a torn section and viciously wrenched it open. The golem jumped off the drum just before a deafening boom sounded. The oil container exploded into toxic black flames that blotted out the blue sky.

"Ray!" Celestine yelled up at the golem. "Can you see a way to stop this monster with your own eyes?"

*Shut up, witch!* Vex bellowed as he appeared atop another oil drum, backlit by greasy soot and jagged white flames. *Your precious Ray is useless now! Give up. The city will burn. Oil will clog all the ports.*

"Ray!" Celestine persisted as Oryn steered his vessel in front of the golem's massive face. "Stop this monster from pouring oil into the ports and tide pools. Stop it from destroying your good repairs from Demon Three Eyes' last mess. Can you see what to do?"

The monster paused. In a shocking, unexpected move, it raised its arms to its face, and with Leger's dexterous fingers, it gouged Ray's eyes out of its own blubbery head. The monster's tortured wail was loud enough to be heard across the city. It plunged Ray's eyes into its gaping maw, chewed, and swallowed them.

Such perfect sabotage! Celestine knew this must be Ray's doing. For now, there was no way Vex could rescue the eyes and put them back in the golem's head. And its other blinking eyes seemed almost blind.

The beast clambered awkwardly atop another oil drum, ripped shards of metal, and tossed them every which way, including some sheets of coppery orange.

"Can we use the metal the beast keeps tearing off?" Celestine asked Oryn and Luna. "Maybe to stab it with? They're sharp, like serrated knives."

"That's it!" Oryn whispered excitedly. "Some of it looks like copper, the perfect conductor of electricity! Thanks for the idea, Celestine."

They discussed an impromptu plan involving all of them.

"Stars help us. I pray it works," Luna whispered.

With thunderous clatters, the beast battered the top of the drum with its ruined ladder. Gigantic flames spread from the last drum to this one. Loud firecracker pops pierced her ears, and she imagined they were the golem's water-filled feet bursting rather than what she suspected: another drum had burst. There was a huge discharge of oil, and the drum erupted into flames. The combined force of spewing oil, pressurized air, and fire drove the light vessel up and spinning out of control. Just as the vessel was diving downward to crash in the fire, Oryn managed to swoop it up again to safety.

Even Vex careened wildly in the sooty oil cloud. His contorted body looked like a huge black insect against the fiery sky. With a sickening thud, he crashed onto another drum. Stumbling to his feet, he shook a fist at them as they swerved lower to attack him.

"Bastards!" he yelled. "Take this!" He raised both arms and sent a jet of toxic liquid their way. Whatever was in it attracted flames that clung to it like a rope on fire. When the raging line of flames reached Oryn's light vessel, they crackled through the ship's hull and caught Oryn's legs on fire. He howled with pain, but Celestine quickly cast a spell to send a swirling batch of magical powder that wrapped around his legs to help douse it.

Vex was aiming his arms at them, preparing to shoot another focused spray of toxic liquid their way when Celestine turned to Luna and Oryn. "Ready?"

Oryn nodded. He raced them away from Vex and launched into a furious flight to collect the coppery debris the monster had flung around the oil field.

Luna leapt from the ship and flew far enough away from Vex to be protected from his direct attack, ramping up her magical water energies to conjure an unforgiving squall of thunder and driving rain.

The already-angry sky darkened even more, pierced by yellow flashes from the oily flames. Spinning in his vessel to be a harder target for Vex to hit, Oryn began to conjure lightning. With great, concerted focus, lightning shuddered through his powerful arms and burst from his fingertips like fire-dragon tongues. Celestine readied the two best of the jagged sheets she'd collected as Oryn aimed the ship's prow straight for Vex. Luna positioned herself in the sky, copper shards in hand.

Vex came soaring toward them, flying in the darkening sky with the force of his evil magic. "Idiots, you are nothing!" he shouted, raising his arms to launch more flammable liquid poison.

Before he could, Oryn flew the vessel close enough to touch him. Celestine and Luna reached out and pierced Vex's guts with their serrated copper sheets, burying them deep enough to do serious damage and shock his system. Blood gushed from his belly, and he made awkward attempts to pull out the jagged metal, but the serrated edges had locked onto his flesh.

Oryn flew by again, firing molten lightning from his fingers into the embedded copper. The powerful electrical charges electrocuted Vex over and over. He fell from the sky and crashed onto an unexploded tank. Oryn tracked him and kept up the killing zaps until Vex looked like charred meat. His body spasmed, his eyes rolled up in his head, and his head dropped onto the oil drum with a thud.

Oryn hovered close and kept shooting volts through the copper until Vex's body was limp for five whole minutes. "We did it," Oryn whispered. "Frying hell, we did it!"

"Teamwork," Luna whispered, lowering herself into the light vessel and folding her damaged wings.

"Go, us!" Celestine agreed. "We really pulled it off!" She hugged them both.

A movement from high above distracted her from the relief of killing Vex. She squinted up to a point above the heavy haze. A pirate ship with Jekyll Clan symbols on the sails like the one in Ray's den painting floated by. She was sure of it! Ray's voice played in her ear. *I'm done here. Good job, wolf woman.* She distinctly heard his gusty laughter, and then the sky again turned dark with smoke and approaching dusk.

The three of them were startled by a deafening bellow that filled the air. Celestine and her friends turned to see the golem, who had been so intimidating, so brutal, stagger and fall between two oil tanks, still aflame. Its bloated body deflated like a monstrous water balloon popped by a spear.

# SEVENTEEN

Celestine, Luna, and Oryn called 911. They waited until many, many units, sirens blaring, arrived at the oil fields. The firefighters asked them questions. Celestine, Oryn, and Luna pointed to Vex's scorched body and the collapsed golem. Its huge belly had deflated, and it had shrunk at least five feet in height.

But with its transparent skin showing fish bones, swamp debris, and many eyeballs staring blankly, it was a shocking, monstrous specter of the sort that no human had ever laid eyes on. They stopped asking Celestine questions and gaped at the golem before turning on their hoses and getting to work. Questions would no doubt come later.

Next, Celestine got in touch with Detective Wade and informed him of Vex's and the golem's demise. Wade thanked her and activated every stripe of emergency vehicle to all parts of Savannah. Finally, the trio made their way to Oryn's, who had the biggest place and a garage for his light vessel. Despite their hard-fought victory over Vex and his monster, they were already in mourning for the untold victims of the golem's violence, including two of the Tunnel Supes. Blackfire and Helen had perished while foraging in an industrial area near the oil fields. Ice Eyes had texted Oryn the bad news.

Desperate for a bite to eat, some healing of their own, and eventual sleep, Oryn brought out blankets, water, a block of cheddar cheese, and bread to the garden. They huddled around the patio table under the flickering light of the will-o'-the-wisps. First, they lit candles and invoked a teary spirit ceremony for Helen and Blackfire.

Then, with what looked like the last of his strength, Oryn had Luna stretched out on his garden chaise and performed his healing magic on her badly blistered wings. Celestine, who was the least injured, cast her earth magic on Oryn's singed legs as he took a turn in the chaise. She conjured magical mud compresses with tincture of tannin that she neatly removed afterward without having to wipe off globs of muck.

Celestine ducked into Oryn's kitchen, washed her hands, and returned to the patio. She settled in next to Oryn at the patio table, broke off a crisp end of the sourdough bread, chewed, and swallowed it in one famished move. "My god, that whole thing was touch and go."

"We survived," he said softly, and gave her shoulders a squeeze.

"I guess it's hard to beat water, fire, and air magic all at once," Luna remarked with a snort from across the table. They all laughed.

"It's going to be a challenge for Wade to explain the golem and Vex Blade to people," Celestine said.

Oryn nodded. "Yeah, even to a city that accepts ghosts, hoodoo superstitions, and the benefits of haint-blue paint on their porches to block bad spirits."

"I wonder if he'll ask us to help explain the golem to people?" Luna mused.

Celestine cringed. "Tricky proposition because we want to start the PI business, but we also want to do it under the cover of a legit art gallery."

"You ladies should be proud of your newfound fame," Oryn said with a wink. "You saved Savannah. They witnessed it. In plain sight."

"You played a huge part, Oryn." Celestine gave him a hug.

"I second that." Luna sighed. "It's all too much to figure out right now." She took a long drink of water. "I'm just glad to be alive and part of the team."

"You did amazing work," Oryn said.

"You sure did," Celestine agreed. "Trapping the golem in ice. Genius. I admit, I was worried about you strengthening the water monster in that reservoir until I got where you were going with it all."

"I can see how it would look counterintuitive," Luna said. The air had cooled, and night had crept in, the air smelling of oil fire. They wearily rose to clean up from the snack.

Inside, Oryn showed Luna to his downstairs guest room, decorated in pear greens. Then he turned to give Celestine a long overdue hug. "I have another guest room upstairs. Would you... Where would you like to sleep?" he asked her shyly.

Even in her dilapidated state, she thought this was glaringly odd. After all, they had kissed, had told each other their feelings, had made love. "With you, of course." She studied his green eyes to see if something had changed.

In response, he kissed her hard. They took their time

with it, easing into an open-mouthed kiss that spread fire through her tired body.

He led her upstairs, and she realized she had never seen his bedroom. It was roomy, with two large picture windows. She noted, with a grin, the haint-blue trim on the wooden frames. The walls were painted deep blue with ferns and other plants bursting from side tables. They fell onto the bed and into each other's arms.

He pulled back to arm's length to gaze at her. His eyes looked troubled, their irises flickering green to gray.

"What?" she asked, tensing slightly.

"You asked me questions a couple times, about my family, my faerie line, my tribe."

"Right. I remember." She also pulled back, her jaw tightening in dreaded anticipation. "You never answered me."

He gave her a solemn look, though his eyes resumed their flickering emerald starlight. "I didn't want to frighten you. Or turn you off."

"Oh." She stiffened under his touch. "What is it?"

"Remember when we were talking about vision quests?" She knit her brows in confusion. He tried again. "You said there might come a time when you needed to cross over into the world of spirits, the departed, to envision Ray and his clan on the sea. Try to witness what happened between the Jekyll and Demon Three Eyes clans?"

"Yes, when I took the poultice. When I wondered how far it could take me."

"Exactly. And I said maybe you could... but that it would be perilous. Especially for a supe who's not fae." His gaze was unsmiling.

A shudder passed through her. "I'm not sure where you're going with this."

"Well, I come from a fae line that exists in another realm. In an ethereal land similar to yours where dead people go, to transform into souls of light..."

"Huh? Like a sort of heaven or hell?"

"Not exactly, but yes, an alternative realm, another world entirely." Oryn's eyes dimmed to desolate dove-gray pools. "It means that my time here on Earth is limited... unless I switch over."

Her chest lilted with a faint hope. "Is it possible?"

"It might be, though it's forbidden in my fae line. I'd risk death. It is a dangerous act."

Celestine gasped. The oxygen felt sucked from her lungs. "Hold me for now, Oryn. Don't let go."

He wrapped her in his arms and held on. The press of his strong body on hers was some comfort, though the possibility of it being snatched away was horrifying. She felt a dampness on her bare shoulder and knew he was also undone, weeping silently. "I'm sorry I didn't tell you sooner," he whispered.

"I should be mad, but that doesn't feel right." She brushed her fingers through his hair. "I'm just trying to understand how intense it is, what the layers of reality are. Would your fae relatives kill you for betraying them or would the transformation itself be the deadly factor? And why did you cross over to, um... Earth?"

"I don't know what my dynasty would do exactly, or whether the change would kill me, send me to an unknown realm or render me human." He sighed. "I didn't exactly cross over. I can move and talk and function in this reality; I just can't fully *exist* here. I know it's hard to comprehend."

"It is." She was in shock. It was hard to talk normally.

"I'll keep trying. Look, neither of us knew where our relationship would go."

"No," he whispered, kissing her cheek. "It happened so fast. My feelings for you overwhelm me. But it isn't fair to lead you on. To not be able to be here for you always."

She pushed past the idea of abandonment. Of being without him. "Shh, I want you. I choose you. What is *always* anyway? I want you now. Nothing else matters. What do you want?" She gazed at him with overflowing passion.

"I want you. Even if that means our *always* is only one day at a time." He wrapped her in his arms, and she gave herself to his lips, his body, their magical souls merging.

# CHAPTER
# EIGHTEEN

The gallery wouldn't be open for business for another half hour, but it already thrummed with jazz guitar that swirled around Luna's dozen sea-glass sculptures. They looked like glittering mermaid castles—some green, some blue, others in multicolor purples, pinks, corals, and pearly grays. Each sculpture had its own pedestal that Riley had cobbled together using foraged driftwood.

Three of Riley's drawings enlivened the side wall—one of Blackfire, another of Helen, and a dragon scene from his graphic novel in progress. On the opposite wall, Celestine had mounted three of Aline's detailed botanicals—studies of sea lavender, crepe myrtle, and bunches of butterworts with blue-flag irises she'd discovered on a hike in the Okefenoke Swamp.

Aline had taken gallery promo photos earlier in the afternoon, of Celestine outside in her slinky black cocktail dress and spiky heels, her long hair wound up with purple and black ribbon studded with costume beads.

"Stand under the Shadow Salon sign and give me some

sexy supe attitude!" Aline instructed cheerily.

Celestine was proud of how Shadow Salon had come together in the mere few months after solving the mystery of who'd stolen dear Ray's eyes and murdered him in cold blood. After Vex and his water monster had terrorized the city, killed dozens of civilians, and spilled toxic sludge across land and rivers, it was a huge consolation to donate Ray's willed money. His fifty thousand dollars went to the Save Savannah's Coastal Waters nonprofit group, and she matched that with fifty thousand dollars of the money Ray had willed to her to help in the cleanup efforts.

She walked to the back of the space and through a door. Oryn, Riley, and Luna had helped her convert Ray's den into the gallery's back office. She had kept his comfy couch and one of Ray's boat paintings but added a roomy desk, some trendy black leather chairs, and side tables for art clients.

Also for those who might hire her and Luna for private investigative services.

Celestine took a seat at the desk and shook her head in amazement at the framed newspaper headline on her wall. She still couldn't believe it referred to her, Luna, and Oryn.

Triple Threat Vanquishes Monsters Intent on Destroying Savannah

After all of Celestine's and Luna's fervent longing for privacy, for remaining undercover, they'd all skyrocketed to fame as the supernaturals able to dole out savage karma to two heinous villains, one monster bound to the other. Their brilliant strategy was lauded in the news and with the people. Celestine snorted softly. All the better to get clients coming in for PI work *and* art sales. A win-win after all.

Luna burst into the office. "Hey! I came as early as I could. Do I look okay?" She twirled around. "Like a proper artist having her debut show?"

Celestine studied Luna's chic white silk jumpsuit with a cutout for her wings, her shiny blue boots, shell necklace, and thick shell bracelet. She wore one dangly pink sea-glass earring and one blue one. Hot-pink lip gloss and blue-cat eyeliner. "You look freaking amazing, Luna. You're going to be a hot commodity."

"When I do PI undercover, I'll have to conceal these badass wings under my denim jacket." Luna snorted a laugh, and the two women hugged.

Aline marched in, checking off things on an iPad, a stack of gallery price lists tucked under one arm. She had on a stretchy teal pajama set with a matching scarf artfully whisking up her wild hair. On anyone else, pajamas at a formal Savannah opening would be an absurd faux pas. On Aline, it was perfect. "I'm ready for the crowd. You?" She looked from Celestine to Luna and back again.

"Bring it on!" Celestine exclaimed, jumping to her feet.

Guests sifted in slowly at first, and then they began pouring in. Celestine greeted Professor Gray in his rumpled teacherly jacket and wind-blown hair.

"It's so enterprising of you to open a gallery and feature SCAD students," he said as she shook his hand. "Ah, I see Riley's and Aline's work. Do you have any of your prophetic drawings? You know, that helped you solve the Bartello case?"

"No, those are private." She grinned as if to remind him that they were private in the art class and should remain private no matter her fame. "But there's plenty to see! Enjoy."

He nodded and walked toward Riley at the center of the growing crowd.

Someone gave Celestine a gentle tap on the back. She turned around, shocked to see Ardenia Culpepper dressed in her trademark jodhpurs, this time in black velvet. She had her hair swirled in a dramatic updo, and her bow-tie lips were perfectly painted in a dark crimson. "Oh! Ms. Culpepper, welcome to Shadow Salon."

"Call me Ardenia. I'm sure you're surprised to see me here."

"I am," admitted Celestine.

"I want to thank you."

Celestine raised her brows, and Ardenia went on. "It's because of your understanding of the ethereal world that my house is no longer haunted. I'm not as brave as you. All I wanted to do was get rid of that cursed pitcher, but I didn't even have the nerve to throw it back in the swamp."

"I get it. Not everyone is cut out for communicating with the dark side. You just thought you were on a mud lark." Celestine gave Ardenia a sympathetic grin. "How's your business going?"

"It took a dive after folks found out the three-spouted pitcher had been in my collection. You know how superstitious some are."

Celestine cast Ardenia a pointed look. "Quite superstitious."

"But after the Bartello case was solved and the villains were apprehended, clients started to come back. They are fascinated to hear the story of how you took the pitcher and unraveled the mystery." Ardenia's face took on an excited glow. "Why, that pitcher was like Aladdin's lamp in reverse, with the bad guys trapped inside."

"People like scary stories best when they know it's safe again."

"One hundred percent. My clients are still drawn to my exotic curios, my travels to remote locations." She laughed.

"Funny that I unearthed the strangest piece right here in Savannah."

"Yes. Do you ever collect paintings or sculptures?" Celestine asked her.

"Not fine art, exactly. I'd like to start, though. Could you introduce me to your Shadow Salon private investigation partner?" Ardenia cast a curious look at Luna in front of the multicolored sea-glass sculpture. She was talking to a potential buyer, with Aline pointing out details on the price list.

"Oh, how did you hear about the PI service?"

Ardenia raised her tweezed brows. "Word gets around."

*It sure does!* "Well, tonight, Luna Finley is also my featured artist." Celestine walked Ardenia over.

"Your featured artist," Ardenia echoed, gaping at Luna's healed wings, once again fluffy and magnificent. "How was it to fight that monstrous water creature?" Ardenia asked. "Those frightful staring eyes! Those lines of rotting teeth!"

"Just another day at the office," Celestine joked.

Some memories she preferred to keep to herself. In the crowd, she sensed some supernaturals mixed in with mundanes, which she had wanted all along. The diverse mix. She tried to parse them out. There was a vamp by the drinks table in a tailored black suit smelling of fresh blood. And a fae—not Oryn—with the trademark forested scent, but it was sweeter than Oryn's, as if this one liked to drink honey. She locked eyes momentarily with a female supe of undetermined species, only knowing that irises burning this blue was next-level supe. And there was a fellow earth mage in the crowd, chatting with Riley. Right away, she picked up on the guy's grounded spirit, his granola-and-nut vibe.

Oryn, who had padded in after the gallery was abuzz

with people, stepped over to Celestine while she was between chats and gave her a kiss. "How's my favorite person?" Dressed in a silver suit and a dark-green shirt with buttons open to his chest, he smelled of pine and midnight flowers. His golden hair set off his cut jaw and expressive eyes that gazed at her with hunger.

"Good!" Celestine showed him her copy of the price list with red dots on some items. "We've made four sales for Luna and two apiece for Riley and Aline."

"Impressive." Oryn gave her another kiss and a warm hug. "I'll mingle and let you do your thing. Dinner and a massage later?" He wiggled his hands at her.

"Mmm, yes, Mr. Magic Hands."

As she watched Oryn weave through the crowd, another man looked over at her. Quite tall, with fiery red hair and goatee, he wore old-fashioned round wire spectacles and a Vintage brown pinstripe suit with epaulets, as if dressed intentionally in costume. In style, she guessed him to be an actor or perhaps a theater director. He looked to be in his late thirties or forties. With his intense hazel eyes and trimmed goatee, he reminded her of a photo of the handsome, talented Chekhov on the cover of his play *The Seagull*. Apprehension filled her as he came toward her.

"Excuse me," he said. "Can I speak to you and your... business partner?"

"About the artwork? Do you collect? Are you interested in buying a piece?"

"No, sorry." He wiped his brow as if something was bothering him. "I heard about your other business—the private detective service." He muttered this under his breath as if he knew it wasn't appropriate to mention during a gallery opening.

"Ah. Can it wait until the end of the opening?"

"I need to get back. I... can't stay long." He peered over his shoulder as if someone had followed him.

Goosebumps rose along Celestine's arms. This man was in serious trouble; his energy was dense. Her supernatural antennae stood at full alert. "Hang on, I'll get my partner, Ms. Finley. She'll be heading up the first official job while I get the gallery off to a robust start. We'll just make this look like a quick art conference."

The man nodded and began to pace back and forth in front of Aline's plant paintings. If Celestine didn't whisk him into the back room fast, his obvious panic might unnerve the customers.

In a flash, she, Luna, and this odd gentleman were ensconced in the office, peering at one another. "I forgot to ask earlier. Your name?" asked Celestine, sitting next to the man.

"Timothy Calhoun."

"Your business?" asked Luna, seated behind the over-sized desk. This job, if they took it, would be run by Luna, as per their recent agreement.

"Headmaster of the Calhoun Conservatory."

"Conservatory?" asked Celestine.

"We are a private post-high school boarding school that focuses on high-level theatrical training. Acting."

"The issue at hand?" Luna continued. Her wings framed her in white splendor, her face set in a determined poker stare.

"Something is terribly amiss at the school." His mouth hung open as if he was afraid to continue.

"Such as?" Luna pressed, leaning forward.

"My library books are missing, the theater and sets have been vandalized, the dorms as well. Someone beat me up in my sleep. But there is no obvious perpetrator."

Celestine noticed a faint blue bruise on his left jaw as Luna continued her questioning. "Surely you can discover the offender on normal security devices. Aren't those the sort of problems that mundanes deal with?" she asked him. "I mean, you know what we do?"

"Supernatural PI."

"Yes. So...?"

"Look, I've been to the police. They've done an investigation and come up with nothing." He brushed a hand through his thick red hair. "It sounds crazy, but I almost sense there's a curse on the school."

Goosebumps rose on the back of Celestine's neck. A curse. Definitely their territory. She looked over at Luna. "What exactly convinces you it's of a supernatural origin?"

"Entire stacks of plays disappeared from my locked office last week. *It's locked*," he repeated. "No one has the key. An hour later when I came back and unlocked the office, there they were, but torn in half with indecipherable red grafitti all over them. And then, right in front of my eyes, they spontaneously caught on fire and I heard a voice saying, 'I'm the Red Specter, your worst nightmare." Calhoun brushed sweat off his brow. "Look, I'm not crazy. I've run the place with no issue for years."

"I hear you," Luna said quietly.

"I looked out the window, behind the bookshelves," he went on. "Nothing. Then a red mist seeped up from the floor. I ran downstairs and studied the ceiling below. There was no reason for this bizarre red vapor. When I went back up to my studio, it was gone." He threw up his hands.

Celestine glanced over at Luna again, writing notes in an iPad. "Your thoughts?"

"We'll take the case," Luna replied.

# PREVIEW OF BOOK 2, THEATER OF CURSES

**Tim**

*It was happening again.*

An abrupt rustling. A dry crackling of paper. Tim's pulse jumped. Startled from his writing, his eyes darted to the bookshelf against the right wall of his long antique table. Nothing amiss, though these days it was getting frighteningly common to encounter a tangle of plays splayed across his floor, pulled out by who? For what reason? Not even a fierce wind could do this. The only window was catty-corner to the bookshelf, at the far end of the room and the air flow rushed toward the office door, not the bookshelf. At first it seemed random as new playbooks were thrown down along with his extensive collection of historic and rare finds.

He kept the office locked. So, it couldn't be a disgruntled student's doing. He ran a prestigious conservatory for aspiring actors, and tempers flared at not getting a plum part or a perceived criticism of one's acting ability. The few other teachers at the school—Ms. Charlotte the pretty drama coach and costume specialist, Mr. Dawson, the wiry exercise instructor, and Mr. Ward, the school's morose psychologist—only had keys to their own offices.

Tim sighed deeply. He resumed typing notes on the script his students would soon be performing—*The Romance of the Recording Angels*. He tweaked the characterization of some side characters and intensified the racy blocking of Nora Fields and Kane Barnes, the lead actors in their dramatic first encounter. After all, audiences loved romance edged with risk. And though the Calhoun Conservatory had been generously endowed by his ancestors and was a famous feeder of young talent to Broadway and film, it depended on donors in the here and now. The first live performance was in sixty days' time. These incidents had him worried that he'd have to delay it.

A louder rustle. He swung around to the slap of dozens of rare historical plays slamming to the floor. He leapt from his chair and hurried toward the chaos. As he did, a red-tinted mist stinking of operating room chemicals wrapped around him. The odor brought him back to his own near-death surgery after an injury turned septic. Choking, he tried to bat away the sour fumes. A sharp tearing drew his attention back to the heap as unseen hands ripped the top script in half. It was one of the dozen copies of *The Recording Angels* he'd made for the students.

And then, some unseen force punched his left jaw followed by a violent shove. He stumbled backwards. With no time to regain his balance or even brace for the fall, the back of his skull clanked hard against the floor, taking away his breath. His eyes watered as he tried to stay conscious.

1.

"Ms. Luna Finley, meet Nora Fields, the lead actress in

our forthcoming *Romance of the Recording Angels* play." Mr. Calhoun, wide-eyed and with a faint bruise on his left cheek quickly introduced them in the school's foyer. "Come to my office when you are done. Nora will show you the way." With that, he turned on his heels and scurried away. Luna's belly did an uneasy flip at his hasty retreat.

"So, you've had disturbing incidents in the dorms?" Luna asked Nora.

Nora, a finely-boned brunette with tawny skin and compelling black eyes nodded. "Costumes were damaged, scripts had pages torn out and nonsensical red graffiti suddenly appeared in the cafeteria. Everyone denied painting it. I'll show you." Nora's strappy yellow sundress rustled as she led Luna through the conservatory halls. She waved on a couple of her classmates, Bonnie, a long-legged blonde woman and Fisk, a husky freckled guy to join them.

Luna wasn't all that much older than Nora and her classmates—maybe all of six or seven years—and a wave of nostalgia for her own youth hit her. Her world had grown darker and more complex since the murder of her own parents by a crazed follower, and her stressful escape from her coastal home up north to save herself. She related to these young actors, whose sense of peace had already been shattered.

First, the group went into Bonnie's dorm, where she showed Luna her torn costume, a full-skirted mint green tulle gown. "When I went to bed one night I hung it in the closet, and it was fine. Woke up the next morning and it was ripped to shreds. Her face reddened. Clearly, Bonnie had treasured this dress and felt violated.

Luna took a moment before she photographed it for evidence to deeply sense it for dark elemental magic. Easier done if she could touch the fabric but that would put other energies and fingerprints on it. The tulle didn't contain even weak traces of air, water or earth magic. Confusing, but there were supernaturals that wielded magic by other means, such as demons. She backed away.

*Chapter continues...*

Subscribe to Catherine's newsletter for news of exact spring 2024 release date for Theater of Curses, Book 2 in the PI urban fantasy Shadow Salon series!

# ACKNOWLEDGMENTS

Thanks to the elegant, historic and spooky city of Savannah, Georgia for inspiring all the magic. The need to research my next book is the perfect excuse to keep on visiting, exploring and getting to know great people. As always, I want to thank my NYC and Cape writing groups, who tirelessly and loyally read and discuss my work. So, thanks to Holly Kowitt, Mary Kate Pagano, Emily Damron, Colin Keenan, Shawne Steiger, Maggie Powers, Margarita Cardenas and Karen Winters Schwartz. Thanks to my card reader, Holly Buczek who helps spark my inner sight to conjure the characters and villains that parade my way, demanding voice. Thanks to Pikko's House for sharp editing skills, and to my incredibly talented cover artist, Christian Bentulan.

And most of all, thanks to all of my readers, whether long time or new to me!

# ABOUT THE AUTHOR

Catherine Stine is a *USA Today* bestselling author of paranormal, urban and historical fantasy, all with romance and suspense. *Witch of the Wild Beasts* won a second prize in the Romance Writers of America's Sheila Contest. Other novels have earned Indie Notable awards and NYPL Best Books. She lives in New York State, grew up in Philadelphia and was born in Virginia. Before writing novels, she was a painter and fabric designer. She's a visual author when it comes to scenes, and sees writing as painting with words. She loves edgy thrills, perhaps because her dad read Edgar Allen Poe to her as a child. Catherine enjoys spending time with her beagle Benny, writing about supernatural creatures and meeting readers at bookfests. Subscribe to her newsletter to find when she'll be at an event near you.

Made in the USA
Columbia, SC
28 August 2023

22193831R00137